# LOVE ME TENDER

## THE BLISS COVE SERIES (BOOK 4)

## NINA LINDSEY

SNOW QUEEN

PUBLISHING

# CONTENTS

Cover designed by Najla Qamber Designs
www.najlaqamberdesigns.com

Published by Snow Queen Publishing

This book is a work of fiction. All names, characters, locations, and
incidents are products of the author's imagination, or have been used
fictitiously. Any resemblance to actual persons living or dead, locales, or
events is entirely coincidental.

# BOOK DESCRIPTION

## LOVE ME TENDER
*A Bliss Cove Romance*

Rory Prescott is desperate for a place to stay before she leaves Bliss Cove for her lucrative new tech job. Tavern owner Grant Taylor is desperate for a date to his brother's wedding before his mother tries to marry him off next.

Grant makes Rory a deal -- he'll let her stay in his cottage if she'll pretend to be his girlfriend. Though the two friends bicker over everything from her love of gummy worms to the horrible singing fish he has on the tavern wall, **"pretending" to like each other isn't a stretch**.

As they share close quarters, argue about cell phones, and exchange more than one hot kiss, **their fake relationship soon becomes passionately real.**

But Grant's family battles and Rory's impending career move shut down any possibility of a happy ending. Their hot, tender romance is about to crash and burn...unless they're willing to risk everything for love.

## BLISS COVE SERIES

WE FOUND LOVE

LOVE WALKS IN

AND I LOVE HER

LOVE ME TENDER

WORDS OF LOVE

BOOK OF LOVE

MESSAGE OF LOVE (COMING IN 2022!)

# CHAPTER 1

*Can't wait to have you on board, hot stuff!*

The email message was followed by a winking smiley-face emoticon with its red tongue hanging out.

Rory Prescott wanted to punch through her 27-inch, ultra-high-def 5K computer screen, pinch the little winkey-face between her fingers, and squish it to death.

Instead she typed *"Never call me that again,"* resisted the urge to add *"asshole,"* and hit the send button.

She pushed away from the desk and shoved her feet into her ratty old boots. Grabbing her jacket, she strode out of her one-room apartment and into the fall evening. The crisp, salty ocean air, as familiar as the smell of home-baked cookies, washed over her. A gray layer of marine fog covered the sky.

Tugging her long black hair from her jacket collar, she walked swiftly toward Starfish Avenue. With the start of fall, the tourists had all departed from the coastal northern California town of Bliss Cove, while students of the private Skyline College had returned for the new school year. Now that October was approaching, the town had settled into its usual autumn rhythm of cooler days, busy students, and preparations for the upcoming Harvest Festival.

She turned off Starfish Avenue and walked to a cluster of wood-and-stone buildings located near a redwood grove that spread out into the surrounding forest. White lights twinkled over the ivy-covered main building, which bore a crooked sign reading Mousehole Tavern. Inside, people clustered around the red-and-white checkered tables, laughing and chatting. "Stairway to Heaven" drifted from an old jukebox, and a fire crackled in the stone hearth dominating one wall.

Pulling off her jacket, Rory tossed it onto a coat rack. Her boots clomped on the worn wooden floor as she made her way across the room. She scanned the crowd before her gaze landed on Grant Taylor, the owner of the Mousehole, who was mixing a drink behind the bar.

The tension in her shoulders eased a bit. Though Grant's back was to her, the sight of his big, solid frame was a welcome reminder that some things in life, and some people, were constant.

"Scotch, straight up." She slapped her hand on the bartop.

"Whoa." Grant turned from setting a drink in front of another customer and squinted at her. "What's wrong?"

"Why does something have to be wrong? I just want a scotch."

Grant tossed a towel over his shoulder, his eyebrows pulling together beneath his wavy brown hair. Though at thirty-five, he wasn't that much older than Rory's thirty, he'd always had a penetrating way of looking at her, like a wise old owl who saw more than he let on.

Sometimes she didn't mind it because no one got past her shield if she didn't let them, so it didn't matter what Grant thought he saw. Other times, she wished he'd just give her what she asked for and go away. She liked knowing he was always here, but she didn't want him getting too close.

"Five years I've owned this place," he said, "and you've never ordered a scotch."

"How would you remember that?"

He tapped his temple. "It's my job."

"Scotch. Straight up."

With a shrug, Grant poured her drink and set it in front of her. Somewhat unnervingly, he stood there watching as she took a swallow. The liquor burned down her throat.

"What?" she snapped.

He folded his arms over his broad chest. "You okay?"

"Of course I'm *okay*." Rory pulled her phone out of her back jeans pocket. She was always okay. As the middle sister of three, she was the independent one, the peacekeeper, the sister who didn't need anything.

Acutely aware of Grant's stare, she ducked her head and pulled up an app on her phone. He turned and walked away. At least the phone trick always worked to get rid of him. Technology was to Grant what DEET was to mosquitos.

Rory scrolled the local apartment listings. None of them would offer her a short-term lease. All of the B&Bs and the Outside Inn had been booked up for weeks, thanks to the influx of students, the upcoming parents' weekend at Skyline, and then the Harvest Festival.

Tossing her phone down, she swallowed more scotch. She could leave Bliss Cove early, but she needed to give her mother time to find and train a replacement at the Sugar Joy Bakery. And truth be told, Rory needed time to get used to the idea of leaving again.

Two years. She had moved back to Bliss Cove from San Jose after her father had died almost two years ago.

She'd expected to stay for a couple of months. She'd help her older sister Callie deal with the paperwork, support their devastated mother, and work to keep Sugar Joy open when Eleanor Prescott wanted to shut the bakery down for good. Then their sister Aria left town, and Rory had felt obligated to stay for just a little longer.

"A little longer" had turned into two years. Rory had been working part-time at Sugar Joy and spent the rest of the time writing technology articles and staying up-to-date on all the changes in the high-tech industry. She'd taken online courses and completed several remote contract jobs.

Now Sugar Joy was thriving, and Eleanor was involved in a relationship with a very nice man, Henry, whom she'd met last spring. Aria and Callie were both blissfully happy in their work and personal lives. The pain of Gordon Prescott's death was giving way to *life* again.

All of which meant it was time for Rory to leave Bliss Cove and return to her own version of life.

Even if it did involve little toads who thought it was okay to send her suggestive messages and winkey-face emoticons *when she had just been hired to work on their team.*

She downed the rest of the scotch as Grant appeared in her peripheral vision again.

"Another, please." She indicated the empty glass. "And a fried onion."

Frowning, he refilled her glass. "Is this dinner?"

"Well, it's not brunch."

"I do serve excellent food here." He rested his hands flat on the counter and leaned in to study her with his shockingly green eyes. "Not that you'd know since you never eat it."

"Last time I checked, fried onion blossoms were still on the menu." Rory hauled the glass toward her. "Are you bringing me one or not?"

Irritation flashed in his eyes, but he shoved away from the bar and strode to the kitchen. Rory ignored a stab of guilt and checked her phone again. After buying the Mousehole five years ago, Grant had revamped the basic menu of burgers and fries. He'd retained upgraded versions of the Mousehole classics while adding stuff like filet mignon and grilled salmon. The only item that stayed the same was the world-famous artichoke soup, whose secret recipe was handed down from owner to owner.

Rory didn't like artichoke soup. And she had no interest in Grant's fancy gourmet food.

"Rory! I have some wonderful prospects for you."

Rory turned to find Destiny Storm, the owner of Moonbeams on Mariposa Street, wafting toward her like a peacock in a shiny turquoise caftan with her curly black hair piled on top of her head.

A strong believer in fates, furies, and One True Love, Destiny had decided the love lives of the Prescott sisters were in dire need of an upgrade. Now that both Callie and Aria were living in committed bliss, Destiny had turned her attention to the "tragically single" Rory.

Because Destiny was Aria's close friend, and because she did like the other woman, Rory had agreed to let Destiny set her up on a casual date or two. She hadn't been on a date in ages, and it would be good practice for when she moved to San Jose.

If she didn't want to end up submerged in work 24/7 again, then she'd have to actively seek out a new social circle. That would not be an easy task in the frequently smarmy and chauvinistic world of the tech industry.

Considering how badly her career had bombed the last time she'd been in the Bay Area, she needed to ease her way back into dealing with men in general. Little Jerk with the winkey-face had reminded her of the type of pig she'd have to occasionally contend with in the workplace. Maybe a date in Bliss Cove would remind her that romance and her career were two separate things entirely.

Destiny leaned one elbow on the bar, her eyes bright with anticipation. "I want you to come in for a reading so I can better assess your energies, but I have a strong intuition about you and Max Weatherford."

"Didn't we already talk about this? I can't even keep a houseplant alive. I'm pretty sure I'm not compatible with a man who doctors pets for a living."

"Ah, you don't know the power of opposites." Destiny raised a knowing eyebrow. "You and Max can learn a lot from each other. I gave him your number, so you should expect a text from him soon. Now if you'll excuse me, I have a date of my own."

With a wink, she fluffed out her hair and sauntered over to a table where Joe, the owner of Metalworks Hardware, was pulling out a chair.

Rory shrugged and turned back to her phone. A date with a good-looking man, even if he did enjoy being around animals, wouldn't be a hardship.

*No short-term leases.*

The text popped up in response to yet another one of her

queries about available apartments. With a groan, she dropped the phone on the bartop.

"That's why I don't have a phone." Grant set a plate of golden-brown, crispy goodness in front of her. "Gives you nothing but misery."

"You know what gives you nothing but misery?" Rory plucked off a piece of onion and bit into it. "Being born a hundred years too late."

He shrugged. "I'm not miserable."

"Please. Anyone who owns a singing fish has issues."

"If we're talking about issues," he said, "what's with the scotch and the groaning?"

"None of your...wait a second." She lifted her head, hope flaring. "The cottage in the back. Is anyone renting it?"

"The one behind the house?" He jerked his thumb over his shoulder and shook his head. "I don't rent it out."

She blinked. "What do you mean? Someone's always been able to rent the Mousehole cottage."

"Not since I bought the place."

"Why not?"

"I live alone." He started polishing highball glasses and setting them on a shelf.

"The cottage is a totally separate building."

"It's close enough that someone would be around."

"And you don't want anyone *around*."

"I prefer it that way, yes."

Ignoring a strange dissatisfaction with his response, Rory tore off another onion slice. "Would you reconsider for two months?"

"No, but why do you ask?"

"Because I accepted a job with Digicore Corporation in San Jose." She wiped her greasy fingers on a napkin.

He glanced up sharply. "You're moving?"

"In two months. It was supposed to be sooner, but they haven't yet gotten funding in place for the project they want me to work on. So I have to wait." She pushed a swath of hair back over her shoulder. "I hadn't expected to stay in Bliss Cove this long, and it's past time for me to leave."

"What's the job?" Grant grabbed a rag and scoured the top of the bar. The sinews in his forearm flexed with his rapid movements.

"Software engineer. I'll be working on cloud systems."

"Weren't you doing some programming contract work?"

"Yes, but this is a full-time job with potential for advancement." Her mouth twisted. "At least that's what they told me."

He tossed the rag aside. "You don't believe them?"

"Another beer over here!" a guy called from the other end of the bar.

"Hold up, Pat," Grant snapped before settling his gaze back on Rory with the *I'm waiting for an answer* look she'd come to recognize.

Maybe the scotch had loosened her tongue because she found herself confessing. "I've worked in the high-tech industry since I was a teenager. All through college, I worked different jobs and internships. I've probably worked for five or six different companies over the years. I've dealt with every situation you can imagine. So while I would very much like to think they'd consider me for advancement, even leading my own project, the stark reality is that women are frequently passed over for that kind of thing. Even women as good as I am. And believe me, I'm damned good."

"I believe you." He leaned back against the counter, his shoulders tense. "So why are you taking the job?"

"Because I miss the work, and I'm the best person for it." She took another sip of scotch. *And because, really, I can't just take contract jobs and work at Sugar Joy forever.*

"I love the coding and analyzing," she continued. "I'll get great benefits. I guess I'm still holding out hope that I'll soon have *the* perfect job, you know? The one where I can use all my skills and even lead my own project. Plus, I've learned how to deal with the shitty stuff."

A frown carved deep lines on either side of Grant's mouth. "What's the shitty stuff?"

"Come on, man, I'm thirsty!" Pat yelled.

With an irritated sigh, Grant pushed away from the counter and strode to the end of the bar to refill the other man's glass. He paused on the way back to put more peanut bowls on the bar—another Mousehole tradition he'd kept.

"Have you ever thought about serving sugared nuts, Grant?" Madeline Fox, who owned the bath-and-body shop Naked, approached the bar and perched on a stool. "I have an excellent recipe for roasted nuts with sugar, cayenne, and cinnamon. Spicy and sweet is the best combination, don't you think?"

Rory barely managed to withhold a snort.

"I can see why you'd like it, Madeline." Grant set a bowl of plain peanuts in front of her.

"Why's that?" Madeline plucked a nut from the bowl and began shelling it with her perfectly manicured fingers.

"Because you're spicy and sweet, aren't you?" Amusement crinkled Grant's eyes.

"In the right circumstances, I certainly can be." Madeline winked at him.

Rory yanked another slice off the fried onion. With her thick blond hair and long legs, Madeline was sexy as hell, but Rory had seen countless women hit on Grant Taylor to no avail whatsoever. He was unfailingly polite and courteous, and he frequently flirted right back, but he never took them up on their overt offers.

Unless he did, and Rory had just never seen it happen. Besides, what man could resist the siren call of Madeline Fox with her knockout body and expert knowledge of the girly stuff that had always eluded Rory?

Her stomach tensed. Must be all the grease from the onion. Grant was right. She should eat more salad. Or at least *a* salad.

Madeline leaned closer to Grant and whispered. He turned and pushed the button on the plaque of an ugly plastic fish hanging on the wall.

The warbly strains of Elvis's "Love Me Tender," sung in a nasally voice with bubbles popping in the background, began playing. The fish came to animatronic life, mouth gaping open to form the lyrics, and its scales shimmering with silver lights.

Madeline clapped. Cheers and laughter rose from the other bar patrons as the fish performed its nails-on-a-chalkboard rendition of the classic song.

Rory gripped her glass and suppressed the urge to throw it at the grating little robot. Grant had put the fish up on the wall after he'd bought the tavern. Upon request, he'd push the button that made the fish sing, or he did it to amuse people.

Women, specifically.

He refilled Madeline's wineglass and said something that made her giggle. With a wave, she picked up her glass and sauntered back to her table.

On a purely objective level, Rory got why women flirted shamelessly with Grant all the time. With his thick, wavy brown hair and chiseled features enhanced by an ever-present stubble, he was aesthetically very appealing. Not to mention, he was tall and broad-shouldered with a deliberate way of moving that spoke to an innate confidence.

He also knew how to cook—Rory had heard, anyway—and he treated his customers as if they were guests in his home. He looked people in the eye and listened—really *listened*—to their stories and tales of woe. He was every man's buddy and every woman's dream guy.

The interesting part was that no one really knew much about him. He'd moved to Bliss Cove five years ago after buying the Mousehole, and he'd eased seamlessly into town life without so much as a wrinkle.

Next thing anyone knew, he was serving *steak au poivre* and fine wine alongside cheeseburgers and artichoke soup, offering his opinion on local politics, showing up at town events, and talking to residents as if he'd lived there forever. He pitched for the Bliss Cove Rockets, volunteered at a nearby food pantry, and was known for being an easy touch when it came to school fundraisers and sponsorships.

The only frustration he caused was among single women who couldn't figure out, or become part of, his love life. He'd dated occasionally, and rumor had it that he sometimes hooked up with women in neighboring towns, but he never seemed to be part of a couple.

Must have something to do with him not wanting anyone *around*.

Well, Rory could relate. Which made her the perfect candidate for renting the cottage.

"Grant, my lease expires on Thursday." She tapped her finger on the bar to emphasize her point as he approached her again. "The job doesn't start until after Thanksgiving. I need a place to stay until then."

"What about your mother or sisters?" He grabbed her crumpled napkin and tossed it in the trash before giving her a clean one.

"I can't stay with them." Rory ate another piece of onion and held out her hand, ticking off all the reasons on her fingers. "Mom's still with Henry and I'm sure he stays overnight, even if she'd never admit that. Callie's course load is crazy with the start of the new semester, and Jake is using the spare bedroom as an office to work from home. I can't impose on Aria and Hunter with everything they have going on. None of the apartment owners will give me a short-term lease, and the B&Bs and the Outside Inn are booked for parents' weekend and then the Harvest Festival. I can't couch surf with friends either, not with my computer and stuff."

"So get rid of the computer and *stuff*."

"I *work* on my computer, you luddite."

He shrugged. "That could be part of the problem."

"It's only for two months." She forced down the rising desperation in her tone. "I'll be quiet as a mouse."

"Funny." He started mixing a drink for another customer.

"The cottage might not even be habitable. I can't remember the last time it was cleaned."

"I don't care." Rory pushed her plate away in exasperation. "I'm not fussy. I wouldn't even be *around* much. I'm still working at Sugar Joy, and at night, I'm just on my computer. I even have headphones, so you won't hear anything if the windows are open. In fact, I'll keep the windows closed. And the curtains drawn, so the glow from the computer screen doesn't intrude on your hobbit hole."

He shot her a look that was a mixture of amusement and irritation. "No."

"Grant." Bracing her feet on the stool rung, she leaned across the bar and grabbed the front of his forest-green T-shirt. The soft, warm material crushed in her fist. "Let me rent the cottage."

"I don't rent the cottage." He put his hand over hers to pull her grip away. His fingers engulfed hers, shocking her with sudden awareness.

He stilled. She clutched his shirt. Energy suddenly charged through the air. Her knuckles pressed against the incredibly solid wall of his chest. His body heat burned through the cotton. He tightened his grip on her hand.

Never before had she noticed how big his hands were. His inner wrist pressed right against hers. She swore she could feel their pulses beating together. His blood thumped swift and heavy beneath his skin.

*What the…?*

Forcing her fingers to unclench, she yanked her hand away and sat back down. Her heart was beating oddly fast. She took a healthy swallow of scotch, which did nothing to quench an unexpected surge of desire.

Grant flicked his gaze over her, as if he knew exactly what that brief contact had done to her. Acute self-consciousness flooded her, burning her cheeks.

*Ugh.* She hated reacting like a girl.

Rory shoved off the stool and dug her wallet out of her jeans pocket. She tossed a twenty on the counter. "I gotta go."

She grabbed her jacket and fled.

# CHAPTER 2

"*H*ey, boss, we putting salmon on the menu?" Winslow, one of two cooks at the Mousehole, peered at the specials board, which they revised every morning according to what local foods were available.

"I'm going down to the harbor now to see what they've got." Grant tossed a dishrag into the laundry. "Tony, you got things covered here?"

His manager nodded, waving a hand for him to leave. Grant headed out the back door to the one-bedroom house located behind the tavern. He pulled the salt-and-pine air into his lungs.

One of the reasons he'd bought the Mousehole was its location close to downtown yet isolated in a grove of redwood trees that stretched toward the forested hills. Not to mention, the house meant he was only a few feet from work.

After taking the mail out of the box, he went inside and tossed his keys on a table. He shuffled through a few bills, pausing to look at a postcard from his friend Kate Rochester, who'd worked at the Sugar Joy bakery a couple of years ago before she'd left to embark on adventures with her new husband.

Pleased, Grant read Kate's happy message about her discovery of *pane di segale* during a trip to Rome. He pinned the postcard to his bulletin board and pushed the blinking light on the answering machine. His younger brother's voice crackled through the tape.

*"Hey, man, I know you're not looking forward to coming up this weekend...considering I'm marrying a goddess, thanks for that...and since I don't want anything to mess this up for Alice, I need to talk to you. Call me."*

Suppressing a sigh, Grant picked up the phone and dialed. "What?"

"I'm fine, thanks," Nathan replied. "How are you?"

"Sorry." Grant pulled a hand down his face. "But your message sounded ominous."

"It was supposed to, Prince Charming."

"Oh, no."

"Oh, yes. First of all, one of Alice's friends came down with mono, so the wedding planner is having a fit over the fact that we have an extra seat and no one to put in it. Therefore, Mom is lining up women for you like they're in a beauty pageant, which she was planning to do anyway but this seating thing has her even more militant. I overheard her talking about moving you to another table so she could seat you between two eligible women. And don't forget Vivian's going to be there. Without a date, according to Alice."

Grant sank onto the edge of the sofa. "I can't do this."

"You have to. Mom will lose her shit if you don't show, and that will seriously fuck things up for Alice, which means I'll have to kill you. My bride is expecting this to be her perfect day, and there is no way I'm letting my big brother ruin it because he's too pansy-assed to face a group of stunning single women."

And *Vivian*. Who apparently was still eligible. Considering her pedigree, that was a surprise.

"Yeah, okay. I'll be there."

"Grow a pair, man. It's just a few hours, right?"

More like a full weekend, but if it were up to his mother, he'd be engaged before he left San Francisco on Sunday night. Some of the women would have the same idea—not because of him, but because of his family. When you were the eldest son of the founder of the Intellix Corporation, a multi-national computer technology company, people tended to notice that first.

In some ways, that was a good thing. He'd learned early on to figure out who wanted something from him, which made it easier to weed out the few real friends he'd had. But over the years, his guard had gotten thicker and heavier, reinforced by his parents and then by the woman he'd expected to marry.

"I'll be there," he assured his brother. "But I take no responsibility for Mom's actions."

"Dude, Mom doesn't even take responsibility for her actions." Nathan laughed. "That's why she's Queen Busybody. The wedding stuff has her anxiety about you kicked up to level eleven. You were supposed to be married first. And what, you're pushing forty now?"

"I'm thirty-five, dickwad."

"Tick tock, man. When Alice was showing Mom her wedding gown choices last year, she said Mom was worried that if you ever get married at your age, there's no way your bride will be able to wear white."

"For fuck's sake. Is Alice wearing white?"

"My bride is an angel. Of course she's wearing white."

"You are so whipped."

"Like cream, bro. Being whipped is underestimated. You should try it sometime."

"How about I just come to your wedding and keep the peace?"

"That'll do, pig."

A grin tugged at Grant's mouth as he hung up the phone. His little brother had been the one reason he'd second-guessed his decision to leave both his family and San Francisco. But after years of trying to toe the family line had culminated in his disastrous relationship with Vivian and an excess of his mother's interference, his instinct to start over— to do what he wanted, instead of what everyone else wanted —had taken precedence.

But his family was still his family. He no longer cared about disappointing his parents, but not for anything would he let his brother down. He'd suck it up and get through the gauntlet of eligible women his mother was lining up for him.

Too bad he didn't have a girlfriend he could bring along. A *plus one* buffer who'd also take care of the seating snafu.

*Unless...*

He glanced at the clock, grabbed a hoodie from the back of a chair, and headed outside. He hurried toward Starfish Avenue, where a mid-afternoon crowd was going in and out of shops and cafés. Turning on to Dandelion Street, he approached the courtyard where the Sugar Joy bakery was located.

Rory was helping a guy who stood beside the counter. Impatiently, Grant stopped to wait.

"Regular or decaf?" She grabbed a mug and looked at the guy expectantly.

"What kind is it?" he asked.

"Dark or light."

"I mean, the dark. Is it Columbian, French Roast, what?"

Barely rolling her eyes, she picked up the bag of coffee and studied the label. "Arabian Mocha-Java. Full-bodied with complex overtones."

"Can I have a sample?"

Rory flicked her gaze to Grant. He shrugged. He'd dealt with more pretentious assholes than he could remember.

She poured coffee into a cup and handed it to the guy. He took a sip, swished it around his mouth, and nodded. "Okay, give me a large."

"A large it is." She poured the coffee and rang up the purchase. "Thanks a bunch, sir."

Only she could make a thank-you sound like, *"Now fuck off."*

After the customer took his cup to a table, Rory lifted an eyebrow at Grant.

"Got any single-origin, semi-aged, organic Sulawesi-Kalosi?" he asked.

She rubbed her cheek with her middle finger.

Grant grinned. "Be grateful he didn't order wine. I could tell you stories."

"I'll bet you could."

"Why'd you leave so fast last night?"

"You noticed?" She crossed her arms and tilted her chin.

"I thought you were too busy chatting up Madeline Fox to notice anything or anyone else."

"I'm an excellent multitasker."

"Multitasking leads to mistakes and shoddy work. You should try focusing instead." She turned to pick up an empty baking tray. "What are you doing here, anyway?"

"I need to talk to you." He let his gaze slip to her ass, which looked round and perfect in frayed denim shorts with the little bow of her apron tied right at her lower back. As usual, he also appreciated the shape of her long legs and the contrast of her scuffed leather boots.

"So talk," she said.

"You off soon?"

"Wow, this talk requires me to get off? I'm intrigued." Rory glanced at the clock. "Ten minutes."

"I'll wait."

*Maybe he could convince himself not to think about Rory getting off. Or him getting Rory off.*

Christ. Heat pooled in his groin.

He backed away, fumbling to sit in one of the overstuffed chairs by the fireplace. Of course he'd *noticed* Rory since she came back to Bliss Cove. He wouldn't be a living, breathing male if he hadn't. With her long black hair, pale skin and thick-lashed dark eyes, she'd caught his attention the second she'd first come into the Mousehole. And yeah, he often admired her body in worn jeans or ragged shorts and a seemingly endless supply of T-shirts displaying a computer pun or the logo of a classic rock or reggae artist.

When they'd first met, he'd appreciated her on a purely male level while also experiencing a tug deep inside, an urge to make her smile. But after their initial encounter, Rory had quickly proven to be a pain in his ass. She was glued to technology, she had the diet of a frat boy, she bitched at him every chance she got, and she attracted too damned much attention when she was sitting at the bar.

Grant eyed her as she stood on her toes to put a box on a shelf. She moved with swift economy, like she didn't want to waste any energy. Her tie-dyed shirt rode up, exposing the pale skin of her lower back.

He shifted, crossing his ankle over his thigh. She was an irritant, like a pebble in his shoe. He couldn't *help* noticing her.

Although, unlike a pebble, she was sometimes kind of entertaining, and she had an incongruity that he found intriguing—computer geek and sexy renegade rolled into one. He could see her slouched at her computer in a Bob Marley T-shirt and knee socks, backtracking algorithms and generating permutations. Did she wear glasses?

*What the...*

This was a bad idea. Why would he think she—

"Okay, I'm done." She appeared at his side, her apron off and a ratty black backpack slung over one shoulder. "What do we need to talk about?"

"Come on." He stood, jerking his thumb to the door. "I'm going over to the harbor to check on the day's catch."

"Fresh air and sunshine?"

"I'll protect you." He held the door open for her and they started down the street.

"So what's this about?" She glanced at him. "You never want to talk to me."

"I always talk to you."

"But you don't *want* to."

"Who says?" He shot her an affronted look. "You're the one who comes in bitching about everything from the uncomfortable booth to the singing fish."

"That booth by the fire *is* uncomfortable, and the singing fish is a travesty."

"Good thing it's not your tavern."

"Is that what you want to talk about? My distaste in your decorating choices?"

"Are you still looking for a place to stay?"

Wariness flickered over her expression. "Why?"

"Are you?"

"Yes."

"You can stay in the cottage at the Mousehole."

She narrowed her eyes. "What do you want?"

"That's what I need to talk to you about." Stopping, he turned to face her. He should've figured out how to word this. She'd either be offended or think it was a joke. "My brother is getting married this weekend. He's five years younger than me, which only reinforces the fact that our parents expected me to get married first. So, of course, my mother is lining up a bunch of single women for me to meet."

"Seriously?" Her mouth twisted. "Like a haram or a slave auction? Sounds like a dream."

"They'll all be women from the right families, good social connections, that kind of thing. But part of the reason I left the Bay Area was to get away from set-ups like that. I don't want to deal with it for an entire weekend, but I have to go to the wedding. I'd also like to be happy that I'm there for my brother. So if I show up with a girlfriend, I'll get my mother off my back, I won't have to entertain a harem, and everyone will be happy. I might even have a good time."

"You want me to be your plus one."

That was another thing he appreciated about her. She always got to the core of what you were saying. No need to mess around.

"Just for a weekend," he explained as they continued walking toward the harbor. "The wedding is on Saturday and my mother always has other stuff planned, so we'll drive up Friday, stay a couple of nights, and come back Sunday afternoon. Done."

"And I get the cottage rent-free until after Thanksgiving?"

"Yes." He almost held his breath. It was a perfect plan. She was totally different from the women he'd dated before, so that would prove he really had no intention of returning to the fold. No one, not even his mother, would expect him to entertain other women if he was with his girlfriend.

"Okay." Rory hitched her backpack farther up her shoulder.

Grant blinked. "Okay?"

"Okay." She shrugged and crossed her arms. "Linda can take my shifts at the bakery, and Mom won't mind if I take a weekend off. In fact, she'll be thrilled. I'll go to the wedding with you."

"That's…that's great." A surge of relief filled him, strong enough to be surprising.

"My lease expires on Thursday," she reminded him.

"I'll get the cottage ready, and I can come help you move." Belatedly, he thought he'd need to figure out where the keys were. "You want a contract?"

She extended a hand. He gripped her fingers, recalling the press of her knuckles against his chest. She had a good, solid handshake. Her palm was warm against his.

Pulling her hand away, she kept walking. "When can I move in?"

"I just need a couple of days to clean the place up." He stopped and lifted a hand to the dockworker who was hauling in the crates of fish and crab. "Hey, Jim. Got any salmon?"

"Set aside some for you." He nodded to a bin by the side of the dock. "How much you want?"

"Ten pounds."

"Give me a second, and I'll wrap it up." Jim disappeared into a warehouse.

Rory was looking out at the ocean. The water sparkled with sunlight. Seagulls coursed across the blue sky and pecked at scraps on the dock. Farther down the beach, music and noise rose from the boardwalk and carnival.

She turned, catching him staring at her. A current crackled in the air between them before she pulled her phone from her pocket.

"So what do I need to know?" Leaning her elbows on the dock railing, she unlocked the screen.

"First that you need to put that thing away." He walked to stand beside her.

"I'm taking notes. It'll be suspicious if I don't know the basics, right?"

"I don't see much of my family, so it won't be a surprise if my girlfriend doesn't know everything about me."

He felt her glance. "What's the story there?"

Grant flexed his fingers against the railing. "My father wanted me to go into the family business, so to speak."

"Let me guess. He's not a restaurateur."

"No." He tightened his grip on the railing. He'd always liked the way Rory looked at him—with amusement, exasperation, irritation, fire. He didn't want her to look at him *differently* just because his father owned a monolithic tech company. He sure as hell didn't want her treating him any differently.

"So you're the black sheep?" she asked.

"I'm the disappointment. Nathan is the good one. He's a company VP and a genuinely nice guy. Our parents always expected us to work for the company. I don't think Nathan ever imagined doing anything else."

A crease appeared between her eyebrows. "Nathan is your brother's name?"

He nodded. He could almost hear the pieces clicking together in her sharp brain.

"And you're Grant Tay…*oh!*" She thunked her palm against her forehead. "You're Edward Taylor's son. Nathan is your brother. I've read articles about your family. Nathan must have been the one to donate all that money to the Mariposa Renovation Fund…how did I not make the connection before now?"

"Because no one would expect Edward Taylor's son to own a small-town tavern. Not even you."

"Still, I should have figured it out." She shook her head, her ponytail swinging. "No wonder your father wanted you to go into the family business. And no wonder you didn't want to."

"What does that mean?"

"Well, if you wanted to cook and own a restaurant, that doesn't seem very compatible with application software and mainframe databases."

"In my family, it wasn't." He shrugged. "I never wanted to work for Intellix. Never wanted to have the kind of marriage my mother and other people wanted for me either."

"Did you have to pick between your life and theirs?"

"I guess so. It wasn't so dramatic that my parents threatened to disown me or anything. I still see them sometimes and keep in touch. But my mother is still trying to get me to change my mind, and my father just uses the opportunity to remind me I'm the bad son." He shook his head in self-disparagement. "Not that I feel sorry for myself. I'm doing what I want, and obviously I love my parents and brother. We just get along better at a distance."

Admiration sparked in her eyes. "Good for you for figuring that out."

His chest unknotted. Edward Taylor was a big name in the tech industry, but Rory seemed surprised rather than shocked and impressed by the fact that he was Grant's father. Even though she didn't know all the details of his estrangement from his family, she didn't think he was an asshole for walking away from them.

"You still want to go through with this?" He gestured between them.

"Sure." She shot him a grin. "Pretending to be Grant Taylor's girlfriend will be the most interesting thing I've done in ages."

He laughed. "Wait until the wedding. *Interesting* won't be the word for it."

# CHAPTER 3

*R*ory flopped down on her mattress and pulled a pillow over her tired eyes. She'd gotten the contract job done, but she'd had to work to concentrate. Thoughts of Grant kept slithering into her mind, as they'd been doing since they'd made their agreement two nights ago.

The whole "be my girlfriend" proposal had been far less of a surprise than the revelation of his pedigree. If someone had told her months ago that Grant Taylor, technophobe, nutrition-police owner of the Mousehole, was actually Grant Taylor, heir to the Intellix Corporation, she'd have laughed until she cried.

But there had been no mistaking the wariness in his tone when he'd told her the truth, or the undercurrent of things left unspoken. Though he might have had a life of privilege, no one was exempt from the pain of rejection—especially by one's family.

It was the polar opposite of her own home life and her parents' unending support of whatever path she and her sisters chose. When her sister Aria had suggested in high school that she might want to become a circus acrobat, Eleanor Prescott had signed her up for gymnastics. When Rory had shown an early interest in computers, Gordon Prescott had checked out a bunch of "introduction to coding" books at the library and read them with her in place of bedtime stories.

Of course, Callie had been such an exemplary oldest child —brilliant student, perfectionist, successful overachiever following in their father's footsteps—that Rory was pretty sure she and Aria could have done anything except land in prison to make their parents happy and proud.

*Poor Grant.*

Okay, *not* "poor Grant." He'd made his choice. He was doing what he wanted to do. She wasn't going to get all squishy just because he'd confided in her. He'd had to tell her the truth so they could pull off this fake relationship successfully. Maybe that was the reason he'd asked her—his parents would probably approve of him dating a computer geek.

Faint tension threaded her chest. She pressed the pillow harder against her eyes. It didn't really matter *why* Grant had asked her and not, say, Madeline Fox. The important thing was that she was getting a place to stay, and she'd have plenty of time to get organized and ready for her move back to San Jose.

A banging sound ricocheted through the room. She pulled her head out from beneath the pillow. Who the hell was knocking at the crack of dawn?

"Go away!"

The knock came louder, like a battering ram. Probably the manager coming to evict her. Maybe even the police. *Bang. Knock. Bang.* What was he using, a sledgehammer?

With a groan, she shoved off the mattress and stumbled to the door, pushing her hair away from her face.

*"What?"* Snarling, she yanked open the door, lifting a hand to block the sharp bite of the sun.

A large male figure darkened her doorstep, his face cast in shadows and the sun glowing behind him like an aura or a nimbus or whatever those holy things were.

"You said you have to be out of here by noon."

The familiar deep voice penetrated Rory's fatigued brain. She squinted, making out Grant's green eyes glittering through the shadows.

"What the...what time is it?"

"Nine."

"Nine? Why are you here so early?"

"Because moving usually takes a few hours." He bent to pick up a stack of empty cardboard boxes and pushed past her.

Still muddled, Rory stepped aside. Grant strode into the apartment and set the boxes down. Hands on hips, he swept his gaze over the room with its mattress on the floor, strewn clothing, and crumpled bags of chips and fast-food.

"Where's your stuff?" he asked.

Rory closed the door. "My stuff?"

"Your *stuff*." He extended a hand to the mattress. "Furniture, books, pictures. *Stuff*."

"This is my stuff." She dragged her hands through her tangled hair. "Look, you don't have to..."

He stalked into the kitchen and yanked open the cupboards to reveal a half-eaten jar of peanut butter and a bag of pork rinds. "Did you move everything to your mother's? Or put it in storage?"

"No. This is all I have." Impatience flicked through her. "I just have to pack up my computer."

She jabbed her thumb at the shiny, huge computer that presided against the wall.

Grant frowned. "You've been living here for two years, and this is all you have?"

Rory grabbed a few crumpled panties from the floor and tossed them into her open suitcase. "Grant, I work at Sugar Joy and I work here. I don't need plants and books and *stuff*."

"But you criticize the fireplace booth and tell me my singing fish is ugly?" A thunderous look descended on his face.

*Uh oh.*

Rory scratched her head. "You have customers at the Mousehole. It's a public place. I just live and work here alone."

"You don't even have sheets on your mattress."

"One less thing to wash."

"That's incredibly gross." His gaze slipped from the mattress to her.

"You're not the one sleeping here, so what's it to you?"

Belatedly, she realized she'd just brought up the image of Grant in her bed. Heat rose to her face. She bent to throw the other strewn articles of clothing into the suitcase. A waft of air suddenly made her remember she was wearing her usual sleepwear of an overlarge T-shirt with nothing underneath.

Jerking upright, she pulled her shirt farther down her thighs. "Look, I can do this alone."

"I know you can, but you don't have to." He picked up a box. "It'll be faster if we do it together, and my truck is already downstairs."

Internally, Rory conceded that the faster she was out of here, the better.

Grant peered at the computer. "Do we have to take this apart?"

*God in heaven.*

"Don't touch that," she said firmly. "You can deal with my other *stuff*."

She pulled the empty original boxes from her closet and set to work dismantling her computer, monitor, speakers, and laptop. In less than fifteen minutes, Grant had taken a box of her meager food items, her suitcase, and her mattress downstairs.

He stood in the open doorway, hands on his hips. The stupid sun spilled into the room again, burnishing his hair with a golden sheen. Rory's stomach flipped. She didn't often see him outside the Mousehole.

He was wearing cargo shorts and a T-shirt the blue shade of a robin's egg. The color was magnificent against his tanned skin and darker, hair-roughened forearms. She wondered if he knew it.

Since when did she notice things like that anyway?

"Why didn't you tell me you were coming so early?" She closed the box containing her monitor. "Don't touch that."

He backed away from the power cord. "Nine is not early."

"It is when you were up until four working. Don't touch that." She wrapped up and boxed the cords and her laptop, setting them beside the door. "Don't take any of this down without me. I need to get dressed."

"Does your mother know you live like this?"

"Does your mother know you're incredibly judgmental?"

"I'll take that as a no." He folded his arms, his mouth twisting.

"So will I." With a huff, she grabbed jeans and a T-shirt from the floor and strode into the bathroom.

As she pulled her clothes on, she realized that she didn't have many...okay, *any* dressy-type stuff at all.

"When do we have to leave for San Francisco?" Fastening her hair into a ponytail, she left the bathroom and picked up her monitor box.

"Tomorrow at noon."

"I have to stop at Callie's. I don't have anything appropriate to wear to a wedding."

"You don't say," he replied dryly, as he took another box and followed her downstairs.

"If your family is trying to set you up with women of good breeding and all that, I'm guessing it's going to be a high-class wedding."

He set the computer boxes in the truck bed and secured them with bungee cords. "It's an expensive one, if that's what you mean."

"Are you in it?" She followed him back upstairs.

"No."

"Why not?"

"My brother knew I wouldn't want to be." He picked up the last boxes and surveyed the room. "Do you want to take the desk apart?"

"No, it came with the apartment. The desk chair is mine, though."

"I'll take it last." He started back downstairs.

"I'll meet you back at the Mousehole."

Rory made a quick stop at her sister's house. Neither

Callie nor her husband Jake were at home, so she grabbed three dresses and matching shoes from the closet and put them in her car. Hopefully, Callie wouldn't notice before she was able to return them.

She drove to the tavern and parked in the back next to Grant's car and truck. He'd already transferred her meager belongings to the cottage, which was small and spare with weathered hardwood floors.

One room with an attached bath and a kitchenette, there was a queen-sized bed and nightstand, a couple of stools lined up under the counter, and just enough room for a narrow sofa in front of a stone fireplace.

"I thought you said this place wasn't even habitable." She ran her hand over the back of the sofa.

"You should've seen it two days ago." He set her suitcase on a chair. "All the cobwebs are gone now."

Rory blinked. "You mean you fixed it up for me?"

"I paid someone to fix it up for you. I'm many things, but a slumlord isn't one of them. Keys to the tavern are on a hook by the door. Help yourself to whatever's in the kitchen since there's no fridge here." He pointed his thumb toward the window, where the front porch of his house was in view a short distance away. "If you need anything, I'm right over there."

He left, shutting the door behind him. Rory watched him cross to his house, his stride long and certain, as if he'd taken that dirt path countless times.

*I'm right over there.*

In the two years that Rory had been back in Bliss Cove, Grant Taylor had always been *right over there.*

She'd first met him less than a month after her father died.

The relatives who'd come to stay with them in the immediate aftermath of the accident had all returned to their own lives by then, but shockwaves of grief would ricochet through their family for weeks to come. Eleanor was insistent about wanting to shut down Sugar Joy, but she'd had no response to her daughters' questions about what she would do instead.

After a painful, emotional afternoon trying to help her mother clear out some of Gordon Prescott's clothes and belongings, exactly two weeks after the funeral, Rory had taken a long evening walk and ended up at the Mousehole. She'd heard the tavern had been sold, but she'd never met the new owner. The moment she saw Grant behind the bar—something about the way he moved, like he was at home there—she knew who he was.

She'd hitched herself onto a barstool. She was exhausted to the marrow of her bones. Hollowed out. She still couldn't believe her father had been here one minute and was gone the next. The fifth part of their lifelong quintet had left a jagged hole in their lives.

Grant placed a cocktail napkin in front of her. He pulled his eyebrows together, scrutinizing her intently before turning to the ugly, mounted plastic fish she'd never seen before.

He pushed a button on the plaque. The fish turned its head and opened its gaping mouth. A nasally, high-pitched rendition of Elvis's "Love Me Tender" rasped out.

Rory swallowed a bubble of laughter. "What the hell is that?"

"Singing fish. It usually makes people smile. Or at least, realize that they still can."

"It's pretty awful."

He clutched his chest. "I can't believe what I'm herring."

This time she did laugh. Grant winked at her and walked away.

A few minutes later, he returned with a plate and a bowl, both of which he set in front of her. A golden-brown sandwich made with thick-cut bread sat on the plate beside a bowl of shimmering, crimson soup that smelled heavenly.

Rory stared at the food as if it didn't make sense. "What's this?"

"Tomato soup and a grilled cheese sandwich." He tossed a dishrag over his shoulder. "What'd you want to drink?"

"Uh, water, I guess." She picked up a spoon. "Why…"

"Just thought you might need some good food. It's more appealing than a singing fish, anyway."

Rory ate every bite of the delicious food and felt a little better. She hadn't gone back to the Mousehole for another couple of weeks, too caught up with trying to help at Sugar Joy and finish a remote contract job a former boss had given her.

Then she'd seen a news piece about the medical software system that had killed any hope for her own MedCure product, and her heart had shriveled into a hard little ball. She'd returned to the Mousehole and perused the menu for the grilled cheese sandwich and tomato soup.

"It's not on the menu," Grant told her when he came to take her order.

"But you gave it to me the last time I was here."

"I had a pot of the soup back at the house, and I made you the sandwich." He shrugged. "It used to be what I ate when I was feeling down. Still do, as a matter of fact. You looked like you could use it."

She hadn't wanted to ask him to make it again, so instead she'd thanked him and ordered the fried cheese curds.

"How about a salad with that?" he'd asked.

"How about a beer?"

Though he muttered a noise of disapproval, he went to the kitchen to place her order. As he passed the bar, a pretty brunette—Sally Gaines, who'd been in Aria's graduating high-school class—stuck her leg out to block his path.

Her long, shapely leg enhanced by a blue jeweled sandal. Sally curled her hand around Grant's arm and said something that could have been *"Do you have any more ketchup?"* but was probably closer to *"I'm wearing a lacy thong. Want to see it?"*

Grant detached himself from her and rounded the bar. He pressed the button on the singing fish. "Love Me Tender" rang out. Sally laughed gaily, like a little music box.

In that instant, Rory's amusement over the fish turned into outright dislike.

Still, over the months, she continued to find comfort in the Mousehole—the cheerful conversation, the clinking of plates and silverware, the music coming from the old juke-box, the big stone fireplace. It was a reprieve from everything else in her life, even her mother and sisters.

She liked Grant's constancy, too. He was always at the bar or taking and serving orders, bussing tables, seating guests. Even if he was cooking in the kitchen, he came out often to chat with customers or deliver a dish in person.

He knew everyone's favorite drink, how they liked their steaks and burgers, what ingredients they wanted left out. And though he expressed his disdain for Rory's love of fried foods, he always made sure her order was extra crispy and extra-large.

Now, even though Rory knew it was past time for her to leave Bliss Cove, she couldn't banish the reluctance and fear tugging at her gut.

When she was living in the bustling, chaotic, traffic-fueled Bay Area again, immersed in work and gnawing on Twizzlers, with her family too far away for weekly dinners... Grant would no longer be *right over there*.

# CHAPTER 4

*R*ory rubbed her sandpapery eyes. The numbers scrolling across her laptop screen were blurring into a sea of unintelligible data. Her stomach growled.

Stretching to pull the knots out of her neck and shoulders, she shut down the computer. Three-forty-three in the morning. Grant had said they should be on the road by noon, so she could catch a few hours of sleep before then.

First, food.

She picked up her phone and grabbed the tavern keys off the hook by the door. Since the cottage only had a hot plate, Grant had told her to store her food in the Mousehole kitchen and to help herself to whatever was in the restaurant fridge.

After pulling on her sneakers, she hurried outside and over the flagstone pathway. The moon glimmered through a layer of clouds. Cold night air brushed over her bare legs and cut through the thin cotton of her T-shirt. She unlocked the kitchen door and flipped on the lights.

Though small, the kitchen had an impressive array of state-of-the-art appliances, gleaming stainless steel counters, and an industrial gas stove, grill, and deep fryer. Everything was spotless and well-organized—knives, pots and pans, utensils, spices, mixing bowls. A desk with a landline phone and calendar sat along one wall.

Rory peeked into the walk-in fridge, which was beautifully stocked with fresh produce, cheese, meats, seafood, and a ton of other delicacies that somehow went into all the tavern dishes—Kalamata olives, hummus, capers, heavy cream, roasted peppers. Too bad she had no idea how to fry one of the onion blossoms.

She helped herself to a carton of sour cream and found the paper sack of food she'd brought from her apartment. Pulling out a crumpled bag of fried pork rinds, she sat on a stool at the counter to eat and check her phone messages.

The door leading to the front of the restaurant opened. Rory looked up, her heart jumping. Grant strode into the kitchen, wearing black pajama pants and a T-shirt, his hair finger-combed and messy.

"Do you ever go to bed at a normal hour?" he asked.

"Do you ever shave?"

He rubbed his stubbly jaw. "After I shower, yes."

"Me too. Except I shave *in* the shower." She dug into the bag for another pork rind.

Grant frowned, as if he were trying to figure out how they'd gotten from her bedtime to her shaving in the shower.

"Have you slept at all?" He skimmed his gaze over her gray *Byte Me* T-shirt and bare legs.

"Considering you're still up too, that's a hypocritical question." She dipped a pork rind in the sour cream and shoved it into her mouth.

"My manager closed last night, so I left early and got to

bed at ten." He tossed a stack of papers and a pen onto the desk. "I woke an hour ago and couldn't get back to sleep. Came here to get some work done."

"Is that expenses and payroll?" She eyed the papers disparagingly. "I don't suppose I need to tell you there are a million computer programs that would make that a lot easier."

"My system works for me. What the hell are you eating?"

"Midnight snack." She dragged another rind through the sour cream. "Want some? Oh, shit, sorry. I should have used a bowl."

He shook his head. "When was the last time you ate something that required a bowl? Or a fork?"

"I don't like bothering with dishes." She held up a pork rind. "Hence, my appreciation for finger foods."

"Did you eat dinner?"

"I don't think so."

"How are you still alive?"

"Preservatives."

Muttering under his breath, Grant strode to the walk-in. He emerged with a carton of eggs, a brick of cheese, and an armful of vegetables. He dumped everything onto the counter, grabbed a mixing bowl, and turned on a stove burner.

"What are you doing?" Rory licked a drop of sour cream off her finger.

"Making you some real food." He scowled at the bag of pork rinds. "Throw those away. For a smart woman, you make terrible nutritional choices."

"It's called prioritizing. I once worked at a start-up where the launch deadline was so crazy I almost never left the office. Our whole team was surviving on candy bars and this nutritional paste that came in these little tubes...*but* we worked our asses off and crushed the launch. You do what you gotta do."

"Please don't tell me you still eat tube goo." Grant set a few sausage links into a pan and took a chopping knife out of the wooden block.

"No, I've upgraded to Top Ramen and pork rinds." She leaned on the counter, watching with growing fascination as he sliced swiftly into a red bell pepper. "Where'd you learn to cook?"

"Kitchens all up and down the Pacific Coast." He skimmed the blade over the interior of the pepper to scrape away the seeds, then began chopping it. "I've worked as everything from a busser to a head chef."

"What made you decide to buy the Mousehole?"

His mouth twisted. "Cowardice."

"I don't believe that." Not him. She was the coward, hanging around Bliss Cove much longer than she should have because she hadn't wanted to battle the chauvinism of the tech industry again.

Grant sliced into the other half of the pepper. He continued chopping, one hand tight on the handle, the other holding the top of the blade.

He always moved with such confident ease through the tavern, whether he was mixing drinks or serving artichoke soup. Customers gravitated toward him, enjoying both his food and the welcoming atmosphere he created.

Rory had never seen him cook before, though. He was like an orchestra conductor, his movements sharp and skilled as he sliced and diced peppers, onions, mushrooms, and some green grass-like things. He tossed butter into a sizzling pan, cracked eggs one-handed, and grated cheese so fast his biceps flexed.

Actually, all of his muscles were involved in the cooking process. His shoulders and back rippled as he turned back and forth between the stove and the counter.

He reached for the salt on an upper shelf, and his T-shirt stretched over his broad chest. When he strode back to the fridge for a carton of milk, Rory couldn't help letting her gaze drift from the triangle shape of his back to his firm ass.

When he was at the counter, his forearms were the star of the show. Whether he was slicing a mushroom or shaking a pan on the stove, his corded forearms tensed, the sinews and tendons flexing with every motion under his taut skin. Light shone from above, turning the dark hairs to gold.

A little fire sparked to life in her belly. She'd never thought she could get turned on watching a man cook—but then again, she'd never watched a man cook before. As Grant tossed vegetables into the pan and sliced through a thick loaf of crusty bread, she couldn't imagine any other man in the world cooking quite like *this*.

Delicious smells filled the kitchen. He grabbed a white plate from a stack and slipped the bubbling omelet and three sausage links onto it. He pulled golden-brown toasted bread from the oven and slathered it with butter.

After setting the plate in front of her, he held up a hand. "Wait."

Her stomach growled impatiently.

He handed her a fork and knife. "Eat."

Rory dug eagerly into the omelet, inhaling the scents of melted cheese and butter before putting the first forkful into her mouth.

"Wow." She spoke while chewing the delicious bite. "This is amazing."

"Don't talk with your mouth full." He leaned against the counter and folded his arms. "I thought your taste buds might be deadened from all that junk."

"Surprise." She sank her teeth into the thick toast. "Do you cook like this for yourself?"

"I usually eat whatever's leftover in the kitchen."

She nudged the plate toward him. "Have some."

"It's all yours."

"I knew there was a reason I liked you." The food was so good and Rory was so hungry that she didn't bother minding her manners—she shoveled the omelet into her mouth, wiped strings of cheese off her chin, licked crumbs from her fingers. Grant set a frothy glass of milk in front of her, and she downed half of it in three gulps.

He put two more slices of thick-cut buttered toast and two sausages on her plate without her needing to ask. By the time she was scraping her plate clean, she was drowsy and delightfully full.

"That was awesome. Thanks."

"You should eat healthier." He set her empty plate and glass in the sink. "My father was a workaholic...well, he still is, but he had to make some changes after he had a heart attack."

"Is he okay now?"

"It was years ago, but yeah, he's better. My point is that you need to take care of yourself."

"Well, owning a restaurant is no low-stress job, from what I hear."

"No, but the Mousehole was already established when I

bought it. Most of the staff stayed on. I made a bunch of changes, but it wasn't like starting from the ground up. And I still work out and eat right, that kind of stuff."

Rory rested her chin on her hand as he started washing the dishes. He always wore T-shirts at the Mousehole, usually dark green or blue, but this shirt was a faded, russet-red that had been washed so many times it was practically a second skin, the soft material shifting and tugging with every movement. His drawstring pants rode almost dangerously low on his hips, and by the way...*was he wearing anything underneath?*

She wiggled on the stool and pressed her thighs together. An even more urgent question appeared in her head. *Had he wondered the same thing about her?*

"What about a girlfriend?" The question popped out. Heat crawled up Rory's neck.

He shot her a look over his shoulder. "What about a girlfriend?"

"As far as anyone can tell, you haven't had one since you moved here."

"I didn't know people were speculating."

"Oh, please." Rory tugged her nightshirt farther down her thighs. "You're one of the most eligible bachelors in a fifty-mile radius. People have been speculating about you from day one. Oh. Is that why you didn't want anyone to know you're Edward Taylor's son?"

He gave a nonchalant shrug, even as tension threaded his frame. He set the dishes in the drainer and turned to face her. "Partly, yeah. I also don't see much of my family anymore, so it's easier not to be Edward Taylor's son."

Rory frowned. "Why don't you see them?"

He expelled his breath in a sigh. "Unfortunate history. It's not so much that I care if people know…I am who I am, but being a Taylor doesn't have anything to do with my life here."

"And if people do know, they'll probably look at you differently," Rory guessed.

Grant studied her through a hooded gaze, then nodded slowly.

"You didn't," he said.

"I didn't what?"

"Look at me differently." He dried the knife and pan and returned to put them in their places beside the counter. "When you figured out who I am. You've been a steady pain in my ass this whole time. Not a single blip on the radar."

"I am known for being dependable."

"With good reason." He turned to face her, his eyes creasing with amusement.

"So why'd you ask me to pretend to be your girlfriend?" A pang of irritation shot through her. "Why not Madeline Fox, whom I'm sure you would never refer to as a *pain in your ass*."

"I need reliable, not impulsive and unpredictable."

"How do you know I'm not impulsive and unpredictable?" *And how do you know that she is?*

"You work at Sugar Joy five days a week, two morning shifts and three afternoon shifts." He ticked the reasons off on his fingers. "You have weekly dinner nights at your mother's every Wednesday, you have drinks with your sisters and friends at the Mousehole every Friday, and you spend the rest of the time on your computer. Not a lot of room for impulsivity, if you ask me."

"I didn't ask you," Rory grumbled, unexpectedly stung by his assessment of her life.

"Yeah, you did. Don't tell me I hurt your feelings."

"Please. You could never hurt my feelings." She crossed her arms and glowered at him. "It was impulsive of me to agree to go with you to the wedding."

"You agreed because I'm giving you what you want in exchange." He stepped closer, his green eyes searing right through her. "If you're being impulsive, you don't have a plan or agreement in mind. How did you get cheese in your hair?"

Lifting his hand, he pulled a strand of stiff, melted cheese off her hair.

"I impulsively threw it in there." Rory was still sulky. Maybe because she was beginning to think he was right.

"You're mad at me." He wrapped her hair around his finger and gently tugged.

"Well, considering you just told me I'm a monotonous, unexciting, pain in your ass who should be thrown in the gallows for my eating and sleeping habits, I think you have some kissing up to do unless you want me to renege on our *agreement*."

Grant smiled slightly, interest sparking in his eyes. The scent of cooking still clung to his shirt—butter, herbs, peppers.

"Kissing up, huh?" A faint husky note roughened his voice.

Her heart jumped. She shot him a cool look from beneath her lashes, acutely aware that not only did he still have her hair looped around his finger, he'd lowered his palm to the side of her neck. His thumb rested right at the hollow of her throat.

Once again, she could not believe that she had never before noticed how big his hands were. He could cover every inch of her skin with a few sweeping glides of his palms. She attempted to control her breathing.

"In the form of an apology." She tilted her chin, feeling every inch of her nakedness under her shirt. "From what I can tell, owner of the Mousehole, you're no spontaneous thrill ride yourself."

A smile tugged at his mouth. "I'll have to prove you wrong."

"Good luck."

"Only you could make that sound like a challenge." He rubbed his thumb against her throat.

"It was."

"I accept." He skimmed his gaze to her lips.

Anticipation flicked through her. She'd never seen eyes that shade of green before—like a leaf or a clover, or those grass-like things he'd chopped and added to the omelet. He could hypnotize her with those eyes. Maybe he was. She was getting a little dizzy. Or maybe that was from having a real food for the first time in days.

Had they ever been this close before? He was a solid wall of male strength—all muscles and sculpted tendons and whatever else men like him were made of. Testosterone and kerosene.

He stood like some sort of architectural support system—his feet planted securely apart, his body as stable as a pyramid, holding her in place by the weight of his hand alone.

Wait a second. This was *Grant*. Her sparring buddy who hated her phone, grumbled about her love of fried cheese curds, and kept a singing fish on the wall just to spite her.

Why was she suddenly getting all soft and fuzzy inside because he had his hand on her neck? And because he was looking at her like he wanted to eat her up? And because he smelled so good that she wanted to bury her face in his shirt-front and inhale a deep lungful? Or twenty.

He edged his body between her knees. Her pulse pounded. She didn't know what to do with her hands. She lifted them almost as if she was going to touch his chest. Then she dropped them back into her lap and curled her fingers into her palms. He swept his thumb over her throat in a slow, sweeping movement that she felt clear down to her toes.

She was totally unaccustomed to men like him. Her previous boyfriends, not that she'd ever called them that, had been from the opposite end of the spectrum—thin, pale computer geeks with poor eyesight who took the term *social awkwardness* to a new level and considered her a weird, mutant species.

Grant didn't look as if he thought she was weird or mutant. He looked at her as if he thought she was…edible.

A shiver raced down her spine. Her breathing went totally awry. Her nipples hardened against her shirt. She desperately wanted to squirm. He dropped his gaze to her mouth again and slid his hand up to cup her chin, tilting her face toward him.

"What're you doing?" Her voice came out on a whisper.

"Proving you wrong." He lowered his head toward hers. "Welcome to a spontaneous thrill ride."

His lips touched hers. Before she could even grasp the reality of *Grant kissing her*, everything went tense and bright, like golden threads were spinning in her veins.

She forced her hands to unclench and curled her fingers into his T-shirt. The warmth of his body heat clung to the soft cotton, and her knuckles pressed against his hard abdomen. He increased the pressure of the kiss, one hand under her chin and the other coming to rest on her bare thigh.

Heat flamed inside her. *Spontaneous thrill ride.* All right, then. She could prove she was impulsive, too. She opened her mouth and tightened her thighs around his hips at the same time.

A shudder rippled through him. He eased his tongue into her mouth, alternating the intensity of the kiss from gentle to rougher and back to gentle again. His breath was warm. He was hard. The evidence of his arousal was a thick, heavy ridge that Rory could practically feel throbbing between them.

Her heart hammered. She drove her fingers into his hair, holding him against her. She had never been kissed like this before.

Spontaneous thrill ride aside, Grant kissed her to *perfection*, as if he knew exactly what she liked and wanted—easy, hot, slow. He teased her gently, didn't hold her too tightly, and asked for rather than demanded her response.

And, oh god, she responded. Every nerve ending flared like a Fourth of July sparkler, showering her with stars. She stroked his tongue with hers, licked his lower lip, trailed her mouth over his stubble-rough jaw. A hot, restless desire pulsed through her, inciting the urge to slide her hand right into his pants and—

"Wait." Pulling in a breath, she pressed her hand to his chest. His heartbeat thumped against her palm.

He tightened his grip briefly on her thigh before backing away, his breathing hard. A flush crested his cheekbones.

They stared at each other, a touch of shock threading the air. Without his body heat, Rory's skin prickled with cold. She tugged her shirt farther down her thighs and struggled for another breath.

If his kiss was a thrill ride, what would sex with him be like? A rocket launch to another stratosphere?

She'd never considered herself to be particularly adventurous, but at the moment she was ready to leap into zero gravity and start exploring brand-new worlds. With Grant.

*And...reality check. Right now.*

"Good to know you can rise to a challenge." She forced a smirk, pushed herself off the stool, and started toward the door.

"Rory—" A rough note edged his voice.

"Thanks again for the food. I'll be ready to go by noon." She hurried back to the safety of the cottage.

She'd better get her shit together fast. Twice in one week now, she'd run away from him, all flustered and hot. If she kept unraveling every time he touched her, she'd never be able to convince anyone that she was his girlfriend.

That was their agreement, after all. A game of pretend. Her body would do well to remember that.

# CHAPTER 5

*G*rant threw his travel bag in the car and slammed the trunk. Despite a three-mile jog and some heavy lifting at the gym, he was knotted with tension. After his encounter with Rory in the kitchen last night—well, early this morning—he hadn't been able to sleep at all.

Which might have been for the better since no doubt he'd have dreamed about her. Not chaste dreams either. He felt the hot, erotic images seething just beneath his consciousness, waiting to break through when his guard was down.

His mind would flood with images of Rory in her gray *Byte Me* shirt that didn't conceal the curves of her breasts. He'd had a terrible time trying not to stare at her long, bare legs and an even worse time trying not to wonder if she was wearing underwear.

She wouldn't be wearing anything in his dreams, though. In fact, she'd pull her shirt over her head and stand naked in front of him, all pale curves, hard pink nipples, and smooth skin.

When he'd kissed her last night, he'd expected her to taste

sharp and fiery, like pepper. Instead, kissing her had been like diving headfirst into a sweet, tart meringue that melted on his tongue and incited a greedy craving for more. And more. And *more*.

He let out his breath in a rush. Stupid of him to have kissed her. It'd make things weird between them, and he couldn't afford *weirdness* this weekend. Maybe he should apologize or—

"You have to get into the car to drive it." Rory's voice sliced through his thoughts.

He looked up to find her striding toward him from the cottage, a travel bag in one hand, a plastic cup and straw in the other, and a paper fast-food bag under her arm.

Despite the evidence of culinary garbage, his insides clenched at the sight of her in torn jeans, a brown leather jacket, and a green shirt that somehow made her eyes bluer than ever. Her hair hung in damp curls around her shoulders, and her face had a freshly scrubbed, pink sheen.

"You're late." Tightening his jaw, he pulled open the passenger door for her and unlocked the trunk again.

"It's noon." She handed him her travel bag.

"It's ten past noon." He tossed her luggage in the trunk and eyed the fast-food bag. "What's that?"

"Beef burrito and chicken enchilada. Cherry coke to wash it down."

"You're not eating that in the car."

She frowned. "So you'll have to wait until I finish it, and then we won't leave until *twenty* past noon."

Grant cursed inwardly. "Don't spill anything."

"I'm a very neat eater."

Right. She'd gobbled up his omelet like a starving

woman, getting cheese in her hair, butter on her cheek, and milk on her upper lip. He'd gotten incredibly turned on just watching her.

"Let's go." He strode to the driver's side. "I want to avoid traffic."

"You need me to program my GPS?" Rory leaned into the car to put the drink in the cup-holder and the bag on the floor.

"I do not."

"Did you eat lunch? Sorry, I should've asked if you wanted me to get you something."

"No. Get in the car."

"Hey." She grabbed the open door and pulled herself up onto the running board, shooting him a glare from across the car roof. "Is this how it's going to be? You're all irritable and annoyed because you started something last night that we can't finish? Don't give me that shit, Grant. A hot kiss doesn't negate the fact that I still hate your singing fish and think you're a disgrace to society for not owning a cell phone. But I'm putting all that aside this weekend to pretend I love everything about you. So I'd be most appreciative if you'd start acting as if you like me in return."

Twin blue flames flared in her eyes. Sunlight sparked off the car roof.

"Get in." He pulled his keys from the pocket of his jeans.

With a huff, she swung herself into the car and slammed the door. He got into the driver's seat and started the engine.

Rory shoved the seatbelt lock into place and folded her arms over her chest. Grant guided the car onto Starfish Avenue.

"I don't need to act as if I like you," he said.

"Whatever."

"I *do* like you."

Surprised silence for an instant before she muttered another, "Whatever."

But this time, there was a smile in her voice. Okay, not exactly a smile, but…less of a frown.

His shoulders relaxed. Even though she was irritating, he'd always felt at ease with her. Aside from being a no-bull-shit straight-shooter, Rory was one of the few women who hadn't hit on him over the years or, worse, tried to finagle something from him. She didn't want anything…except to see him get rid of his singing fish, which was probably one of the reasons he kept the piscine warbler around.

He started toward the coastal highway leading north. He'd called his mother to tell her he was bringing a date to the wedding, and her response on his answering machine had been predictably delighted. *I cannot wait to meet her!*

If his mother hadn't been preparing to ambush him with a barrage of eligible women, he might have felt guilty about lying to her. But with Rory as his buffer, he'd not only keep his mother happy, he might even enjoy himself.

He breathed in her smell, something like coconut and bananas. Last night, her scent had been masked by the aromas of cooking. He hadn't expected the sun-averse Rory to smell warm and tropical.

Then paper crinkled, and the odor of processed beans assaulted his nose. He shot her a narrow look as she slathered the soggy burrito with packaged sour cream and crammed a bite into her mouth.

Grant shifted, tightening his grip on the wheel. The "food" was disgusting, but just a glimpse of Rory eating caused heat to collect in his lower body. It was so damned sexy the way she licked her tapered fingers, made little chewing noises, and darted her tongue out to catch a smear of sauce on her lip. She was making him hungry in more ways than one.

"Want some?" She waved the burrito under his nose.

"No, thanks."

"You know, food snobbery is kind of elitist." She pursed her lips around the straw of her drink.

"I'm not a food snob. I just want people to eat *good* food. Trust me, I can make a burrito that will turn you off of all other burritos. Especially fast-food ones."

"Oh, sounds like another challenge." She popped the last of the burrito into her mouth and unwrapped the enchilada. "Though I don't really like the idea of being turned off."

He chuckled. "In this case, I'd recommend it."

"Okay, so prove it the next time we're in the kitchen." She took a bite of the enchilada and spoke around the mouthful. "But I'm actually quite nondiscriminatory when it comes to Mexican food. Or any food, really."

"After you eat more of my food, you'll develop some actual taste." He slanted her a glance. A smear of sour cream decorated her cheek. "That's the second challenge for me. When do you get one?"

"Isn't pretending to be your girlfriend a challenge?"

"It's an agreement. Giving up your cell phone would be a *challenge*."

She laughed and sucked up more cherry coke. "I'm not giving up my cell phone."

"What do you think would happen if you did?"

"Nothing would *happen*." She crumpled up the enchilada wrapper and stuffed it into the bag. "I just need my phone."

"Why?"

"Because I'm a woman who lives in the twenty-first century. And if you have such issues with my phone, you should've asked Madeline Fox to go to the wedding with you."

"Third time you've mentioned Madeline."

"So?" Irritation edged her voice.

He shrugged. "You still sound jealous."

"Well, I'm not. I know what you're doing. You asked me because your parents will be somewhat mollified by the fact that you brought a computer geek home. Even though I'm not in the right *social sphere*, I work in the right industry and know about things like algorithms and mainframe databases. You've probably never brought home a girl like me before, but your parents will approve, right?"

Grant didn't know what to say. Of course she could talk shop with his father and most of the other wedding guests, but he hadn't asked her *because* she was a computer geek.

He'd asked her because—

"Yeah." He flexed his hands on the wheel. "They'll approve."

"Exactly. So stop hassling me about being a tech girl." With a *tsk* of exasperation, she drained her cherry coke and stuck the cup in the cup-holder. "But for the record, you'd better tell me what you've had going on with Madeline."

"What makes you think I had something going on with her?"

"Oh, please. Everyone knows she has the hots for you. Well, most of the women in Bliss Cove have the hots for you, but Madeline makes no secret of it. I saw the way she was looking at you. Like she wanted to eat you up."

Grant's jaw tightened. That was the way he'd felt about *Rory* last night. He could have devoured her.

"Just because she was looking at me doesn't mean we've ever had a thing."

"Have you?"

"No."

"Never?"

*"No."* He shot her a glare, suddenly annoyed by her prying. "I've never dated Madeline Fox or hooked up with her. I've never wanted to."

Rory slipped on her sunglasses and looked out the side window. Though she spoke under her breath, he distinctly heard her murmur, "Good."

RORY DIDN'T USUALLY LIKE LONG CAR RIDES—THE HEAT, THE sun, the smell of asphalt—but the three-hour drive with Grant ended up being quite enjoyable.

Once he stopped griping about her phone and she stopped wondering about his sex life, they had lengthy conversations about movies (he was a fan of dramas and thrillers, she preferred raunchy comedies), Greek mythology (ingrained in her since childhood), *Game of Thrones* (they had to agree to disagree), and whether or not the Bliss Cove Library was haunted (Rory = *not a chance*, Grant = *absolutely*).

He indulged her reggae playlist, asked about her sisters, and refrained from comment when she bought a candy bar and a bag of Sour Patch Kids during a gas stop. By the time he pulled into the parking lot of San Francisco's Ritz-Carlton, she believed this whole weekend would be easier than she'd thought.

Only when she was standing in the bathroom of the fancy hotel, pulling her hair into a sedate knot at her nape, was she beset by an attack of nerves. She was pretending to be the girlfriend of the son of the man who'd founded Intellix…and the rest of his family and guests at his brother's wedding.

While Rory prided herself on her many talents—a natural facility for math, data processing, a good memory, the ability to see through bullshit—*acting* had never been one of them. She'd never even been a tree in an elementary school play.

"You okay in there?" Grant called.

"I'll be out in a sec." Skimming her hands over her hips, she studied herself in the mirror. Callie's pale blue sheath was both elegant and understated, and the matching cashmere cardigan would hide the circuit board tattoo decorating her upper arm.

She swiped on her lipstick and walked out of the bathroom. The door adjoining their rooms was open, and Grant stood at the mirror in his room, knotting his tie. He turned, scanning her from head to toe so thoroughly that her self-consciousness kicked into gear.

"You look great," he said.

"So do you."

Her remark was an understatement. She'd never seen him in a suit before. He looked almost like a stranger—his crisp white shirt fit him to perfection, and his silk tie nestled right in the hollow of his strong throat.

"Guess we both clean up pretty good." He pulled on his suit jacket and buttoned it. "Ready to face the gauntlet?"

"Do we get to raid the minibar when we get back?"

"Definitely."

"Then I'm ready." She picked up her sweater, inhaling as she passed him so she could catch the scent of his aftershave.

As they walked down to the hotel's dining room, he settled his hand on her lower back. Rory's heart jumped. His broad palm burned heat clear up her spine.

"Okay if I touch you in public?" He gave her a rueful glance. "Girlfriend and all."

"Uh…sure." Her voice came out breathless. She was still trying not to think about their intense kiss last night—or how much of a bummer it was that they'd started something they couldn't finish—and she hadn't considered how they'd act around other people. But as a couple, they had to touch each other.

Rory was definitely a fan of consensual touching, but given her reaction to *Grant's* touch, she hoped she wouldn't make a fool of herself by getting all breathless in public.

Conversation rose throughout the massive, high-windowed dining room. Linen-draped tables glittered with crystal glasses and silverware, and elaborate bouquets bloomed from vases. Grant curled his fingers gently through hers.

"Rory, my mother Joanna and my father Edward." He extended his other hand to the handsome, well-dressed couple getting to their feet.

"We are so delighted to meet you, my dear." Joanna Taylor was a lovely woman with perfectly coiffed blond hair and fine, elegant features. She squeezed Rory's hand between hers. "It's been forever since Grant has come home, much less brought anyone with him."

"I'm glad it was me, then." She smiled and turned to

Edward Taylor to shake his hand. Tall and broad-shouldered, he was an older version of Grant, his face settled into strong, distinguished lines enhanced by a neat, graying beard. "Nice meeting you, even if you could scale up the Intellix database architecture by making the grid computing more transparent to the user."

Silence fell. Her face heated. She opened her mouth to apologize when Edward laughed. The tension broke, and the other guests joined in the laughter.

"Did I mention that Rory is a software engineer?" Grant's eyes twinkled at her.

"Then I'd like to find out what she's doing with you." Edward pulled out the chair beside him and motioned for her to sit. "Where do you work, Rory?"

"I'm going to start at Digicore after Thanksgiving." She sat down and glanced warily at Grant, but he looked both comfortable and relaxed as he took a seat next to his mother.

"Hmm." Edward nodded and picked up his drink. "Digicore isn't the best or the biggest, but they're doing some interesting work."

"That's why I accepted the job."

Edward introduced her to the other guests at the table. Though Rory might have found it intimidating to talk to the founder of Intellix, it was entirely different talking to Grant's father. He was curious about her work, her ideas, and how she would change the Intellix database system to make it run more efficiently.

"No more shop talk, you two." Joanna leaned over from the other side of the table, her eyes bright. "Tell us how you met Grant."

"At the tavern." Rory took a sip of wine and shrugged.

"It's not very interesting, I'm sorry to say. My mother owns a bakery in Bliss Cove, and I moved back a couple of years ago after my father passed away. I knew the Mousehole had been sold, but I hadn't met Grant until I stopped by again."

She wouldn't tell them about the grilled cheese sandwich and tomato soup. She hadn't told anyone how he'd made her feel better with that one gesture. Did he even remember it?

"When did he ask you out?" Another woman—Grant's aunt—asked eagerly.

Rory glanced at Grant. "About...how many months ago?"

"Three or four, I think."

"I will never forgive you for not bringing her to meet us sooner." Joanna gave her son a chiding look. "Why did it take you so long to ask her out? You're lucky she was still available."

"I was lucky, indeed." He met Rory's gaze, and a sizzle lit the air between them.

Her belly fluttered. What was wrong with her? It was as if that kiss from last night had settled in her bones, silver and bright like the moon, and was radiating all sorts of never-before-felt sensations toward him.

So strange. She'd always been a woman who could separate the physical from the emotional. She preferred it that way. Her tech jobs had allowed so little room to breathe, and while she loved the mind-bending work, the challenges and problem-solving, she'd always needed to find supplementary ways to exert her body.

She'd run track in high school and college, played volleyball, spent a lot of time hiking and jogging. She'd been discriminatory about her sexual partners, but the act itself had been more of a release than a loving, intimate connection.

Too many encounters with sexist pigs who wanted to demean or dismiss her had left her wary of men in the tech industry. And after the crash-and-burn end of her last career venture, she hadn't sought any kind of *release* during her relatively stress-free stay in Bliss Cove.

Which meant that it really had been a long time. At least a year. Maybe that was why she was getting all hot and bothered about Grant. That, and the fact that the man knew how to kiss. Extremely well. It made her think he also very likely extended that expertise to other sexy acts.

"...for the database design," Edward was saying.

Rory refocused on the conversation. She was here to play a role, not to start imagining what Grant would be like in bed.

While they hadn't discussed what would happen if someone found out that she wasn't really his girlfriend, she wanted the weekend to be a success. Whatever reasons Grant had for his family issues, she wouldn't be the one to make them worse.

"So sorry we're late!" A stunning redhead in what had to be a designer suit sailed up to the table trailed by a handsome young man who had a softer, kinder version of Grant's hard features. "I can't believe the last-minute issues that are coming up."

"Sweetie, that's why you have a wedding planner." Joanna rose to exchange air kisses with the woman. "You should be relaxing on the eve of your wedding. Come and meet Grant's girlfriend."

"Grant has a girlfriend?" Her eyebrows shot up to her hairline.

"Not only that, he brought her along." Joanna waved her hand as if she were a showcase model displaying Rory, the brand-new car. "This is Rory Prescott. Rory, this is our lovely bride Alice, and Grant's younger brother Nathan."

Rory greeted them both, and Grant rose to embrace his brother. Nathan shot Rory a curious smile.

"Funny that you didn't mention her," he remarked, slapping Grant on the back.

"He likes to keep me to himself." Rory winced at the suggestive tone to her voice, but she had little doubt that Nathan suspected she was a decoy. "Thanks for accommodating a plus one. I'm looking forward to the ceremony."

"Not as much as we are." Alice smiled at her fiancé, who responded with a look of such besotted devotion that even Rory's steel-clad heart softened a little.

She enjoyed the rest of the dinner more than she'd expected to. Talking with Edward, and Intellix VP Nathan, was both enlightening and interesting, and Joanna was a master hostess who kept the conversation pinging back and forth about everything from the best hotels in Monte Carlo to the ERA of the San Francisco Giants.

Though Rory had to sit through Alice's tales of wedding-planning woe (*The photographer had initially double-booked! A storm impacted the Alaskan fishing industry and they weren't able to guarantee enough lobster for the guests, so they were serving King crab legs instead! One of the brides-maids gained so much weight that they had to let out her dress!*), once Alice had garnered enough sympathy, she started telling Rory about her job at the San Francisco Museum of Modern Art—which was far more interesting than lobster and bridesmaids.

"Grant, you still slinging burgers?" Edward's voice boomed across the table, silencing all other conversations.

Joanna's expression grew pinched, as if she were watching storm clouds gather on the horizon.

"Still am, Dad." Grant faced his father, his mouth tightening. "You need me to take a look at the Intellix cafeteria menu? See if we can elevate the packaged sandwiches to something edible?"

*Oh, slam.*

"No, thanks." Edward gave a thin smile. "My team is happy with what we offer. They're busy with real work, after all."

"Edward." Joanna's voice held an unmistakable warning.

"Grant did an amazing job revamping the Mousehole Tavern," Rory remarked casually. "It was written up in *Food & Wine* magazine as one of the best rustic restaurants on the West Coast."

"It sounds delightful," Joanna said.

"The *Mousehole Tavern*." Edward said the name as if it tasted unpleasant in his mouth. He took a swallow of scotch and set his napkin down. "It might interest you to know, Rory, that I raised both of my boys the same."

"*We* raised them, Edward," Joanna put in tartly. "And no one wants to hear your complaining right now."

"I'm just stating the facts. It would be an interesting scientific study. Maybe one involving mice." He guffawed and took another drink. "Two mice...or boys...raised the same way. Had all the same privileges. Attended excellent private schools. Never wanted for a thing. Vacations in Europe. All the best technology, of course. One of the boys goes on to graduate from Stanford with a degree in computer science, makes no noise about starting at the bottom of his father's company, and works his way up to a well-deserved

VP position. The other boy works as a kitchen dishwasher and busses tables. As a career goal, he wants to learn how to cook a steak and scramble eggs."

*So what's wrong with that?* Rory barely managed to bite back the remark.

If Edward Taylor belittled his son's career choice, no wonder Grant had distanced himself from his family. Rory knew all too well what it felt like to be treated as *less*— though thankfully never by her family. That had to hurt like hell.

"Yet you're all about fine dining, aren't you, Dad?" An undercurrent of bitterness threaded Grant's question. "You love to eat, so it's not as if you have anything against chefs as a rule. But the fact that *your son* wanted to work in a kitchen has always had you in a rage."

"Grant, your father's point is that you had a great deal of privilege that was intended to set you on the right path," Joanna said quietly.

"Mom, cooking obviously *is* the right path for Grant," Nathan put in. "Neither one of us was born with source coding in our DNA."

"I'm pretty sure I was." Rory polished off the last bite of salmon, eyeing Edward narrowly. "And don't you think a developer who's not totally committed to his or her work and who doesn't love what they do is far worse than no developer at all?"

His mouth compressed. "You don't have to be born with a talent to learn how to do something well."

"But life is about doing what you love, isn't it?" piped up Aunt Lucy. "Shall we have dessert?"

Conversation rose again, and Rory leaned closer to

Edward. "I know it's none of my business, but he really is an excellent chef."

"You're right." Edward's jaw tightened. "It's none of your business. But do you see that woman?"

He nodded toward Joanna, who was conversing with Lucy.

"She and I met when we were undergrads." Edward's expression softened a bit. "Twenty years old. She was the only person who didn't laugh when I told her I wanted to start a computer company. She married me even though I had nothing. For years, I couldn't even afford to give her a proper wedding ring. But she didn't waver. Stuck by me through it all…the starts and stops, the failures, the times when I was ready to give up. I wouldn't be where I am without her. Intellix might not even exist without her. And she has been heartbroken by Grant's rejection of everything she wanted for him. Everything we've worked to provide."

Edward stabbed his fork into his steak. "I won't stand for it. I'll remind him every chance I get that hurting his mother is unacceptable in every way."

He turned to the person seated on his other side, effectively dismissing her.

Rory caught Grant looking at her. She found it very difficult to believe that he was intentionally hurting his mother. He tapped his watch and mouthed *Let's go.*

"We'll see you all tomorrow." Pushing back his chair, he stood and turned to say goodbye to his brother and Alice.

As Rory said her goodbyes and thank-yous, Joanna rounded the table to her side.

"Tomorrow morning, we're taking Alice to the spa for a few hours so she can relax before getting ready for the wedding," Joanna explained. "Hot stone massage, facial, mud-bath, the works. I insist you join us."

"Oh." Rory shot Grant a desperate look, but he was speaking to his aunt. "I'm not really a spa kind of girl."

"Nonsense. Every woman is a *spa kind of girl*." Joanna narrowed her eyes on Rory's face. "Your skin is lovely, but you might want to get those blackheads taken care of. The aestheticians can also show you how to enhance your features with makeup…red lipstick can be stunning, but with your pale skin, it's a bit harsh."

Rory forced a smile. She'd heard close to the same thing from her own mother over the years.

"A car will pick you up at nine." Joanna patted Rory's arm. "I'll arrange a wake-up call just in case. I do apologize for Edward. He promised he wouldn't cause a scene, but he has a hard time concealing his disappointment."

Something twisted in Rory's chest. "He has no reason to be disappointed in Grant. Neither do you."

"Oh, I know, my dear." Joanna smiled, though sadness touched her eyes. "Sometimes it's just hard to let go of expectations. It breaks my heart that Grant's choices have caused such a rift in our family."

"Maybe…" Rory swallowed the suggestion that surfaced like a piece of sea glass in her mind. She had no right to interfere in Grant's relationship with his family.

"See you tomorrow," she said instead.

After Joanna left, Grant approached. A faint line of concern etched his forehead. "Was she asking about *our* wedding plans?"

"No, but I have to go for a hot stone massage and facial

tomorrow." Rory shifted on her uncomfortable heels. "I hope she hasn't scheduled me for a bikini wax."

He grinned. "Thanks for taking one for the team. And sorry about my father."

"Tantrum aside, I like him." She walked beside him to the elevator. "I'm sorry if I made things awkward by what I said."

"You didn't." He glanced at her. "I appreciated what you said."

"It just doesn't seem like your dad is being fair. Has he ever tried your food?"

"Once when I was working up in Seattle, my mom dragged him to the restaurant where I was a sous-chef. She hoped it would soften him up."

"Did it?"

"He ate everything I made, but didn't actually tell me he liked it." Grant tossed her a rueful grin. "So, no. It didn't soften him up."

"That kind of sucks."

"Yeah." He unlocked the hotel room door and stepped aside to let her enter. "I don't like complaining about it, though. There are far worse things than your parents wanting a certain life for you."

"But it's not what you want." Rory sank into a chair and kicked off her shoes.

"I have what I want now, so it doesn't matter anymore." After tossing his suit jacket on the bed, he lifted his arms above his head for a stretch. His shirt tugged over his chest, and his shoulder muscles bunched.

"What about your mother? It sounds like she was supportive."

He shook his head, his mouth tightening. "I hate that she's

upset by all this, but unfortunately, she was part of the problem. She wanted me to work for Intellix, of course, and she still wants me back in the fold, married to the right girl, attending all her parties and events. Another good son she can show off."

"Sounds like a lot of pressure."

"Yeah." He cracked open a bottle of Jack Daniel's from the minibar and sloshed the liquor into two glasses. He handed her one, his fingers brushing hers. "It's one of the reasons I ended up striking out on my own. I've been working in kitchens since college, but about eight years ago, I found a job at a restaurant in San Francisco. So I was living close to my parents again, and I figured I'd make my mother happy by going to parties and whatnot. Couldn't hurt. At a museum benefit dinner, I met Vivian. We dated for a while and eventually I asked her to marry me."

Rory lifted her eyebrow. "You were engaged?"

He downed a swallow of his drink. "Until I found out that my mother had set us up. She'd known Vivian and her family well and she wanted us to get married. A family connection thing, like joining dynasties. Vivian knew exactly what was going on. I was the idiot who thought we were in love."

Though his tone was self-deprecating, it contained a hint of embarrassment. Indignation filled her.

"She was using you," she said flatly.

"Wasn't the first time." Grant shrugged. "I'd been dealing with that my whole life. Nathan too, though he handled it better. The thing was...when I came back to work at the Golden Fork and tried to make amends with my parents, I thought I'd figured it out. I was cooking at this great restaurant, my mother was happy because I was socializing the way she wanted me to, I got to hang out with Nathan a lot, and for a while my father didn't even mention me working for Intellix. Seemed like I'd found a way to fix everything that was wrong."

A band constricted around Rory's heart. She swirled the liquor in her glass. "But you didn't."

"No." He pulled at his tie, his mouth compressing. "Vivian, her mother, and my mother had set up our meeting, and she was a great actress. Every time I sensed something was off, I talked myself out of my suspicions. I wanted it to work. I also wanted to be married for love, family, building a life together…all that sappy stuff."

"When did you realize Vivian didn't want the same thing?"

"When I found her texts to another man." He swallowed the last of the whiskey and set the glass back on the table. "She made it abundantly clear why she had to be with me and not him, even though he was the one she loved. Needless to say, that was the end of our engagement. My mother tried to talk me out of the break-up, too. She still wanted her plan to work. She's a master at interfering in other people's lives, consequences be damned."

The tightness around her heart intensified. Rory didn't want to embarrass him or make him think she was pitying him by saying *I'm sorry*.

Truth be told, she was sorry he'd been hurt, but she wasn't sorry that he'd escaped Vivian before they'd actually gotten married. She wasn't sorry that he'd fought back against his mother's manipulations.

She rose, rubbing a slight ache in her lower back. "Vivian is going to be at the wedding, isn't she?"

"Yeah." He yanked his tie off, the silk rustling against his tailored shirt. "I don't care about her anymore, obviously, but I'm not setting myself up for a repeat of the whole disaster either. My mother won't be over the break-up until I'm married and settled down. Having you here will get her off my case so she can focus on what's really important, which is Nathan's wedding."

"Well, I'm glad I can help."

"You're doing more than helping." He indicated the mini-bar. "Do you want another drink?"

"No, I should get some sleep." Rory bent to pick up her shoes. "I need to rest up for a morning of facials and mud baths."

"I meant what I said." He walked her to the door adjoining their rooms. "You're a lifesaver."

She lifted an eyebrow. "What flavor?"

"Pork rinds."

She laughed. Grant's eyes crinkled in responding amusement. He lifted a hand as if he were going to touch her—and her entire body went electric with anticipation—but then he dropped his hand back to his side.

"Get a good night's sleep," he said.

"You too." Her voice came out breathless.

She walked to her room and closed the door behind her. She didn't know whether to be pleased or worried about the fact that she and Grant appeared to have more in common than she'd ever realized before.

# CHAPTER 6

"*W*here'd you find her?" Nathan eyed Grant in the reflection of the mirror as he fastened his bow-tie. "Rent-A-Chick?"

"Watch it." Grant scowled. "She's a good friend and my legitimate date."

"I'm not saying I don't like her." Nathan stepped back to admire himself in the mirror. "I'm actually impressed that you came up with a plus one who's both really hot and can talk shop with Dad. That'll stick in Vivian's craw."

"That's not why I brought Rory." Grant pushed to his feet. He'd spent the morning with his brother and groomsmen, but this was the first time he and Nathan had been alone all day. "I'm sick of Mom hoping I'll marry a girl from the right family who will magically get me to move back to the Bay Area."

"I overheard Rory telling Dad she'll be starting at Digi-core after Thanksgiving." Nathan picked a piece of lint off the sleeve of his tuxedo. "Does that mean she's moving to San Jose?"

"Yeah." An odd tightness spread through Grant's shoulders.

Though he'd known Rory was back in Bliss Cove "temporarily," he'd never really considered the fact that she would move away one day. She deserved a great job, and obviously a woman with a brain like hers needed to live in the hub of the tech industry, but…he'd gotten used to having her around.

"So what's going to happen to your relationship when she moves?" Nathan slanted him a curious glance.

Grant shrugged and pushed to his feet. "Guess we'll figure it out. Thanks for your concern. Now go get married."

"Oh, shit." Nathan's mouth opened, and shock dawned in his eyes. "I'm getting *married*."

Grant grinned and clapped a hand on his brother's shoulder. "Good luck, man."

He pulled Nathan into an embrace before returning to his own hotel room to get dressed. He and Rory had agreed to meet in the hotel lobby at four, and he didn't know whether or not to be wary about the recap of her spa day with Alice, his mother, and God knew how many other women. He wasn't worried about Rory saying anything that might give away their ruse, but he didn't want her to be uncomfortable or anxious. He'd have serious issues with anyone who made her feel that way.

After knotting his blue-and-gray silk tie, he went to the lobby. Many of the wedding guests were also staying at the Ritz-Carlton, and they teemed around the lobby in suits and evening gowns like a flotilla of ships. People stopped to greet him with the usual comments and questions—*hello, congratulations to Nathan, how've you been?*

He responded politely, but sensed their inevitable judgements simmering under the surface. *How could he walk away from his family? So ungrateful. Clearly he doesn't appreciate everything he had.*

Still, none of it mattered anymore. He'd made his choice. Even if he'd wanted to change it, which he didn't, entering the tech industry at thirty-five when you didn't even have a cell phone was hardly a bang-up start.

His heart thumped against his ribs. He turned. Rory was coming out of the elevator, stunning in a sequin-and-lace, rose-colored cocktail dress that flowed from a fitted bodice into gentle folds around her knees. Her hair was pulled into a fancy knot with little tendrils framing her face, and she wore a light coating of makeup that enhanced her features.

Beautiful as she was, she didn't look at all like the T-shirt-wearing Rory who complained about his singing fish and lack of technology.

"Hi." She stopped, indicating his suit. "Again, you look good."

"So do you. Very…shiny and sparkly."

"The shine is because I was exfoliated within an inch of my life."

He smiled in sympathy. "Was it horrible?"

"Not really." She extended her bare arm. "My skin is as smooth as a baby's butt. Feel."

He skimmed his hand over her arm. His blood heated. As far as he could tell, her skin felt the same as it had when he'd touched her in the Mousehole kitchen. Velvet, silk, and pure warmth.

Rory pulled her arm away from him and stepped back so abruptly that she teetered on her heels.

"Whoa." He closed his hand around her wrist.

Her pulse raced under his fingertips. She was so damned *responsive*.

He'd always known she had fire because of the spark in her blue eyes and the way she bitched at him, but he'd also seen her reaction to the men who tried to hit on her at the Mousehole. Her cold look alone gave them frostbite. Grant always greatly enjoyed watching the dickwads stammer and slink away from her.

Which begged the question…when was the last time she had a boyfriend? Or a date? Or sex? She'd needled him about his lack of dating, but what about her?

Though he fully intended to find out, half an hour before his brother's wedding was bad timing.

Releasing Rory's wrist, he indicated the town cars and limos clustered outside the hotel's front doors. "The car will take us to the church first, then the reception."

"Great. I hope there'll be cake."

They were whisked away to the cathedral, where large bouquets and ribbons decorated the pews, and guests lined up to sign a leather guest book. An usher led them to their seats in the front row.

The ceremony was elaborate but heartfelt, with his parents heading the processional of a dozen bridesmaids and groomsmen. Alice was resplendent in a white Cinderella gown, and Grant didn't even have to look at his little brother to sense Nathan's joy over marrying her.

While Grant had never been into the show-off nature of weddings, he was very glad he'd come to witness his brother and Alice's happiness. He might've even experienced a tightness in his throat when Nathan choked up while reciting his vows.

After the newlywed couple departed to resounding applause, Grant had to accompany his parents for picture-taking. To avoid Joanna coercing her into the photos, Rory told him she'd meet him at the reception.

During the excessive picture-taking, Grant's impatience stretched thin. He almost wished he had a cell phone so he could text Rory and make sure she wasn't bored or feeling out of place among people she didn't know.

When the photographer was finally done, he hurried to the reception hall, which was housed in a massive classical building with a vast staircase sweeping up to a columned porch. As he'd expected, his parents and Alice's parents had spared no expense for the wedding reception.

The ballroom was like a palace with flowers everywhere —including vast bouquets suspended from the coffered ceiling—chairs decorated with immense gauzy bows, glittering china place settings, and a head table elevated on a carpeted dais. Guests mingled and wandered to and from the open bar as they waited for the sit-down dinner to be served.

When he saw that he and Rory were seated at a table of his father's friends, he sent his brother a silent thank-you for ensuring they weren't at the *single women* table. After greeting the other guests and introducing Rory, he went to the bar to get them both drinks.

"Hello, Grant."

Tension stiffened his spine. Vivian stepped into the space beside him, as lovely and elegant as ever in a blue gown that skimmed her slender figure. Her blond hair was twisted in a French knot, and diamonds glittered at her throat and ears.

"A glass of Merlot and an old-fashioned," he told the bartender. "Hello, Vivian."

"Alice told me you'd be here. It's been a long time."

"Yes, it has." He waited to experience some emotion—anger, hurt, regret—but there was nothing. Not even sadness over what he'd thought he'd lost. He'd never even had *what he'd thought* in the first place.

Vivian stepped forward, extending her arms. He gave her a perfunctory embrace, his nose filling with the smell of expensive perfume before he moved away from her.

"You look fantastic." She smiled and patted his lapel. "It's been far too long since you've been back. Believe me, I've taken notice."

"It's been awhile." He let his gaze slide to the guests milling around the reception hall. "How have you been?"

"Just fine, thanks." She moved her hand down his chest. "You look wonderful. All that cooking and whatnot clearly agrees with you."

He backed up another step to try and politely get her to stop touching him. She stepped forward, her hand now inside his jacket.

"Where's your boyfriend, Vivian?" He pushed her hand away from him.

"You mean Jordy? That didn't last. I told you I was sorry."

"Obviously that didn't make a difference."

"So when are you moving back to civilization, Grant?" She lifted her eyebrows in inquiry. "I miss seeing you around. Daddy has season tickets to both the opera and the Giants, you know. We could have a lot of fun again."

"Oh, *there* you are!" Rory's voice rose above the chatter and noise as she approached.

"Rory." Relieved, Grant grabbed her arm and hauled her closer. "Meet Vivian, an old friend of the family."

"Well, not *old*." Vivian gave him an arch smile, her eyes frosting over as she looked at Rory. "And you are?"

"Vivian, this is my girlfriend Rory." To emphasize the point—Vivian had never been good at taking a hint—he wrapped his arm around Rory's waist and pulled her against him.

"Girlfriend." Vivian's smile remained fixed in place, though her eyes darkened. "Last I heard, Grant Taylor had sworn off girlfriends. To say nothing of *fiancées*."

Grant's shoulders tensed. "Sounds like you heard wrong."

"Or I changed his mind." Rory smiled with a sweetness like honey. "The right woman can do that, you know. Just as the wrong one can scar a man for life. Would you excuse us, please? I'm so anxious to meet the rest of Grant's family. I plan to see a lot of them all in the near future."

She grabbed his hand and tugged him back toward the table. "Well, she's pretty much what I expected."

"Yeah. My only regret is that I didn't figure it out sooner. Thanks for the save."

"Grant!" A matronly woman in a glittering gown swept toward him, brandishing a martini. "How wonderful to see you again. Come say hello to my Thomas. He's visiting from London, where he's working with a large financial company. I know he'll want to catch up."

She grasped his arm firmly. Rory smiled and wiggled her fingers in sympathetic farewell as Mrs. Watterson steered him toward her Thomas.

Even when he was getting bored out of his mind listening

to Thomas drone on about the value of the pound versus the dollar, Grant kept his gaze on Rory.

She wandered the room, plucking hors d'oeuvres off trays, chatting with the bartender and whatever guest happened to be standing alone. At one point, he caught her helping one of the bridesmaids untangle her dress from the arm of a chair where it had snagged.

Despite her tough-girl attitude and her snark, Rory was a softie at heart. She'd always been steadfastly there for her sisters and mother, committed to her work, always showing up when and where she was needed.

Warmth and something else swirled in Grant's chest. Tenderness. Regret over the fact that Rory would be leaving Bliss Cove soon. For some reason, it felt like it was happening *too soon*. As if something wasn't quite finished, though he didn't know what.

He did know that while he no longer felt anything for Vivian, he'd been storing up a lot of feelings for Rory.

# CHAPTER 7

*R*ory watched Grant navigate the reception, his tall, powerful figure weaving around the tables like a blade slicing through cloth.

Though he moved with the same confidence and grace at the Mousehole, a guardedness surrounded him in the reception hall, as if he were protecting himself from both criticism and opportunists. While everyone at the tavern loved him, no one there ever wanted anything from him that he wasn't willing to give.

That wasn't the case here. Vivian aside, other people in his family's circle clearly wanted and expected things from Grant Taylor. Several guests greeted him with warmth and embraces, but an equal number made underhanded remarks (*"Your mother wants you at the altar next." "Your father could use you at Intellix." "Still wasting your talent, son?"*).

To his credit, Grant responded with polite graciousness, though Rory saw the tension lining his shoulders and the stiffness of his spine.

A polished, elegant woman seated at a table grabbed his wrist as he passed, bringing him to a halt.

Rory started to rise, instinctively wanting to be at his side. Then she saw Vivian sitting in the chair beside the woman, and the similarity in their features left no doubt that they were mother and daughter.

She sank back into her chair. One confrontation with Grant's ex-fiancée was enough. Though she was supposed to be his girlfriend, she didn't want to make herself memorable to this circle of people.

Grant spoke for a few minutes with the older woman, who indicated Vivian. He smiled, his eyes emptying. If Rory had any curiosity about his lingering feelings for the other woman, they disappeared in that instant. He didn't even dislike Vivian—not anymore, at least.

Rory reached for her wineglass, dispelling a sudden unease. She would hate to be the recipient of Grant's *indifference*.

He detached his arm from the woman, nodded curtly, and strode back to the table. The tightness in Rory's chest eased as he took his place beside her.

"You okay?" she whispered.

"I am now." He shot her a faint smile.

"Attention, please." A fork clinked on glass, and Edward Taylor rose from the head table. "Before the dancing begins, we'd like to make several toasts to the happy couple."

The chatter died down.

"I've been lucky in many ways." Edward settled his hand on Nathan's shoulder. "I started my company at the right moment in time. I married the love of my life. I was there when the Giants won the pennant"—the guests laughed—"and I've seen more of the world than I thought I would. All of that has been a great fortune. But I won the parenting lottery with my son Nathan. I'm exceeding proud to have a son who is so dedicated, intelligent, and determined to do what's right not only for him, but for his family. Not every son possesses such loyalty and good character."

Rory's stomach clenched. *Really, Edward?*

Joanna, seated at her husband's left, thinned her mouth into a tight line. Nathan pulled at his bow-tie with discomfort.

"Not every son values his upbringing and is grateful for the privileges he's been given," Edward continued. "Not every son recognizes the meaning of the word *family*. But Nathan does. That is just one reason why I'm so pleased that today he and Alice are starting the journey to create a family of their own."

Applause rose along with a few hoots of approval. Edward ended with a toast to the couple and resumed his seat. Joanna grabbed his arm and hissed a few angry words in his ear.

Rory risked a glance at Grant. His face was expressionless, but a muscle ticked in his jaw. She considered asking him to leave, but he would never walk out and disrupt his brother's reception.

Alice's father rose for a speech. Thankfully, no one else lacked the grace to make underhanded comments about Grant, choosing instead to focus on the happiness of the newlywed couple.

Dinner followed—the King crab legs were delicious—then the cutting of the four-tiered cake and dancing. Though Rory warned Grant that she was a terrible dancer, he turned out to possess such expertise that after two spins around the floor, she was ready to audition for Broadway.

"Where did you learn how to dance?" Breathless and flushed, she let him twirl her again.

"Ten years of private lessons." He shook his head with a humorless laugh. "My mother wanted to make sure Nathan and I knew how to dance with a woman. I drew the line when she tried to sign me up for ballroom dancing competitions."

Rory grinned at the thought of a younger Grant dressed in a glittery sequined costume. "You'd rather make salsa than dance the salsa."

He chuckled. "I'm better at the former, too."

"Grant!" Nathan barreled across the dance floor. A trickle of sweat ran down his temple. "You're not going to believe this."

Grant brought him and Rory to a halt, her hand still encased in his and his arm around her waist. "You want to cut in, all you have to do is ask."

"I don't want to cut in." Nathan threw Rory an apologetic look. "No offense."

"None taken."

"Man, you gotta do something." Nathan grabbed his brother's sleeve, his forehead crinkling with desperation. "This is, like, an epic disaster. I know there's been a lot of champagne and stuff, but I don't think she's drunk. I think she's serious."

"Hold up." Releasing Rory, Grant turned to his younger brother. Concern darkened his eyes. "What are you talking about?"

"*Mom.*" Nathan spread his arm out in agitation. "Maybe she's finally gone off the deep end after Dad's little shade-throwing speech, but she just decided that wouldn't it be *wonderful* if she and Dad took a much-needed vacation."

"So what's wrong with that?"

Nathan fisted his hands in Grant's suit jacket, horror widening his eyes. "A vacation with me and Alice *on our honeymoon.*"

"What?"

"Whoa," Rory murmured.

"Right?" Nathan stared at her, still clutching Grant's jacket. "It's insane."

"She's not serious." Grant shook his head in disbelief. "She and Dad are not going with you on your honeymoon."

"That's what I thought at first, but I swear to God, she thinks she had the most brilliant idea since what's-his-name discovered electricity. She was just going off about how Dad's been under so much stress lately and trying to explain why he was such an asshole in his speech, and how much work she's done planning the wedding, then she announces that they're going to Bali for a week for some much-needed R&R and *staying in the same hotel as me and Alice.* I'm about to have a heart attack."

"First, chill out for a second." Grant took hold of his brother's shoulders and gave him a slight shake. "Did you tell her no fucking way? In nicer words?"

"Yeah, I told her no! And she got all pouty and reminded me that she and Dad had sprung for half the wedding and the entire honeymoon and spared no expense at all, which is true, but really? Our *honeymoon*?"

"What did Dad say?"

"Nothing! He got all stone-faced and annoyed, but he didn't say no. *He didn't say no, man.*"

"When are you leaving?"

"Tomorrow morning." Nathan swiveled to look at the head table, where Joanna was busy texting on her phone and chatting with another woman. "She already called Simon and told him to book the flight for her and Dad, and to arrange for them to stay in the suite next to ours. The same flight. The *next-door* suite. I can't take it. I can't even tell Alice. She loves Mom, but aside from being the biggest meddler of all time, Mom has been a total mother-of-the-groom bridezilla or whatever. Alice really needs a break from her. If I tell her Mom's going to be on our honeymoon, Alice will *cry*. She will sob. The only reason I want my wife weeping on our honeymoon is because she can't believe how happy she is."

"Okay." Grant pulled in a breath and squeezed his brother's shoulder. "I'll figure something out."

"What?"

"I don't know yet. I said I *will* figure something out."

"I can't have Mom and Dad anywhere near Indonesia." Nathan scraped his hands frantically through his hair. "I don't even want them in the southern hemisphere. And knowing they're in the same hotel, right next door…Jesus, I probably wouldn't even be able to get it up." He winced. "Sorry, Rory."

"I can see how that would kill the mood," she agreed.

"It will *serial kill* the mood." Nathan clutched Grant's lapels again. "You gotta help me, man. Do something."

"I will."

"What?"

"Still future tense." Grant detached his brother's fists from his jacket and glanced at Rory. "I'll come find you in a few minutes. Sorry about this."

"Let me know if there's anything I can do to help." She gave Nathan a sympathetic pat on the shoulder and returned to the table. Joanna was still chatting happily and busy on her phone—maybe looking up "things to do" in Bali for her and the newlyweds.

Grant would take care of it. There was no question in Rory's mind that he'd fix this for his brother and Alice. The certainty of the thought didn't surprise her. For the past two years, he'd been the most dependable person she knew.

She watched as he stood at the side of the room with Nathan, still apparently talking his brother off the ledge.

A fluttering sensation appeared in her chest. She hadn't quite realized until recently just how much she'd come to count on Grant. Stupid singing fish, artichoke soup, faded T-shirts, and all.

As she was eating another piece of cake, he returned to the table and sat down. Lines bracketed his mouth, and his shoulders were still tense.

"Any luck?" she asked.

"I haven't been able to get my mother alone yet. I don't want to wait until after the reception because she could very well leave for the airport right away. If she—"

"Grant, guess what?" Joanna sailed toward them, dragging Edward behind her. "I finally convinced your father to take a vacation."

"*Convinced* is not the right word." Edward's features settled into a heavy frown.

"That's great, Mom. Listen, I—"

"I've decided that since Nathan and Alice are going to Indonesia, this would be a perfect opportunity for your father and I to tag along!" Joanna held up a hand with a laugh. "I know, I know. It's their honeymoon. But as I explained to Nathan, we're not going to monopolize all their time. I've found a few activities we can do together, like elephant riding and Balinese massages, and perhaps some visits to the temples. But, of course, Nathan and Alice will want to spend time alone, so—"

"Mom." Grant stood so fast that his chair almost tipped over backward. "Nathan and Alice want to spend *all* their time alone on their honeymoon. You and Dad need to go somewhere else. Like Hawaii."

"Exactly what I said," Edward muttered.

"I've been to Hawaii a million times." Joanna sighed and lifted her hands. "Neither your father nor I have been to Bali and, honestly, it's not as if we're going to be staying *in* the honeymoon suite. We'll just be next door. Rory understands, don't you, dear? Oh, by the way, I do hope you'll join us for breakfast tomorrow morning in the hotel restaurant."

Grant closed his hand on Rory's shoulder in a silent signal. She picked up her beaded pocketbook and stood.

"Sorry, Mom, but we're going to hit the road early." He put his hand on Rory's back, steering her toward the coat check. "We both have to get back to work."

"Well, that's disappointing." Her face falling for an instant, Joanna hurried to catch up with them. "How long of a drive is it to...what's it called?"

"Bliss Cove."

"Oh, yes. I looked it up when you first moved there, didn't I, Edward?" Joanna beamed at her husband, who was still beside her like a massive stone statue. "I suggested that we drive to Los Angeles and stop in Bliss Cove on the way, but of course your father insisted on flying. Anyway, I wanted to let you know about our trip to Bali in case you need to reach us."

"Mom, you cannot join Nathan and Alice on their honeymoon." Grant stopped and faced his mother again. A muscle ticked in his jaw. "Besides, I'm sure Dad can't take the time off."

"Nonsense. He's long overdue for a vacation, and my women's club is closed for restoration this coming week. We're going to think of it as our second honeymoon. The timing is perfect."

"Then go somewhere else." Grant's voice hardened. "You have *got* to stop interfering in people's lives like this. Nathan and Alice deserve the time alone. There are countless other places you and Dad can go."

"I don't want to go to Europe again." Joanna rolled her eyes, making it sound as if Europe were the vacation equivalent of watching paint dry. "I'd love to spend a week relaxing by the beach...oh! I just had a thought. I suppose we *could* come and visit you and Rory in Bliss Cove instead."

Grant looked up sharply. Rory's heart stuttered. She'd thought yesterday that maybe if Edward and Joanna actually saw where Grant lived and worked, they might ease up on him. But she hadn't expected Joanna to make the suggestion herself. And right now?

"This week isn't a good time, Mom." Grant sounded as if he were speaking through clenched teeth.

"Nonsense." His mother waved a dismissive hand. "You just told me we need to go *somewhere else*. Well, what better *somewhere else* is there than where you and Rory live? We do see Nathan and Alice all the time, and of course we rarely see you. It's a wonderful solution."

"There's not much going on in town this coming week," Rory said quickly. "You should come around Christmas time. Bliss Cove goes nuts over the holidays. Winter Carnival, Gingerbread House contest, Polar Bear Swim, you name it. Super fun stuff. Well worth waiting for."

"Wait a moment." Joanna furrowed her brow and took her phone from her purse. "Didn't I read something about a Harvest Festival in Bliss Cove this coming weekend? It sounded quite charming."

Rory forced a weak smile. "I almost forgot about that."

"We are not going to Bliss Cove," Edward snapped, his frown slashing lines on either side of his mouth.

"Oh, excuse me." Joanna bristled and shot her husband an icicle-cold glare. "May I speak to you alone for a moment?"

"You may." Straightening his shoulders, he led the way to a nearby column, where Joanna stretched to all of her five-foot-three-with-heels height and began berating him in a low voice.

Grant rubbed his head, as if he were fighting a painful ache. "Rory, I—"

"Edward, how dare you?" Joanna's angry whisper carried to them with crystal-clear acoustics. "You must be under the impression that you have a say in this matter when, after your unpleasant little innuendos for which you still owe both of your sons and me an apology, you have none whatsoever."

She poked her husband in the chest. "After all the work I have done to plan this wedding, you have the nerve to disrespect this family like that. I'm going to be kind and chalk it up to stress, overwork, and one too many cocktails, which is the reason we're taking a vacation. And for the life of me, Edward Taylor, we're going where I say we're going."

Beneath Rory's lingering shock, a faint respect for Joanna Taylor began to form.

"As I was saying, the Harvest Festival looks delightful." Joanna smiled as she swept back toward them. She scrolled on her phone. "Music, hayrides, a parade, arts and crafts... why, there's even a pie contest. How quaint. No elephants, but I suppose you can't have everything. I did rather have my heart set on Bali, but it's not too late to change our plans."

Grant gave a strained smile that came out more like a grimace. "Mom, the inn and the B&Bs are booked for the festival. There's nowhere for you to stay."

"Well, that's not a problem at all." Joanna blinked. "Didn't you say there's a cottage behind your little tavern? We'll stay there."

Rory tried not to groan aloud. Edward grunted a noise of irritation and took out his phone.

"You'd hate staying in the cottage." Grant shook his head. "It doesn't even have a full kitchen."

"Perfect! It'll be like camping."

"You've never camped, Mom."

"Well, it's about time I did, isn't it?" Joanna looked up at her husband again, eyes sparkling. "It sounds like fun. We can get a quilt and roast marshmallows in the fireplace. Won't that be romantic, Edward? I'll text Simon to make the changes in our itinerary."

"I'm sure we can find you somewhere else to stay." A hint of desperation edged Grant's voice.

"I won't hear of it. I insist on staying in the cottage."

"One week." Edward pulled his heavy eyebrows together. "That's all I'm agreeing to."

"With your delightful company, I'm sure that's all the rest

of us will be able to handle." Joanna gave his lapel a sharp tug. "I'd strongly suggest you get into a second honeymoon mentality, Edward."

"With you at my side, what choice do I have?" He pinched her cheek.

A flush rose to her face as she suppressed a smile. Edward winked at her and strode toward the bar. Joanna turned back to Grant and Rory.

"We'll plan to drive down on Wednesday," she announced. "You can show us around, and we'll go to all the festival events, and maybe we can even get tickets to a show at the local theater or whatever. All right?"

Grant dragged a hand through his hair, tightening his fingers around the thick strands as if he were ready to pull them out.

"Well played, Mom," he muttered. "Very well played."

"Drive safely on your trip back." Joanna gave them a bright smile. "I'll send you all the details of our visit tomorrow. This is going to be so much fun!"

"*Fun*," Grant remarked, "is not the word I would use."

With a little wave, Joanna returned to the party in a sweep of taffeta.

As she watched the other woman depart, Rory shook her head with a combination of disbelief and grudging respect. "Damn."

"That's not the word I would use either," Grant said darkly as he strode toward the coat check. "But you got the four-letter part right."

# CHAPTER 8

"We'll tell them we broke up." Grant pulled down the sun visor and guided the car onto the highway leading back to Bliss Cove. "Happens all the time."

The flippant note in his voice sparked Rory with irritation. "Then what if your mother is so upset by our break-up that she books the next flight to Bali?"

"She's not going to Bali." Exasperation threaded his voice. "She never *was* going to Bali. This was a ploy to get both me and my father to tolerate a week-long visit to Bliss Cove because she knew neither one of us would agree to it any other way."

"I realize that, but are you entirely certain she *wouldn't* fly off to Bali if things don't go exactly as she wants them to? That woman is not the type to make a threat and not follow through."

Grant compressed his mouth into a tight line. Despite Rory's anxiety about this curveball and her knowledge that

Joanna Taylor had a ruthlessly manipulative streak, she couldn't help admiring her just a tad.

Clearly, the woman was the power behind the throne. She'd have been a force to be reckoned with in Tudor England. Hell, she was a force now.

"She said she's coming to spend time with *us*," Rory continued. "Even if a break-up doesn't send her off to join the newlyweds on their honeymoon, she'll go on the prowl for you again. In Bliss Cove, there's a good chance she'll meet Madeline Fox, and if Madeline thinks she can get to you through your mother, then look out, Grant Taylor, because there is no way you can battle both of those women alone."

"Of course I…okay, you're probably right."

"And have you forgotten I still need a place to stay?" Wishing she had a bag of gummy bears to gnaw on, Rory unlocked her phone screen and pulled up a game of Clash Royale to give herself something to do. "Everything is still booked for the Harvest Festival through next weekend. What am I going to do when your parents stay in the cottage?"

Grant flexed his hands on the steering wheel. "You can move into my house."

"Your house? Do you not remember giving me your Boo Radley crap about not wanting anyone *around*? You only let me stay in the cottage because you needed something from me. Now you're asking me to move in?"

"Just for a week." Grant threw her a scowl. "My parents will stay in the cottage, you'll move into my house, and we'll pretend like we're living together."

"Whoa there, Buckaroo Banzai." Rory misjudged her opponent's attack. Her tower crumbled. She dropped the phone back into her lap. "I agreed to pretend to be your date for a wedding. I did not agree to pretend to be your live-in girlfriend."

"Okay." He heaved a sigh and rubbed the back of his neck. "I'll give you Bob."

"What?"

"The singing fish. Bob. Do this for one more week while my parents are visiting, and you can have the fish."

Rory blinked. "I hate the fish. Why would I want it? And seriously...*Bob*?"

"It's a pun."

"I don't get it."

"A *bobber* is a float attached to a fishing line."

"I don't fish."

"You were fishing yesterday for information about Madeline." He slanted her a knowing look.

Heat rose her to cheeks. "I don't fish *in the ocean*. So why would I want your stupid singing fish?"

"You can do whatever you want with it. Take it apart. Throw it away. Crush it with a sledgehammer. Pretend to be my girlfriend for one more week, and neither you nor anyone else will have to suffer through Bob's rendition of 'Love Me Tender' ever again."

"Hmm." She pursed her lips. "Tempting. Why didn't you name him Elvis Fishley? Now that would have been funny."

"*And* I'll cook for you." He glowered at her. "If we're not eating out, I'll make you three large, delicious, well-balanced meals a day until you leave."

"Done."

Not a bad deal, all things considered. It wasn't as if she'd have to hang around Grant and his parents every minute. She could pretend she had some coding contract work and other things to do, so it shouldn't be too difficult.

*Except*...

She shifted and fidgeted with her phone. "So your place is a one-bedroom right?"

"You can take the bed. I'll sleep on the sofa."

"Great." She pulled up a new game of Clash Royale.

That was *not* disappointment poking her like a thorn.

RORY KNEW SHE WAS IN TROUBLE WHEN SHE WALKED INTO Sugar Joy for her Monday afternoon shift, and her mother asked, as usual, "How was your weekend, dear?"

"Great, thanks." She hurried into the back to put on a clean apron.

She'd told her mother and sisters she'd be out of town, but she hadn't said anything about the wedding and Grant. While it had been relatively easy pretending to be his girlfriend a hundred miles away from Bliss Cove, there was no way she could dupe her family into thinking they were actually together.

But if she told them the truth, she'd put the entire charade at risk. Her mother and sisters would never tell Edward and Joanna outright that she and Grant were faking it, but any offhanded comment could blow the whole thing up.

This was going to be far more complicated than she'd thought.

"When does Linda start full-time?" She returned to the

front counter, tying on her apron. "I should probably start cutting back on my hours soon. Give her a chance to take over."

"She's already full-time, so you can cut back whenever you'd like." Eleanor set a tray of cookies on the counter. "I know you'll need the time to get ready for your move. Are the arrangements going well?"

"Yes, we've done all the paperwork." Rory started putting the cookies into a basket. "I'm keeping an eye out for an apartment near the Digicore campus so I don't have to commute too far. The head of my department sent me the details of their upcoming projects so I can get caught up."

"Have I told you how proud I am of you?" Eleanor paused to hug her around the shoulders. "And how grateful I am for all you've done? I've known for a while now that it's past time for you to get back to your career, but selfishly I've been happy to have you around. While I'll miss you terribly, I'm thrilled that you've found a job where you can use your talents again."

"Thanks, Mom." Rory forced a smile and returned her mother's embrace.

"Hi, all." Aria Prescott breezed through the swinging wooden doors leading to the kitchen, looking pretty and bright-eyed as always in a pink sweater and skinny jeans. "Did you finish my order for the birthday party tonight, Mom?"

"The cake is ready to go." Eleanor nodded toward a bakery box on the counter. "I made some cat cookies for you, too. I just need to box them up."

"I can do it." Silver bracelets jangling, Aria pulled a tray of cookies from the baker's rack. "I had three adoption applications for two different cats this weekend, and our Saturday game night was booked. I've had to start taking reservations for the Cat Lounge on weekends."

"That's great." Rory put the basket in the display case.

"Mayor Bowers told me the town council approved a budget for Mariposa Street renovations." Eleanor patted Aria's shoulder, her face creasing with a smile. "That's wonderful."

"We're close to finalizing an agreement to renovate and build out the rest of the land," Aria said. "Oh, be sure to visit our Bliss Cove Preservation Society booth at the Harvest Festival."

"I'll give you cookies so you can lure people over." Eleanor pushed the baker's rack back into the kitchen. "Rory, put a fresh pot of coffee on, please."

As Rory started measuring out the coffee, Aria asked, "So, how was your weekend?"

The speculating note in her voice had Rory's suspicions sharpening. "Fine. Yours?"

"I already told you about mine." Aria glanced at her, eyebrows lifted. "But on Saturday afternoon, you were spotted in the passenger seat of Grant's car, heading toward Highway One. He was driving."

Rory's heart thumped. "So?"

"Since when do you hang out with Grant?"

"I don't."

"Then what were you doing in his car?"

"He was giving me a ride home."

Aria crossed her arms, her eyes narrowing. "Your apartment is in the opposite direction of Highway One."

"Thank you, Sherlock," Rory muttered. "Who in the...oh,

hell. Brooke, right? That nosy little reporter needs to mind her own business."

"Bliss Cove happenings *are* Brooke's business," Aria said. "Rory Prescott hanging out with Grant Taylor is newsworthy, indeed."

"I was not *hanging out* with Grant, and there's nothing newsworthy about me being in his car." Rory turned away so her sister couldn't see her telltale blush. "But since you're snooping, I happen to have a date tomorrow."

"You have a *date*?" Aria made it sound like Rory had scurvy.

With a scowl, Rory scrolled on her phone and pulled up Max's confirmation text from early last week. She turned the screen toward her sister. "Max Weatherford and I are having lunch tomorrow."

"You and Max?" Aria squinted at the screen, as if she were trying to figure out if Rory had somehow manufactured the message herself. "But you don't like animals."

"That doesn't mean I don't like *him*." Rory dropped her phone back into her apron pocket. "By the way, what did Hunter think of that urban development software the design firm was using?"

To her credit, Aria rolled with the unsubtle subject change. "I don't think he or the designers at Studio Twenty-Five were very impressed. Not enough functionality for what they want to do."

"Which is what?"

"Well, the whole idea is to create a plan and design that's consistent with the historical architecture and supports rather than overtakes the street itself." Aria taped up a box of cookies. "You have to talk to Hunter about the specifics, but there's a ton that goes into the planning. Data visualization, mapping, geospatial analysis…I don't even know what else. He said he was going to contact you soon to see if you have any other recommendations."

"I'll do some research."

"Awesome, thank you."

Pleased at the idea of finding out more about software systems for a field she didn't know much about, Rory got to work restocking the muffin baskets and helping customers.

After her shift ended at six and she closed up the bakery, she returned to the Mousehole cottage, only to find that all of her stuff was gone.

Whirling on her heel, she crossed the flagstone pathway to the back door of Grant's house. When he didn't answer on the third knock, she found him in the Mousehole kitchen, presiding over a dozen burgers sizzling on the grill.

Just a whiff of charred juicy beef made Rory's stomach growl.

Just the sight of Grant—bare arms flexing, bandana tied around his forehead, skin glistening with heat and sweat—made other parts of her body ache with a different kind of hunger.

"Hey." She poked him in the shoulder. "What'd you do with my stuff?"

"Threw it out."

"What?"

"I moved it into my house, genius."

"Even my computer?"

"Even *your precious*."

She fisted her hands on her hips. "You didn't set it up, did you?"

"I'm not that chivalrous." He flipped a couple of burgers. Steam billowed up from the grill.

Lord, she was starving.

"What about my other stuff?" She was acutely conscious of the fact that she'd left her suitcase open, the messy contents and tangle of bras and panties out in plain sight. Had he touched them?

And how messed up was it that the thought of his big, tanned hands on her unremarkable panties got her all hot and quivery?

"It's still packed. I'm working late, so I'll have to show you tomorrow where to put everything." He slanted her a dark look. "Now if you don't mind, I'm cooking here."

"I see that." She eyed the burgers and tried not to salivate.

Muttering something under his breath, Grant slapped a thick burger onto a freshly baked bun, put it on a plate, and shoved it toward her. "Go away."

"Can I get some fries with this?"

His glower deepened. He stalked to the deep fryer and scooped a batch of fresh, crispy fries onto her plate.

"How about a milksha—"

"Go *away*."

"You said you'd cook me three meals a day."

"Starting on Wednesday when my parents get here." He snapped his eyebrows together and shot her another scowly look. "Do I need to say it again?"

Before he started breathing fire, Rory grabbed a bottle of ketchup and scurried out the back door. His parents were due to arrive late Wednesday afternoon, so they didn't have a heck of a lot of time to make it look like they were living together. Hopefully, Joanna had already realized tech girl Rory wasn't much of a decorator.

The back door to his house was unlocked, so she ventured inside. Might as well get acquainted with the place.

Her heartbeat increased as she closed the door behind her. In a direct contrast to the noisy, bustling tavern, a quiet peace filled the house.

Everything was in shades of taupe, light gray, chocolate. A warm, honey-brown leather sofa and chairs sat in the living room, with a woven throw rug covering the worn hardwood floor. Her suitcases, computer hardware, and speakers were all stacked in front of a stone fireplace.

Shelves full of books lined the room, and framed artwork from local artists decorated the walls. There were paintings of the ocean splashing against the rocks, the dusky shadows of the redwood forests, and a downtown scene signed *H. Higgins*—the lovely, elderly owner of the Outside Inn.

Not unexpectedly, the kitchen was bright and pristine with shiny, stainless-steel appliances, a gourmet coffee-maker, and a polished little table by the windows.

After setting her plate down, Rory explored the rest of the house—the bathroom with its old-fashioned pedestal sink and towels that were fluffier than sheep, a linen closet so neatly stacked with sheets, pillows, and blankets that Martha Stewart would be impressed, and a shoebox bedroom with a huge picture window framing a view of the redwoods. A king-sized bed covered with a navy comforter and several pillows dominated the room.

It was…charming. Not a word she'd ever have associated with Grant Taylor. There was nothing feminine or frilly in the décor, but it had a warmth she hadn't expected.

What had she expected? Sports memorabilia and a plasma screen TV?

She let her gaze linger on his bed. She could easily picture him asleep, the navy sheets twisted around his body like ocean waves. Lying on his stomach with the thick, soft comforter pushed to his waist, his body moving in the rhythm of sleep, clutching a pillow against his muscled chest…

Letting out a breath, she retreated back to the kitchen and sat at the table to eat the burger and fries.

Even with her equilibrium about Grant jolting up and down like an earthquake reading on the Richter scale, she'd successfully made it through a weekend with his family at an extravagant wedding. She could handle another week with just his parents.

The question was…could she handle a week with *him*?

Just being close to him was an exercise in lust and self-control. She'd certainly noticed his good looks and sexiness over the past two years, but she'd never once imagined hooking up with him.

Okay, maybe she'd *wondered* every now and then, but she'd gotten so comfortable with their relationship as it was that some part of her didn't dare shake up the status quo. She was accustomed to him being *right over there*, and if getting closer to him changed that in any way…

No. She'd needed Grant Taylor to be exactly who he was and where he was.

Except now that she was moving and he wouldn't be right around the corner anymore—

A shiver ran down her spine. She'd better not let her thoughts go in that direction when she had other things to focus on. Like ensuring that his parents' visit went without a single hitch.

After washing the plate, she wandered back into the living room. She desperately wanted to set up her computer so she could distract herself with work, but since she had no idea where Grant wanted her to put it, she'd have to wait until tomorrow.

He obviously had no evidence of a computer. Not even a laptop. He had a crap ton of books, though. Callie would like him. Gordon Prescott would have, too.

Tilting her head, she studied the spines of the books—everything from mystery novels to political biographies. One entire shelf held nothing but cookbooks. She opened one by Jacques Pepin and Julia Child, scanning the recipes of everything from whitefish in lemon-butter sauce to *haricots verts*.

As she settled on the sofa with the book, the back door opened. She turned, her belly tensing as Grant strode in, his hair messy and his wrinkled T-shirt clinging to his chest. The smoky scent of the grill still hovered around him, and lines of fatigue etched his face.

He set a tall, frosted metal cup and a paper straw on the coffee table. "I'm going to take a shower."

Before she could respond, he disappeared into the bathroom. A second later, the shower started.

The cup contained a thick, chocolate milkshake. She stuck the straw into the ice cream and enjoyed a long slurp as she continued leafing through the book.

Half an hour later, Grant emerged from the bathroom—Rory attempted unsuccessfully to catch a glimpse of his towel-clad body as he went into the bedroom—and came out in track pants and the forest-green T-shirt that turned his eyes the color of emeralds.

As he pulled a hand through his wet hair, the shirt rode up, exposing the ladder-like ridges of his abdomen and a tempting trail of hair leading right down into his pants.

Rory's breathing increased.

This was nuts. She had to get control of herself. Salivating over him all the time might help her prove to the Taylors that they were a serious item, but it would wreak havoc on her nerves.

She sucked down another gulp of milkshake. "Thanks for this. It's delicious."

He jutted his chin toward the book. "You going to take up cooking?"

"Ha ha. Did you know gravlax is basically just raw fish?"

"Cured raw fish."

"What was wrong with it?"

"What are you talking about?"

"If it needed a cure, it must have been sick." She smirked and closed her lips around the straw again.

"That's the best you can do?" He leaned against the door-jamb and folded his arms.

"Well, it's late." She glanced around for her phone, mildly surprised to discover she'd lost track of it. "What time is it?"

"Twelve thirty." He opened the linen closet. "Your phone is on the kitchen table. I need to work early in the morning, so we'll get your stuff unpacked tomorrow afternoon."

"Okay." Setting the book aside, Rory pushed herself up and retrieved the phone. She started toward the door. "See you later."

"Where are you going?"

"Back to the cottage." She frowned at his snappish tone. "Where are *you* going?"

"To bed."

"Great." She pulled open the door. "Sweet dreams."

"Why aren't you sleeping here?" He was starting to scowl, as if she were intentionally making things difficult for him.

"Your parents won't be here until Wednesday."

"So?"

"So we don't have to pretend until then."

"That doesn't mean you need to sleep in the cottage. All your stuff is already here anyway." He jabbed his thumb toward the bedroom. "Take the bed. I'll sleep on the sofa."

"Why would you do that when there's a perfectly good bed in the cottage?" Rory scratched her chin, suddenly uncomfortable. "I wouldn't feel right about sleeping in your bed...er, I mean *the bed* when you're the one with the early shift."

"Fine, then you take the sofa."

And try to sleep knowing he was just in the other room? Yes, she'd have to get used to that very soon, but no need to prolong the stress. "I'll be fine in the cottage."

"Between now and Wednesday, we need to act like we've been living together for a while."

"Do your parents even know we're living together?"

"I told them the other day." He dropped a pillow on the sofa. "As far as my mother was concerned, I might as well have said you and I were walking down the aisle next."

"That's where I draw the line."

"I would hope so." He tossed the blanket on the other end

of the sofa. "But since we'll need to do a lot more pretending to pull this off, we'll start now. You need to, like, *live* here. Put girl stuff around. Lotions, hairbrushes, clothes, lipstick."

She arched an eyebrow. "Because I'm a girl, I need to clutter up your place with lotions and lipstick?"

"No." He groaned and dragged a hand down his face. "You need to establish a *presence* here. And not with bags of pork rinds and dirty T-shirts."

"Wow. Way not to like me for who I am." She injected a hurt note into her voice, then chuckled when he looked slightly horrified at having upset her. "Kidding. But really, even your parents will expect me to have a computer."

"We'll set it up tomorrow. I need to move stuff off the desk in the bedroom." He flopped down on the sofa and put his feet on the coffee table. "So I know about your career, your terrible diet, and your family. What else do I need to know?"

"That's it."

He slanted her a glance. "I don't believe that."

She shrugged. "You know what I like to eat and drink, who my friends are, what kind of music I like. I work out and jog. I go to concerts when I can. I like hiking. That's the main stuff."

He studied her, his eyebrows drawing together. "Still not buying it. Everyone has secrets."

"I didn't say I don't have secrets. I said that's all you need to know about me to pretend like we're together. Your parents will expect you to bring me a large coffee—no cream, two sugars—without me having to ask. They won't expect you to tell them that I sing karaoke and dance around my apartment in my underwear when I'm stuck on a coding or design problem."

Intrigue sparked in his eyes. "Do you?"

"Like I said…" She grabbed the milkshake cup and turned toward the foyer. "That's all you need to know."

She was halfway out the door when she heard him laugh.

# CHAPTER 9

"Be sure to let us know if we need tickets to any of the festival events," his mother chirped over the phone. "Can't wait!"

"Looking forward to it, Mom," Grant lied. He hung up the tavern's landline phone and turned his attention back to the artichoke soup simmering on the stove.

Though his mother had orchestrated this whole visit in a masterful display of interference, Grant was not entirely convinced that she wouldn't drag Edward to Bali just to prove a point—if she thought she wasn't welcome in Bliss Cove.

Keeping her happily occupied was Grant's main goal. Nathan had practically prostrated himself with gratitude for his rescue from the Joanna Taylor juggernaut, and now he and Alice were ensconced in their honeymoon suite where— Grant was certain—his brother was having no issues with erectile dysfunction.

Also, Rory had considerably eased Grant's concerns about his parents. Not only had she played her role to perfection at the wedding, he'd enjoyed her company. He'd enjoyed *her*, from her good-naturedness about letting his mother drag her along on a spa day to her care over extracting herself from the wedding pictures to her willingness to dance even though she had no idea how.

His instincts had been right about asking her instead of, say, Madeline Fox to pretend to be his girlfriend. Rory made the *pretend* part easy.

Maybe a little too easy.

After adding more salt to the soup, he returned to the dining room. A talkative lunch crowd filled the tavern, and the servers wove between the tables with trays of plates and drinks.

He was halfway to the bar when unease tugged at his gut. He scanned the room, his gaze skidding to a halt on a table by the window. Rory, dressed in a rose-colored blouse with her hair fastened into a tidy ponytail, sat perusing the menu.

Grant's brain clicked into gear. She always looked *good* to him, no matter what she was wearing or how messy her hair was—in fact, he liked her disheveled look a lot—but today she'd clearly made an effort to look extra nice. She was even wearing earrings.

What was she doing at a table set for two? She always either sat alone at the bar or at a corner booth with her sisters and friends.

His unease deepened. He started toward her. The front door opened, bringing a rush of cool autumn air. Forcing himself to veer toward the entering customer, Grant turned.

"Hey, man." Max Weatherford, the local veterinarian and Grant's occasional fishing buddy, extended a hand. "Good to see you. I'm renting a boat this weekend, if you want to head out to catch some salmon."

"Maybe. Thanks for the offer." Grant grabbed a menu from the hosting station. "Table for one?"

"No, actually, I'm meeting a woman for lunch." He tilted his chin toward the bank of tables beside the windows. "According to Destiny and the Oracle cards, I'm supposed to have a lot in common with Rory Prescott."

Grant's back teeth snapped together. "And Destiny is just telling you this now?"

"Yeah." Max shrugged. "Something to do with Mercury in retrograde and Rory's aura."

"Didn't know you believed in that kind of thing."

"I don't, but it's no hardship to have lunch with her."

Grant slapped the menu on the table. Rory looked up, her eyes widening slightly.

"I…uh, I thought since you worked the early shift, you'd have the afternoon off." Her gaze skidded past him to Max.

"Nope." He stepped aside.

"Hi, Max." Rory stood and extended her hand, leaning forward to embrace him at the same time. Grant caught her scent—pineapple and mangoes. No wonder he always wanted to eat her.

"Good to see you, Rory." Max regarded her with appreciation. "You look beautiful."

"I'll get you some water." Grant edged between them, breaking their hand-holding, and picked up an empty glass. "You want a beer, Max?"

"Sure. London porter." Max shed his jacket, waiting for Rory to sit again before he pulled out his own chair. "Anything you want, Rory?"

So the vet was a *gentleman*, too, huh? Grant had seen women giggling over him at the tavern or the docks, but he didn't know much about the guy's social life. Apparently he wasn't attached, if he was out with Rory.

"I've got mine already, thanks." She indicated her pale ale.

Grant strode back to the bar, stopping to take a couple of orders along the way. No harm in making Max wait a few minutes for his beer. Didn't look as if the guy was expecting it immediately anyway, given the way his attention was fixed on Rory.

Why was she smiling? Veterinarians weren't known for being funny, as far as Grant knew.

Turning away, he went back to the bar and refilled a couple of peanut bowls.

"Grant."

"Rory." He set a bowl down unnecessarily hard and started wiping down the counter. "Need another drink?"

"No." She glanced back at Max and lowered her voice. "I wanted to tell you I'm sorry. I agreed to this date last week, long before our...uh, agreement."

"You couldn't have cancelled?"

A frown creased her forehead. "First, I didn't see the point because if I recall, you and I are pretending. Second, Aria's friend Brooke saw me in your car the other day, which means she got all gossipy about us. So my going out with Max will keep Aria off my case."

Grant tossed the dishrag aside and planted his hands on the bar. His muscles were locked tight. He might've been gritting his teeth. "I thought you were moving away."

"I am."

"So why the hell are you dating a guy who lives in town?"

"Max knows I'm moving." She reached for a peanut.

"And I'm not *dating* him. This is the first time we've ever been out together. I haven't been on a date in a while, and when Destiny brought it up, I figured it was about time."

"Why?"

"Because I might actually attempt to have a social life when I move to San Jose." She cracked open the peanut and shot him an irritated look. "What business is it of yours, anyway? I came over here to explain things *as a friend*, not to be interrogated about why I'm on a date."

He folded his arms. "You interrogated me about Madeline Fox. Several times."

Twin spots of color rose to her cheeks. "That's different."

"Why?"

"Because…because…" She huffed out a breath. "Well, you said you never dated her."

"What does that have to do with you going out with Max? And why didn't he take you to a fine dining restaurant on your first date?"

"I suggested we come here because I didn't want to spend a lot of time eating when you and I have to get ready for your parents," Rory snapped in a low voice. "Plus, I didn't think you'd be working now. Why am I finding it necessary to justify myself to you?"

"No idea." Grant put a Corona on the bar and pushed it toward her. "That's for your date. I'll be over in a minute to take your order."

"Grant, if you—"

He cut off her words by pushing the button on Bob's plaque. The fish began warbling out "Love Me Tender." The patrons at the bar cheered.

"Oh my god." Rory pressed her hands to her temples. "Are you really going to be this childish?"

"You eat gummy worms for lunch, and *I'm* the childish one?"

"I am going to *burn* that fish when we're finished with this relationship sideshow." She grabbed the beer and turned on her heel. "Now if you'll excuse me, I need to get back to my *date*."

She returned to her table. Max stood when she approached, and a smile bloomed over her face. Grant clamped down on another surge of jealousy.

For the full hour and a half of Rory and Max's lunch date —not that Grant was watching the clock—they chatted, laughed, and appeared to be having a grand old time. Rather than her usual order of an onion blossom or fried cheese curds, Rory ordered a salmon salad.

Did she think she could impress the doctor of veterinary medicine with her nutrition-conscious choice? Did she *want* to?

"No cheese curds?" He set the salad in front of her with a smirk.

She smiled blandly. "No, thanks."

"What about you?" Grant looked at Max, who shook his head.

"I'm good."

"You're good for getting Rory to eat some fiber." He jerked his thumb at her. "Her diet consists of three food groups—candy, fast food, and pork rinds."

Under the table, Rory kicked him. Hard.

Appearing faintly baffled, Max shrugged. "I'm a fan of all those things, too. Maybe not in the same meal, though."

"Sure you don't want the mozzarella sticks?"

"If we want something else, we'll order it." Rory was still smiling, even though a muscle ticked in her jaw.

Grant held up his hands. "Just let me know."

"Oh, I'll let you know," she snapped.

Grant strode back to the bar. Christ, he was such an asshole.

He told one of the servers to take over Rory's table and went into the kitchen to cook so he'd stop fixating on them. He tied a bandana around his forehead and slapped steaks on the grill. Flames billowed up around the meat.

He'd never seen Rory on a date before. That was why he was being such a jerk. She hadn't hooked up with any of the guys who'd propositioned her at the bar—not that Grant would know for sure, and not that he intended to speculate otherwise—and he'd taken it for granted that he knew what she did and whom she did it with. She was predictable.

Or so he'd thought. She could very well have a secret life he knew nothing about—and why wouldn't she? He had no claim on her. He just *assumed* he knew her schedule because he sometimes saw her during her Sugar Joy shifts, she came into the Mousehole regularly, and she often talked about working on some database coding or whatever.

Feeling somewhat cowardly, he stayed in the kitchen for the rest of the afternoon, which was where he most liked to be anyway. He flipped burgers, grilled salmon, ladled artichoke soup, sliced freshly baked bread.

During the lull between the lunch and dinner rushes, he turned over the kitchen to one of the other chefs and started back to his house to check his voicemail messages. His parents would be arriving tomorrow at noon, and his father never deviated from a schedule.

The cottage door was open. He turned and went inside, catching a whiff of cinnamon.

What the…?

Rory stood on a stepladder, positioning a red-checkered curtain and rod into place over the window facing the woods.

"What're you doing?"

"Dancing the tango." She threw him a narrow look and climbed down, brushing off her hands. "What do you think?"

He didn't know whether to be more surprised by the fact that she'd thought of decorating the cottage—given what he'd seen of her apartment, home décor was not her forte—or that she'd done it so well.

There were red-checkered curtains, a woven rug under the coffee table, and a quilt tossed over the old sofa. She'd put up framed historical photos of the tavern, placed a little artichoke-shaped teapot on the stove, and spread a sky-blue comforter on the bed strewn with fluffy pillows. A little bowl of potpourri sat on the counter, which accounted for the cinnamon smell.

"It's incredible." He rubbed his hands on his jeans, not knowing what to think. "But you didn't have to do all this."

She shrugged. "I don't know much about decorating, but your mother could probably teach Martha Stewart a thing or two. I thought she'd enjoy it more if the place was spruced up a little."

"Thank you." Shame rustled in his chest. He scratched his head. "Uh, sorry for being kind of an ass earlier."

"Kind of? You mean like Voldemort is *kind of* evil?" She closed the stepladder and stored it in the closet. "Look, I tried to explain about Max. I never intended to go out with him again while your parents are here, so just chill out, okay? We're not going to pull off this live-in lovers thing if we argue about the women constantly hitting on you or the *one* date I've had in months."

She'd had one date in months? Interesting.

"In fact, that kind of talk needs to be off-limits, or one of us is going to slip up," she added.

"Okay." He forced himself not to pry further into her comment that she wasn't going out with Max again *while his parents were here*. Did that mean she intended to see him after they left?

Jesus. He had to get his shit together. Less than a week, and already it felt like an earthquake was rumbling underneath his quiet, carefully constructed life.

All he'd done was ask Rory to step in a little farther, to cross the invisible line that had always existed between them, and the next thing he knew, they'd had a hotter-than-hell kiss, she was moving into his house, and he was getting insanely jealous about her lunch date.

"I'm sorry." He held up his hands and approached her. "I've never seen you on a date. Turns out I didn't like it, even if you're my fake girlfriend. I got possessive."

Faint amusement rose to her eyes. "Territorial."

"What?"

"That's what Max said after you left. That you were territorial." She frowned and crinkled her forehead. "Then he said something like—if the Prescott sisters were planets, we'd inspire a whole new international space race."

She shook her head and straightened one of the sofa cushions. "Anyway, I didn't really understand what he was talking about, but clearly he was getting some *back off* vibes from you."

"Good."

Rory looked up sharply, her gaze crashing against his. Tension threaded the air. He flexed his fingers.

"Don't go out with him again." The command came out gruff and scratchy.

She blinked. "I wasn't going to. And not because you ordered me not to," she added.

Grant ran a hand over the back of his neck. "You don't like him?"

"Of course I *like* him." She spread her arms out in irritation. "Everyone likes Max. Not only does he look like Captain America, he helps animals, for heaven's sake, and he's really smart, easy to talk to, friendly, knowledgeable—"

"Point taken."

"If it hadn't been for you glowering at us from halfway across the room, I'd have enjoyed lunch with him. I did enjoy it, in fact. But obviously I'm not looking for a relationship, and even if I were, Max isn't the kind of guy I'd want to be with."

"What, you want a stupid, unsociable, mean boyfriend who kicks puppies?"

Rory laughed. It was a genuine, full-bellied laugh that rang through the cottage and settled somewhere deep inside Grant. Had he ever heard her laugh like that before? Apparently not, if the sound turned him into a bowl of mush.

"Okay, *no*." She shook her head, still smiling. She was pretty with a scowl. She was stunning with a smile. "I meant that, despite what Destiny's Oracle card reading said, Max and I are not romantically compatible. I hate the word *chemistry*, but maybe that's what it was. I liked talking to him about the integration of veterinary software systems, but I didn't want to kiss him."

Grant tried to ignore an upwelling of relief. "If all you talked to him about was software systems, then I'm guessing he probably wasn't dying to kiss you either."

*He*, on the other hand…

"I don't know about that." She gave an offhanded shrug. "Tech talk can be pretty sexy, when it's done right."

"Yeah?" He narrowed his eyes, certain he shouldn't go down this path and already knowing he was going to. "Prove it."

"Well, there's the obvious." She ticked the items off on her fingers. "Hard drives. Hot swaps. The pleasure of big pipes and large bandwidths. Joysticks. RAM. Open source. Penetration testing, and probing for exploitable holes…"

"Hmm." He shook his head and tried not to stare at her lips. "Too easy."

Her eyes sparked with the intrigue of a challenge. She stepped closer and made a horizontal motion between them.

"This space is our shared boundary." She lowered her voice to a husky drawl that would have made a phone-sex operator envious. "When two separate parts of a computer system exchange information, they need to cross the boundary and connect…or *interface*. In technology, interfacing can refer to the way a person experiences a computer and its hardware, output, and functions. Sometimes you can both send and receive data through an interface, like a touchscreen. People do the same thing. They cross a shared boundary to connect." She wiggled her fingers. "And they use touch to create and control responses."

Grant knew he shouldn't have started this, but damned if he was turning back now. He hated retreating.

"Still not feeling it." He shrugged. "If I were nice guy Max, I'd have paid the bill and politely thanked you for joining me."

"Ah, but you're not nice guy Max." Stepping closer, she tracked her gaze over his features. Her brown eyes gleamed. "You're cranky, territorial Grant who thinks a singing fish is a work of art and who turns cooking into a porn show."

For a second, he wasn't sure whether her assessment of him was flattering or not, but he didn't care either way. She was looking at him with such brewing heat, and her lips were so fucking ripe for the taking that his body tensed with both the urge to kiss her and the knowledge that crossing that boundary again was dangerous.

"Touchscreens are input devices." She brushed her fingers against his jaw, her attention drifting to his mouth. "They react to pressure. Some absorb ultrasonic waves created by a touch. Sometimes a touch generates an electrical charge. Input. Output."

Her touch was generating a reaction, all right—waves of lust and a hot charge going straight to his groin. Not only had she just won this challenge, she'd left him in the dust.

Time to catch up.

He took hold of her waist and pulled her closer. Their lower bodies collided. Rory widened her eyes as his growing erection pressed against her.

"Don't even think about telling me I didn't prove it." A husky note still entwined her voice.

"You proved it. Tech talk can be sexy…when you do it, at

least." He slipped his hand under her chin and tilted her face up to his. "But it doesn't make me want to kiss you."

Consternation flashed over her expression. "What does, then?"

"You."

He covered her mouth with his, and the instant their lips touched, a hard surge of relief filled him. Like he'd found something he'd lost...or never had in the first place.

Rory let out a little gasp and curled her hands around his arms as she parted her lips. Their tongues touched. He pulled her closer, digging his fingers into her hips. His head filled with her taste, her scent, the feel of her lush body against his.

If he'd had any more questions about why he was so jealous and possessive of her, the answers flooded over him like the tides—he liked her, he wanted her badly, and she was as responsive as a feather touched by the wind, which was so fucking fascinating when paired with her sharp attitude.

He wanted to know more about her than how she took her coffee, and he ached to find out how explosive they'd be in bed together.

For all her straightforward, tough-girl snark, she was as pliable and sweet as taffy. She wound her arms around his neck, pressed her luscious curves against him, and returned his kiss as if she, too, was increasingly desperate for more.

"For the record," she whispered, her breath brushing his lips, "if I *were* looking for a relation—"

"Hellooo!" Outside, a car door slammed.

Rory's eyes widened. Grant couldn't think past the heavy thump of his heart.

"We're here!" His mother's voice sang through the air. "Are the lovebirds home?"

# CHAPTER 10

*R*ory yanked herself away from Grant so fast she stumbled backward. Her breath rasped hotly in her throat. Lust fogged her brain.

They stared at each other, the air flooding with shock the instant before a shutter slammed over his expression. Just like that, the heat disappeared from his eyes and was replaced with calm poise as he turned to the front door.

"Grant?" Joanna Taylor called. "Are you in here?"

Rory wasn't as good an actor as Grant, so she turned away quickly to try and compose herself. She was throbbing. Her insides ached with desire.

"Mom." His deep voice held just the right amount of surprise. "You were supposed to arrive tomorrow."

"Surprise!" A whiff of Chanel No. 5 filled the cottage as Joanna approached the door. "Your father finished a project early, so I convinced him to come down today. Of course, the big goof had to make several stops to check his messages, but he *promised* not to work while we're here. Rory! How are you, dear?"

Fixing a smile on her face, Rory turned to greet the older woman, who was a vision of casual elegance in a linen pantsuit and chunky gold jewelry.

"Nice to see you again, Mrs. Taylor. Welcome to Bliss Cove."

"Oh, heavens, call me Joanna. Is this the cottage?" Removing her large sunglasses, she stepped inside. A slight frown dipped her mouth. "Oh, my. It is small, isn't it?"

"I did warn you." Grant glanced past his mother's shoulder. "Where's Dad?"

"Finishing a call." Joanna rolled her eyes and set her YSL purse on the counter. She sniffed the air. "Is that potpourri? I'm afraid I'm a bit allergic to synthetic scents."

"Mom." Grant's tone hardened.

"We'll just take it away." Rory grabbed the little potpourri pot and pushed open a window. "How was the drive?"

"Oh, lovely, dear." Joanna ran her finger over a counter in the kitchenette and examined whatever specks of dust she'd collected. "It's wonderful to be reminded of how beautiful the Pacific Coast is."

"So this is your place, huh?" Edward Taylor stepped into the cottage, the breadth of his shoulders and sheer height making the space seem even smaller than it was. "No wonder it's called the *Mousehole*."

"The Mousehole is the tavern, Dad." Grant folded his arms, his jaw tensing. "This is the cottage. My house is over there…" he pointed to the north, "…and the tavern is the building you saw when you drove up. The other building is a rental space for parties and classes."

"It's charming, isn't it, Edward?" Joanna picked up a

corner of the comforter and rubbed it between her fingers. "Let's go take a peek at your house, Grant."

Rory drew in a sharp breath. Grant caught her eye, and an unspoken message of faint panic passed between them. They'd intended to unpack her stuff and set up this afternoon. Instead, all of her boxes and suitcases were still stacked in his living room, and there was zero evidence of her living there.

"Actually, why don't you come to the tavern first?" Grant spread his hand out toward the door. "Have a drink, get something to eat. It's close to dinner. You must be tired from the drive."

"Yes!" Rory spoke with such enthusiasm that Joanna looked at her in surprise. "Go relax for an hour or…um, three. The house isn't quite ready for visitors yet."

"Oh, we don't mind, dear." Joanna waved a dismissive hand. "We're just delighted to be here."

"Come on, Dad. I'll make you a martini. Extra dry with a twist." Grant took firm hold of his father's arm and steered him out toward the tavern.

With a little shrug, Joanna picked up her purse and followed. After Grant set his parents on the path around the tavern to the front door, he poked his head back into the cottage.

"I'll get them situated and meet you back at the house."

"Go," Rory hissed, pulling her cell phone out of her back pocket. "Keep them occupied. I'll take care of the house."

He hurried after his parents.

Dialing Aria's number, Rory ran toward her car. "Aria? I need your help, but you can't ask questions."

"Can I ask what you need my help with?"

"Get a bunch of girly stuff together for me. Some of your

jewelry, shoes, even a dress or two. Novels with people kissing on the cover, maybe a few things from Moonbeams, like scarves and a crystal lamp or something. Do you know what I mean?"

"You mean stuff that you've never bought in your entire life."

"Exactly. Put it all in a box and bring it over to the Mousehole within the hour."

"The Mousehole? But…okay, no questions. I'll be there."

"Don't go into the tavern. Just come around the back to Grant's house."

"Oh my god, you are killing me. Not even one teeny little question?"

"Hurry, please."

Ending the call, Rory started the car and drove to a side street off Starfish Avenue, where Madeline Fox's bath-and-body shop Naked sat housed in a pristine white, glass-fronted building. Given Joanna's worries about synthetic scents, Rory thought she'd better personally scrutinize any and all products brought into Grant's house.

The instant she stepped inside Naked, she felt like a bull barreling through a china shop. Everything was white, soft music played from speakers, and glass shelves held dozens of jars and bottles of lotions, creams, oils, and God knew what else women slathered on their skin. All were packaged with distinctive blue-and-white labels and the tagline *Get Naked*.

"Hello, how can I…Rory?" Madeline Fox looked up from the computer, her perfectly plucked eyebrows rising.

"Hi, Madeline." Trying not to appear too panicked, Rory hurried to the glass counter. "I need some lotions and stuff."

Madeline blinked, then composed her perfect features into

a welcoming smile. "Of course. You've never been here before, have you?"

"No. Anything's fine, really. Just nothing synthetic."

"None of our products contain synthetic ingredients." Madeline's eyes frosted over a tad. "We use fresh, organic fruits, vegetables, and essential oils to craft rich, hydrating products intended for—"

"Sounds fantastic." Rory dug her wallet out of her pocket. "Give me some lotion, shampoo, makeup and stuff."

"Is this for a gift?"

"No, it's for me." Rory pulled out her credit card.

"Oh. Well, that's wonderful. Have a seat." Madeline indicated a stool in front of a lighted mirror. "We always begin with a holistic diagnostic so we can personalize your products to your skin type, lifestyle, environment and the—"

"Madeline." Rory forced a smile. "I am in a crazy big hurry here. I don't need a holistic diagnostic, really. I just need a bunch of lotions or whatever. *Please*."

Madeline pursed her lips, seeming not to know whether to be irritated or amused. "All right, but I'm going to give you products from our Natural Beauty line so that you don't end up with competing scents or applications."

Rory tried not to grit her teeth. She held up her credit card as if it were a tablet of the Ten Commandments that had to be obeyed.

Madeline smiled and strolled to a shelf. As Rory checked her phone for the time, Madeline brought an array of bottles and jars to the counter.

"So for your morning regimen, begin with the lime-scrub cleanser." Madeline unscrewed the lid and thrust the open jar under Rory's nose. "It's very light and refreshing."

"Great." She took a whiff and wondered if Grant had key-lime pie on the menu today. "As I said, big hurry here. Wrap it all up."

Ten minutes and a ridiculous amount of money later, Rory rushed back to Grant's house just as Aria was pulling up in her old van. Her sister hauled two cardboard boxes out of the back.

"I have a thousand questions." Eyes bright, she hurried up the front steps as Rory unlocked the door. "No, a *million*."

"Suppress them." Rory dropped the Naked bag in the foyer and took the boxes from her sister. "And please don't tell anyone about this."

"You went to Naked?" Aria peered into the bag. "What did you get? Is that lip gloss and body wash? What is going on?"

"Those are questions."

"First, you were spotted in Grant's car." Aria lifted her thumb. "Then you call and tell me to bring girly stuff to Grant's house." She held up her forefinger. "Then you buy lotions, lip gloss, and body wash at Naked, of all places, when you usually just get whatever soap is on sale at the drugstore, and for some reason you're bringing it all into Grant's living room."

She extended another finger. "Callie might be the one with the PhD, but it doesn't take an advanced degree to figure out that something very interesting is going on here and that it has something to do with Grant."

"No questions, Sherlock." Rory gave her sister a quick hug. "Now go away."

She shooed Aria out the door and sprang into action. Since her own belongings were meager, she hauled all of her boxes into a utility closet near the back porch. In the bedroom, she yanked open drawers of Grant's neatly folded clothes and stuffed them with her T-shirts, jeans, and underwear.

She could not, for the life of her, stop herself from noticing that he wore boxer briefs, mostly black with a few dark gray pairs, and that his shirts smelled like him when he wasn't cooking—citrus and salt.

She ran her hand over his T-shirts, all of which were soft as clouds and felt as if they were shaped to his chest and shoulders. If she were the poetic type, she'd even have sworn that his body heat still clung to the material.

Not that she was fondling his clothes. She slammed the drawer and hung a few of her shirts in the closet. The front door opened.

Her heart almost stopped. Were the Taylors already finished with dinner?

"Rory?" Grant's voice.

"In the bedroom, sweetie!" she called cheerfully. "Haven't I told you to pair your socks *before* you put them in the laundry? And have you seen my hairbrush? The one with the pink handle."

"My parents are still at the tavern." He stopped in the doorway, his face set with a frown. "What'd you do with your stuff?"

"I put the boxes in the utility closet. No way will I have time to set up my computer." She threw a pair of her jeans shorts and a shirt at the foot of the bed to make it look like casual disarray. "You'd better go back there and keep them at bay. Text me when...oh, crap, will you please get a cell phone? Give me another half hour. Go, go!"

Waving him away, she grabbed the boxes and Naked bag from the foyer and returned to the living room. Aria had nailed it—sheer flowy dresses, candles, "live your best life" type magazines, romance novels, tubes of lip balm, jewelry, beaded sandals, even lacy stockings and lingerie.

Rory scattered everything in various places around the house as if it were her personal clutter. She replaced a couple of Grant's black-and-white photos with paintings of fairies and pinned a funny cat calendar to a wall in the kitchen.

She put the Naked shampoo and conditioner in the shower, uncapped the jars of moisturizer, and set the other toiletries on the counter beside Grant's shaving cream and razor. She found a new toothbrush in the cabinet and plunked it next to his in the holder.

"Honey, we're home." Tension underscored his greeting.

Rory swiped her lips with sticky, strawberry-scented gloss, pinched her cheeks to make them red, plastered a smile on her face, and sailed into the living room.

"Welcome!" She spread her arms out. "How was dinner?"

"Wonderful, dear." Joanna beamed. "Edward found his steak a bit tough, but the garlic whipped potatoes were exquisite."

"Good martini, too." Edward scanned the room.

"Great!" Rory wondered if she'd feel the need to speak with exclamation points for the rest of the week. "So, come on in and have a seat. Would you like to look at Oprah's magazine, which I subscribe to along with this one...*Home and Garden*. Or perhaps you'd like to read this book...um, *Love in the Jungle*? It's one of my favorites. Oh, here, let me light this lovely, vanilla-scented candle."

Her palms were starting to sweat.

Behind his mother's back, Grant made a slashing motion across his throat even though his lips twitched. "Or we can head downtown, and I'll show you around Starfish Avenue."

"It's getting a bit late, and I want to see the town during the day." Joanna wandered to the open bedroom door and peered inside. "Why, this is quite spacious, isn't it? Not large enough for a family, of course, but rather perfect just for you two. Rory."

She gestured for Rory to come closer. After tossing Grant a puzzled glance, Rory joined Joanna at the doorway.

Bracketing her mouth with her hand, Joanna whispered, "Not to meddle, but it's a bit uncouth to leave your under-clothes lying on the floor."

Rory's gaze shot to the crumpled blue panties prominently announcing *Juicy* right across the bum. *Thank you, Aria.*

"Must've fallen out of the laundry basket." Her face heat-ing, she grabbed the panties and shoved them in her pocket. "So, would you like something to eat or drink?"

"We just ate and drank, dear." Joanna smiled, though her sharp assessment of the bedroom appeared to miss nothing. She strolled around the rest of the house, remarking on the "charming" fairy paintings, the state-of-the-art coffee-maker and bag of French Roast, which was Edward's favorite, and the size of the "gorgeous" back porch with its Adirondack chairs.

As Joanna walked out to admire the view of the redwoods, Grant brushed his fingers against Rory's arm and whispered, "Thank you."

Her whole body tingled, whether from his gratitude or his touch she couldn't say.

"It must be so lovely to have coffee on the porch every

morning." Joanna walked back into the kitchen with a wistful sigh.

"You've got the balcony at home," Edward remarked.

"I don't have a view of the redwoods at home." Joanna gave him a pointed look.

"Sure you don't want to see the downtown area tonight?" Grant asked.

"Not me." Edward pulled out his phone and swiped the screen.

"I think we'll go back to the little cottage and unpack." Joanna studied a sculpture of a cat holding a flower. "I'm a bit tired, so we'll get an early night's sleep and be ready to sightsee in the morning."

"I'll get your suitcases from the car." Grant shot out the door faster than the human bullet.

"Let us know if you need anything." Rory took Joanna's arm and guided her outside. "You have my cell number, right?"

"Yes, though I'm surprised you haven't convinced Grant to get a phone yet. Isn't that right, Edward? How does he get by without a cell phone?"

Edward grunted. "Won't last long, with Rory moving up to the Bay Area soon."

Concern furrowed Joanna's brow. "How will you and Grant make that work, Rory?"

"We'll figure it out." She and Grant would need to come up with a game plan for that fictional scenario, too. She opened the cottage door and ushered them inside.

"It's freezing in here." Joanna shivered and huddled into her coat. "What on earth…?"

"I opened the windows to get rid of the cinnamon smell."

Rory hurried to shut and lock the windows against the autumn chill.

Grant set two gigantic suitcases on the bed. "I'll build a fire, Mom."

"No, dear, the smoke would be horrible. I'll just wear my coat."

"You got one of those coffee-makers in here?" Edward opened a kitchen cabinet, and a loose hinge popped off. The door tilted. With a frown, he shut it. "Better get that fixed."

"You can have breakfast at Ruby's Kitchen," Grant said. "Anything else you need?"

"No, it's just that we're used to having coffee *before* we get ready for the day." Joanna shivered again and folded her arms. "But we'll make do."

"Where's the TV?" Edward sank down on the narrow sofa and looked around as if expecting the TV to materialize by voice command. "I watch CNN every night before bed."

"There's no TV here, Dad."

"Use your laptop, Edward." Joanna patted the mattress. "Does this have a cushioned topper? Because, you know, your father has back problems."

Grant pinched the bridge of his nose. "No topper, Mom."

"Well, we'll manage. The bed is a bit small, though." With a laugh, she walked over and squeezed her husband's shoulder. "I hope we can fit. It will be like sleeping in a tent, won't it?"

Rory caught Grant's eye and jabbed her thumb toward his parents. His mouth compressing, he shook his head.

She frowned and made a frantic gesture to convey: *Otherwise, you'll never hear the end of it, and do you really want to deal with your parents being unhappy for the next week on top of convincing them that we're a devoted couple? And did you forget about Bali? I'm pretty sure the suites at the resort are a crap ton more luxurious than anything Bliss Cove has to offer, and despite her manipulations, I've little doubt your mother would be thrilled to exchange a mattress without a topper for Egyptian cotton sheets and feather pillows.*

Apparently Grant got all that because he expelled his breath in a long rush of surrender.

"Mom." Thin patience stretched his voice. "Why don't you and Dad sleep in the house? Rory and I will be fine out here."

"Oh, no, dear." Joanna shook her head emphatically. "We couldn't possibly kick you out of your own home."

"I could," Edward remarked.

"Really." Grant twisted his neck, as if it was stiff with tension. "You'll be much more comfortable in the house."

"Well, if you insist…" Joanna bit her lower lip worriedly. "It would be nice to have some space and a comfortable bed. And it's not good for your father's eyes to watch CNN on his laptop."

Time for an exclamation point.

"Of course not!" Rory smiled and glided across the small space to the door. "Grant, bring your parents' suitcases into the house."

"Where's my other one?" Joanna tapped the Louis Vuitton case. "And my toiletries bag? You did tell Marcus to put them in the car, didn't you, Edward?"

"Far as I can remember."

"I'll get them, Mom." Grant hefted the suitcases to the house, then returned to the car to get the rest of the luggage— which was more than all of Rory's assets combined.

After he'd situated his parents in the house, ensuring they had everything from the TV remote to instructions for the coffee-maker, he and Rory grabbed a few clothes and toiletries. They walked back to the cottage.

"You didn't have to do that," he said.

"Doesn't matter." Rory shrugged. "I'm not big on creature comforts, and it's no surprise that your mother is. When I got my first job in San Jose, the housing was so tight and expensive that I rented an unfinished basement room. Had a cot right next to the washing machine and dryer."

"That can't have been comfortable."

"It was fine." She sank onto the edge of the bed and pulled off her shoes. "I spent most of my time at the office, anyway. I had super clean clothes, too."

He chuckled and opened a cabinet. "You want some tea or coffee?"

"I thought there's no coffee-maker here."

"There isn't." He indicated the hot plate. "The coffee's instant, and I can boil water. Or I can grab some from the tavern along with a piece of pie."

"No, but thanks."

Rory dragged her hands through her hair. A wave of fatigue hit her. She recognized it as a ghost from all her tech jobs—the intense, frantic work of finishing a project had invariably been followed by a crash after she'd met the deadline. Though getting ready for Edward and Joanna's visit wasn't the same thing, it was definitely *work*.

She flopped down on the bed. "Hey, this is pretty comfortable. Your mother should have tested it out."

He didn't respond. She glanced up. He stood beside the kitchenette counter, his arms crossed and his pensive gaze on her. The cottage was small by any standards, but with him here, it seemed to shrink to minuscule proportions. Even now, only a few steps' distance separated them.

"You're getting the short end of this deal," he finally said. "Are you sure Bob the Fish is worth all this trouble?"

"I'd let your mother take me away for a spa weekend, if it meant I could get rid of Bob."

She pushed herself up onto her elbows. "Well, maybe I wouldn't go that far, but I don't mind helping you out. I do intend to start cashing in on my free meals soon, though."

"Just say the word." Unfolding his arms, he opened a small closet and took out two pillows and a blanket. "If you don't want anything now, I'm going to head over to the tavern for the rest of the night shift. I'll be back around midnight."

He dropped the pillows on the bed at her side.

"Hey, Grant?" She sat up, running her hands over her thighs. "Why cooking?"

He twisted his mouth with discomfort. "It sounds like another poor little rich kid story."

"But it's not. It's your story."

"When I was a kid, I had a nanny. Of course." He rubbed a hand over his hair. "Lupe. I spent more time with her than my parents, both before and after Nathan came along. My parents had a trained chef on call, but Lupe did a lot of our daily cooking for us, so I was in the kitchen every day. I did my homework at the kitchen counter, then she'd take me to baseball or football practice before we came back to start dinner. She'd always let me help, no matter what we were having. Before long, I was learning how to make everything from pot roast to chili rellenos. I loved being in the kitchen—the smell of frying onions, the sizzle of oil, the thunk of Lupe's knife as she chopped peppers. Best time of my day."

"That sounds nice."

He shrugged. "I had it good compared to a lot of people. And there was…well, whenever Lupe served my parents and whatever guests they had over…they were always so happy. Their faces would light up over perfect sea scallops or tamales. Everything was good. I guess I wanted to make people feel that way, too."

"Aww." She nudged his leg with her stocking foot. "That's so sweet."

A faint flush rose to his cheeks. "Yeah, well, don't tell anyone."

"So Nathan never got into cooking?"

Grant shook his head. A shadow passed over his face. "He had some health issues and set-backs when he was a kid, so our mother kept him pretty close. He had his own nanny who was also an RN. He's fine now, but despite what my father told you, we weren't actually raised the same way."

"What happened to Lupe?"

"She married a man who owned a real-estate company. When he retired, they moved down to San Diego to be closer to family. We're still in touch." Pulling his keys from his jeans pocket, he started toward the door. "Call me at the tavern if you decide you want anything. I'll bring it over."

"Grant."

He turned to face her, his strong features unreadable except for a touch of wariness lingering in his eyes.

"You do make people feel that way," Rory said. "Like everything is good, even when it's not."

*Does anyone do that for you?*

Their eyes met. A force vibrated between them, like a sharp current of electricity flashing across the night sky.

Rory had lost track of the number of times she'd gone to the Mousehole after a long day or just to get away from her apartment. More often than not, she'd walked in feeling tired or cranky—not to mention ravenously hungry. After chatting with Grant and sometimes pestering him, and hanging out with her sisters and friends, she always left feeling better than she had when she'd arrived.

She had no doubt that all of Grant's other customers felt the same way, and it was because of him.

"Well." He opened the door, his gaze shifting away from her. "Thanks for putting up with this whole mess. It's funny, but I kind of wish—"

He stopped and shook his head. "Get a good night's sleep, Rory."

Then he was gone. The door closed behind him.

*I kind of wish we'd crossed the line sooner.*

Rory flopped onto her back and stared at the ceiling. Maybe that wasn't his wish, but it was starting to become hers.

# CHAPTER 11

The smell of French Roast coffee wafted through his sleep. Peeling his eyes open, Grant focused on Rory sitting on the table in front of him, holding a take-out cup.

"You look super uncomfortable," she remarked.

"Looks are not always deceiving."

With a groan, he straightened his cramped legs. He sat up slowly, twisting his stiff neck. The narrow sofa was neither wide enough nor long enough to allow for a good night's sleep, but the cottage was too small for a big, cushy sofa that could also double as a bed.

Rory held out the coffee. He grunted a "thank you" and took a gulp. Aches and pains aside, waking up to Rory bringing him coffee wasn't a bad thing at all.

She was fresh-faced and scrubbed, her long hair curling in damp tendrils around her face and shoulders, and her blue eyes were bright. Clearly she'd slept just fine. She also smelled fantastic, like key-lime pie. She probably tasted like it, too.

A drop of water trailed from her hair into the V-neckline of her powder-blue shirt. He wanted to lick it up.

Warmth flickered through him. At least one part of his anatomy hadn't been affected by his twisted-pretzel slumber.

"You should've slept in the bed." Rory pulled her hair into a ponytail and took an elastic band off her wrist. "There's room, and I think we could get past the weirdness of sharing a bed."

*Weird* wasn't the word he'd use when it came to sharing Rory's bed.

"I'm okay." He stretched his arms to the sides, hoping he could make time for a workout to loosen up his muscles.

"Besides, if your mom comes knocking on the door before we get up, she'll wonder why we're not sleeping in the same bed."

Grant glanced at her. As rationales went, that one was pretty weak. And while he was…somewhat secure in his ability to control his attraction to Rory even if they were sharing a bed, he couldn't help wondering why she was pushing the issue.

The sofa was damned uncomfortable, though.

"Thanks for this." He lifted the coffee cup, figuring they wouldn't have to cross that bridge until tonight anyway. "What time is it?"

"Seven."

"Have you seen my parents yet?"

"No, but the lights in your house were on when I went to Java Works to get the coffee." She reached for her cell phone and showed him the screen. "I also made an itinerary…tentative, in case your parents have other ideas about what they want to do, but I figured we need to keep them as busy as possible. Boredom is a surefire path straight to Bali, and from the looks of Nathan's social media pages, he and Alice won't want anything bursting their glowing bubble of happiness."

Grant scrolled through the itinerary, which included everything from a tour of the local mission to guided nature hikes and a whale-watching boat ride.

She'd planned for his parents to meet Mayor Bowers, eat at all the local restaurants, attend a Bliss Cove Theater production of *South Pacific*, take an *en plein air* painting class on the coast, spend an afternoon at the boardwalk, and participate in all the Harvest Festival events. She'd even scheduled "down time" if Joanna and Edward wanted to go back to the house and rest.

An emotion he couldn't define nudged at Grant. It was warm and soft, like a fuzzy little puppy had just settled on his chest and tucked its head underneath his chin.

"This is great." He handed the phone back to Rory, deflecting a stab of irritation that he couldn't think of a better word. "Thanks for taking the time to do that."

"I figure the more they're enjoying themselves, the less time they'll have to think about leaving early and catching a flight to Indonesia." She rose and picked up another coffee cup from the counter. "I'm just on-call at Sugar Joy now, so I can show them around if you have to take a shift."

"I worked it out so I can drop in when needed." He stood, lifting his arms above his head for another stretch. His back muscles lengthened. "The other guys will cover the shifts and call me if they need me. I'd better keep a close eye on Mom and Dad all week."

He headed to the bathroom for a quick shower. A fragrant

mist coated the air, smelling like limes and other citrusy scents.

The shower contained matching bottles of shampoo and body wash. He'd never have pegged Rory as a woman who liked fancy personal-care products—he didn't remember carting anything except bar soap out of her apartment—but maybe it was one of her "secrets."

He wanted to know more of them. In fact, thinking about Rory and her secrets while he was soaping himself down brought up vivid fantasies that had sparked last night when he'd come back from work and found her sleeping.

Though he'd felt like a pervert, he hadn't been able to stop himself from looking at her. With her hair spread over the pillow, one slender arm stretched to the other side of the bed, and her body moving in the steady rhythm of sleep, she'd been like one of those fairy-tale princesses that she probably hated.

But *damn*. She'd been wearing a peach-colored tank top that hugged the generous curves of her breasts and displayed her pale shoulders. Her skin was burnished by the moonlight.

He'd been struck with an intense urge to press his lips against her neck, tangle his fingers into the straps of her tank and ease them down over her breasts. She'd be soft all over, and based on her responsiveness to their kisses, she'd react like a firecracker to his touch. He could practically see her writhing underneath him.

Turning the shower water to cold, he stuck his head under the freezing spray and told himself to get a grip. Even though they'd been blindsided by his parents' visit, Rory was being so damned good about it all that he felt even worse for his lustful thoughts.

Not that it had been easy to stay away from her over the past two years. He'd always been conscious of not dating women in Bliss Cove, especially the ones who frequented the Mousehole. It avoided complications if things went wrong, and even if they didn't, he had no desire to become the target of local gossip.

The boundaries hadn't prevented him from finding female company—he'd had his fair share of relationships, albeit short-term, and no-strings-attached affairs with women in neighboring towns or up in Santa Cruz.

God knew he'd enjoyed himself, and he'd liked the women a lot, but he'd never felt...*this* toward them. He'd never wondered what might have happened if they'd stayed together. He'd never wondered if he should rethink his "no commitment" stance.

If any woman could make him wonder that now, it was Rory. Which was so completely stupid because she was leaving Bliss Cove soon, and she wasn't a woman he'd ever consider for a short-term relationship or a no-strings affair.

The realization felt like the earthquake tremor was pushing toward the fault line.

He got out of the shower and grabbed a towel. Better shove all those thoughts down deep and focus on getting through the next week. Ignoring the fact that it was increasingly easy to "pretend" like Rory was his girlfriend. His live-in lover.

A knock came at the bathroom door. "Your mom just texted that she and your father will be ready for breakfast at eight. She wants to go to the market later so she can get some food for your kitchen. She's not very impressed with the stock in your fridge."

"Are you still wondering why I don't want a cell phone?" Grant hitched on his jeans and pulled a T-shirt over his head before opening the door. "Now that she has your number, there's no escaping Joanna Taylor."

"I actually find her impressive in a sort of Machiavellian way." Rory shoved her phone into her back pocket. She slipped her gaze over him in that way she'd been doing since the first time they'd kissed. She hadn't looked at him that way before then—at least, not that he'd noticed.

"I'm going to swing by Sugar Joy to make sure Linda's doing okay on her first full week." She started toward the door, her ponytail swinging. "I'll meet you over at Ruby's Kitchen at around eight-fifteen. Do you want me to call ahead and ask Ruby to save us that nice booth by the corner window?"

"That would be great, thanks. I'm going to get a few things done at the tavern, then we'll head over."

He went into the tavern kitchen to make sure everything was ready for the morning prep. The Mousehole opened at eleven, and he double-checked the schedule, completed some paperwork and orders, and did a quick inventory before going to get his parents.

"Good morning!" His mother answered the door, looking like a classic movie star in a Chanel suit and scarf. She reached out for a hug. "We slept marvelously. Must be the sea air. Edward, Grant is here! You'd better not be on your phone."

"Morning." Edward Taylor strode toward the foyer, straightening the cuffs of his shirt. "So begins the first day of our second honeymoon, eh? Is there a golf course nearby?"

"There's mini-golf near the boardwalk," Grant offered.

"Hit the ball into the shark's mouth on the last hole and win a fifty-percent discount on ride tickets."

"That sounds like fun." Joanna picked up a Prada bag and hooked it over her arm. "Where's Rory?"

"She's meeting us at the diner."

"Lovely. I can't remember the last time I ate at a diner. Can you, Edward?"

"The Sunny Side Up on Shattuck Avenue." He slid his phone into the pocket of his suit jacket. "Maybe it wasn't the last time, but I remember it."

"Oh my goodness." Joanna laughed and set her sunglasses on top of her head. "That was our favorite place to eat when we were in college, Grant. The Cal Berkeley students used to go there all the time because their pancakes were so cheap. And huge. They almost filled the entire plate, and they'd give you three of them."

"And they had unlimited coffee refills," Edward added. "It was an undergrad's dream."

"We should visit Skyline College while we're here." Joanna preceded Grant out the door to the car. "I haven't been on a college campus in years."

"Skyline has tours, so it can be arranged," Grant said. "Rory's sister is a professor in the Classics department."

He winced when the statement came out. All he needed was to drag Rory's family into this farce.

"I'd love to meet her." Joanna paused while Edward opened the passenger side door of their car for her. "We'll follow you to the diner, Grant. Your father and I will want the car if we decide to come back."

Grateful for a short reprieve, Grant got into his truck and led the way to Ruby's Kitchen. Rory was already there, having

145

commandeered the booth by the corner window. The instant they sat down, one of the servers swooped in with fresh coffee.

"This is Bliss Cove's most popular breakfast place," Rory informed his parents. "The eggs Benedict are the specialty, but the Belgian waffles are my personal favorite."

"I usually have a soft-boiled egg and grapefruit for breakfast, but the waffle does sound delicious." Joanna studied the menu. "Edward, remember the ER doctor told you to watch your cholesterol."

Grant looked up. "When were you in the ER?"

"Your father had an *incident* a few months ago." Joanna took a sip of coffee. "It turned out to be an angina attack."

"It was nothing." Edward set his menu aside with a frown.

"It was not *nothing*." Joanna peered at him over the tops of her reading glasses. "Angina is a symptom of heart disease, and with your history of heart trouble, you need to take care of yourself."

"Why didn't anyone tell me Dad was in the ER?" Though he knew exactly *why*, he hated thinking that his family, even Nathan, would deliberately keep him out of the loop regarding a health emergency.

"I didn't want to bother you, dear." Joanna closed her menu.

"Telling me that Dad was in the ER isn't *bothering* me." Tension crawled through his shoulders. "You can dislike what I do and where I live all you want, but I'm still part of this family. Nathan didn't even tell me."

"We told him not to." Joanna arranged the silverware neatly at her place. "Don't be upset, Grant. There was nothing you could have done."

"That's not the point, Mom. When something serious happens, I want to know about it."

"Why?" his father asked gruffly. "So you can come running home and be the hero?"

"Bliss Cove is home, but yes, I would have come to visit you." Grant managed to keep his tone even. "But be the hero? How?"

"Maybe by making chicken soup." Edward shrugged and sat back, eyeing him narrowly. "You don't bother *visiting* when everything is fine, but you want to be kept informed when things go bad?"

"I don't visit because you spend the whole time telling me what a shitty son I am for not doing what you want me to do," Grant snapped. "You couldn't even hold it together for Nathan's wedding, could you? You had to let everyone know what a—"

He cut the words off as he felt the warning pressure of Rory's hand on his thigh.

Edward's face darkened with annoyance. "So you figure that visiting me in the hospital would change my mind?"

"Stop it." Joanna threw her husband a fulminating look. "I will not have you two fighting, especially in public and in front of Rory. Both of you need to get it together and be civilized to each other, or I swear I will lock you in a room and not let you out until you've made peace. Now I would like to order and have a nice breakfast. I'm going to take Rory's suggestion of a Belgian waffle, my diet be damned."

Edward huffed, still staring Grant down beneath his heavy eyebrows.

"Either you're part of this family through good and bad,"

he said, his voice low, "or you're not part of this family at all."

"Edward!" Joanna grabbed her purse strap. "One more remark like that, and I'm walking out and not coming back."

"Liz, can you come take our orders?" Rory waved frantically toward one of the servers. "We're really hungry over here."

Liz hurried over, and after they placed their orders, Rory switched the conversation to the history of the Mousehole, which used to be a stagecoach stop in the nineteenth century. Though Joanna made interested noises and acted as if the Belgian waffle were the most incredible thing she'd ever eaten, tension clouded the atmosphere. Edward didn't speak, and Grant struggled to contribute to the conversation.

Finally, he pushed his half-eaten eggs aside and gestured to Liz for the check. Edward reached for his wallet.

"I've got it, Dad."

"No need." His father tossed a fifty on the table. "I'm not a charity case."

"Speaking of charities," Rory said quickly before Grant could respond. "Did you know Grant helped start a non-profit organization to bring healthier food and nutritional education into low-income schools?"

"Really?" Joanna looked at her son with pride. "Why, that's wonderful, Grant."

"It's really made an impact on many of the rural communities," Rory added.

"At Intellix, we work with many tech-related non-profits to help get computers and technology education into underserved communities." Edward put his crumpled napkin on the table and stood. "We're also working on legislation to bring fiber optic lines and broadband services to areas that have minimal connectivity. I noticed the signal at your house is weak, Grant. Maybe we should put Bliss Cove on our list."

He strode toward the door. Joanna muttered something, grabbed her purse, and went after him. Grant pulled a breath into his tight lungs.

"Wow," Rory murmured. "He's like King Claudius. He was the asshole king, right?"

Grant let out a huff of amusement. "That would make me Hamlet, and both of those characters end up dead."

"Okay, forget the Shakespeare references." Rory glanced out the window to where Joanna was delivering another apparently scathing lecture to Edward. "I thought I liked him at first, but my opinion of him has nosedived considerably."

"He gets that a lot, I'm sure."

"Your mother is looking in our direction." Rory edged closer to Grant. "But no one else is, and Liz is behind the counter making a pot of coffee. So for your mother's benefit, I'm going to kiss your cheek and act like I'm being all consoling and sweet, okay?"

"Go for it."

She pressed her soft lips to his cheek and tangled her fingers into the hair at his nape. His nose filled with her scent —limes and sugar, now with an added touch of maple syrup. Sweet, indeed. The length of her thigh pressed against his. Her breasts nudged his arm. He felt her long, silky hair on his neck. She was like a cool glass of water pouring over his blistering anger.

"How'm I doing?" She rubbed her lips across his jaw.

"So well that I'm about to get totally inappropriate for a family diner." He slid his hand over her leg underneath the table and turned his head to kiss her. "Funny thing is, I don't give a damn."

Because having Rory at his side was turning out to be his saving grace.

"Let's go." She pinched the back of his neck and eased away. "Take the high road."

He gave a derisive snort. "The high road is like the edge of a cliff. People fall off it."

"Maybe, but at least they first get to enjoy the view." She nudged him with her hip. "Come on. We have a whole day of Frick and Frack to deal with."

After getting out of the booth, Grant turned to face her. "Look, I know this sucks. You don't have to do this. Go back to the cottage or spend the day with your sisters or something. I'll tell my parents you have to work."

She arched an eyebrow. "Do you *want* me to leave you alone with them?"

He thumped his chest. "Me brave and strong. Me can go it alone."

"I know you *can*, tough guy." She narrowed her eyes. "I'm saying you don't have to. At least if I'm around, it's two against two. Though I'm beginning to think your mother is more on our side than she's letting on."

She pulled on her sweater and tugged her ponytail from the collar. "Besides, the only work I can do is getting up to date on the new projects for Digicore, but I don't have my desktop available. So, instead, I can devote myself to enjoying your father's charm."

"I'd rather you enjoyed my charm."

"You have charm?"

He kissed her again, hard and swift. The taste of her went

straight to his blood. His heart ran around in circles. There might have been internal singing.

When he lifted his head, he hoped his mother hadn't witnessed the kiss. It was one thing for her to see them pretending. It was another thing entirely for her to see something real.

# CHAPTER 12

The Rolling Stones' "Wild Horses" blasted from Rory's media player as she sat on the sofa in the cottage later that evening. She bit into another gummy worm and scrolled through the search results on her laptop, examining the details of the urban planning and development software she'd found.

Hunter, Aria's significant other, had emailed her a list of what he was looking for to assist with the renovation of Mariposa Street. Rory had also contacted several friends and former colleagues for recommendations, though no one knew of a program that fit all of Hunter's and the design studio's requirements.

She set the laptop aside and rubbed her eyes. After the contentious breakfast with the Taylors this morning, the rest of the day had been thankfully conflict-free. It hadn't been all rainbows and chipmunks—Edward had been mostly silent, and Joanna had tried hard to cover for his bad temper—but at least they'd seemed to enjoy touring downtown and the historic Spanish mission.

At four, Joanna had suggested they meet up again tomorrow morning, as she and Edward wanted to try out a Michelin-starred restaurant in Rainwood and do some things on their own. Neither Grant nor Rory had tried to change their minds.

Grant had gone to the Mousehole for the dinner rush, and Rory had returned to the cottage to see what she could find out about the software. Grant had brought her dinner—an astonishingly tender and delicious steak with roasted vegetables and rice pilaf—before going back to the tavern. Tempted as she was to go hang out at the bar and pester him, he'd been on edge all day and probably just wanted to focus on work.

A chill rippled through the air. Zipping up her hoodie the rest of the way, she put the kettle on the hot plate to boil water for a cup of instant coffee.

The Jacques Pepin and Julia Child cookbook that she'd borrowed from Grant was sitting on the counter. She leafed through the pages, struck by the detailed techniques required for everything from deboning a chicken to making sure a sauce didn't "break."

As she was studying a food-porn photo of a glistening caramel flan, Grant came in—sweaty, tired, and surrounded by the smoky smell of charcoal. For some reason, seeing him all worn out from presiding over the grill and stove made Rory's nerves tingle. She was accustomed to him serving food and pouring drinks, but discovering how immersed he got in his first love of cooking was pretty damned sexy.

"Chocolate cake." He set a box on the counter, then pulled off his bandana and wiped his forehead with the back of his hand. "You doing okay?"

"Now that there's cake, of course." She nibbled the head

off a cherry gummy worm. "Your mom texted me that they had a nice dinner at Field & Farm over in Rainwood, and she wants to go shopping tomorrow morning." She hesitated. "Also, she says your dad isn't interested in shopping, so he wants to go fishing with you."

"Hah." Grant started toward the bathroom. "She wants him to want to go fishing with me."

He closed the bathroom door, and a second later the shower started. Rory set two mugs on the counter and added spoonfuls of instant coffee. The water was boiling by the time Grant emerged in navy pajama pants and a T-shirt that clung to the still-damp parts of his torso.

"I could've brought over some coffee from the tavern." He accepted the cup Rory held out to him with a nod of thanks. Now he smelled like soap and shampoo, and she tingled all over again.

"Making instant is more fun." She sipped the coffee. "It's like camping."

A smile twitched his mouth. "She's a piece of work, huh?"

"Yeah, but I like her." Rory rubbed her thumb over the handle of her mug. "When I first met your parents at the wedding dinner, your father seemed to be especially upset because the rift between you was hurting your mother."

"He thinks *I'm* hurting my mother." Grant leaned back against the counter, his shoulders tightening. "Maybe I am. He's always been angry that I didn't marry Vivian, even though my mother orchestrated the whole thing. She wanted me to stay in San Francisco, marry Vivian, and work for Intellix. Obviously I didn't do any of those things, and there was no compromise. Neither of them understood why I'd choose a different life. So, yeah. My father blames me for my mother's unhappiness, and he won't let me forget it."

"He also doesn't see that by hurting you, he's hurting her."

Grant stared at his mug. "There's a lot he doesn't see."

"To be fair, there's a lot you don't *let* people see."

He shrugged and met her gaze. His eyes were so green, shot through with gold. Sunlight in a forest.

"You're not exactly an open book either." He lifted his mug to his lips.

"Is this about me singing karaoke in my underwear?"

A low chuckle rumbled in his chest. "Could be. It could also be about why you've stayed in Bliss Cove for two years and why you're not thrilled about your job with Digicore."

Rory's heart stuttered. Breaking eye contact, she paced to the sofa. "What's that supposed to mean?"

"You tell me." He studied her, his gaze hooded. "It's pretty clear, to me at least, that Digicore may be a job you need, but it's not necessarily one you want."

Unease and something else tangled in Rory's belly—a combination of appreciation and wariness that Grant, of all people, understood what she hadn't even been able to fully articulate to herself.

"Need, want, it doesn't really matter." She sank onto the sofa and dragged her hands through her hair. "I'm taking the job. The pay and benefits are fantastic, and the work itself looks challenging enough to hold my interest. There's a chance I'll get to lead my own projects. Plenty of room for advancement."

"So why aren't you more excited about it?"

*What business is it of yours?*

She stopped the sharp retort. She'd learned a lot about Grant's inner life in the past few days—seen more than she'd seen in two years—and their intimacy was increasing exponentially. There was no reason she couldn't give him the truth. It wouldn't change the facts or her plans.

"Because I've dealt with a lot of shit as a woman in the tech industry, and I don't want to put up with it again." She leaned forward and turned off her laptop to give herself something to do. "But I also hate letting them push me out, and I love the work, so…I have to figure out a way to deal with it. Again."

Grant frowned. "Sexual harassment and discrimination? I've heard plenty of stories. All reprehensible."

"I knew about it going in, and it's no big secret." Rory rubbed her temples against a growing tension. "I've always been the only woman in the room, and when you pair that with a non-inclusive culture and a lot of men…not all of them, of course, but plenty…who use sex as power, you're stuck in a toxic atmosphere. I filed a lot of complaints to no avail, especially if the fucker who put his hand on my ass or invited me to a strip club was a *stellar performer* whom the company didn't want to penalize. I learned quickly that if I wanted to stay in the industry, I had to develop an armor as thick as steel. So I did. I ignored sexist comments, didn't let anyone get close to me, and worked as hard as I could even when I was passed over for projects I deserved."

"Hell, Rory. I'm sorry."

She shook her head. "I did have jobs where I was treated well, and I worked on some incredible systems. A lot of the guys were good people…or at least, not total scumbags. And for what it's worth, I know that Intellix is one of the few companies making a conscious effort to right the balance by hiring and promoting women who've made great contributions to the industry. But several of the places where I've worked haven't done that.

"I did make good money, though, so after I left a job because my boss made no secret of wanting to have sex with me, I took some time to pursue my own project. I'd had an idea about designing a system for integrating medical software. I called it MedCure. After working on it for about a year, I decided to seek funding. I approached a venture capitalist who requested a meeting and a presentation. Turned out he wasn't interested in the system."

Grant's jaw tightened. "What happened?"

"You can guess." Rory sighed, battling back old, raw anger and hurt. "He propositioned me, I rejected him, and he got mad. Not only did he turn down my idea, he blackballed me to other VC firms and blocked other potential funding opportunities."

Grant pushed away from the counter, his shoulders stiff. "And he got away with that?"

"I had a record, so to speak, for filing complaints and being labeled a troublemaker, so, honestly, it wasn't the first time someone had undercut me. That didn't make it suck any less...obviously, it was worse because I'd been trying to strike out on my own...but that kind of shit happens all the time. I can't say I was surprised. Disgusted, furious, disheartened, sad...but not surprised."

"Rory, that's sickening." Grant flexed his hands, anger burning in his eyes. "It's evil, what that asshole did to you. He can't get away with this."

"It's too late, and I'm over it now." She rubbed her chest,

where grief still coiled tightly. "My father died not long after it happened, and that was an infinitely worse blow. But in some ways, his death put the whole mess in the past where it belongs."

Living in Bliss Cove again, close to her mother and sisters and surrounded by everything familiar, had been exactly the balm she needed to soothe all her blistering pain.

"What happened to MedCure?" Grant asked.

"Another company came out with a similar system that took off commercially, so I missed the mark. It was bad timing and worse circumstances."

"And having to go back into that hellhole…is that why you were so angry when you came into the Mousehole last week wanting a scotch?"

"Sort of." Rory leaned her elbows on her knees and sighed. "I wasn't all that thrilled about returning to the corporate world to begin with. Then I got a sexist come-on message from a guy I'll be working with, which made it worse. I'll deal with it again, and I'll file complaints and take a stand, but I wish I didn't have to.

"I haven't been able to tell anyone because my mother and sisters are all being so supportive about the job. In fact, my mom has been gently telling me for at least six months that it's time for me to move on. She's right. I've just been too much of a coward to take the step until now."

"You're not a coward." Grant crouched beside her, and the darkness in his eyes seared right into her heart. "Cowards don't go back into the battle."

Her throat constricted. "I want so badly to get back to the work, to find out what else I can do, to make my ideas come to life, but I'm scared, too. Of losing. Of being considered less. Of doubting myself."

"Being scared and still going forward makes you the bravest person I know." He put his hand over her wrist and squeezed. "Cowards run away and hide. Sometimes in Mouseholes."

"You're not a coward either, Grant." Rory turned her hand so their palms touched. "You stood up for what you want, and now you have the life you chose and created. There's nothing stronger than living an authentic life." She wiped away a stray tear. "I might've gotten that from Oprah."

A smile tugged at his mouth. "Maybe we're both braver than we think."

She looked down at their loosely clasped hands. The calluses on his palm rubbed against hers. He had beautiful hands—long fingers with square, blunt nails and a dusting of dark hair on the back. There was a slight nick on his thumb.

She wanted his hands on her body.

Her heartbeat increased. She lifted her gaze to his, wondering if he could read the desire that had been brewing inside her for so long that she didn't even know when it had started. Maybe the moment he first pushed the button on the singing fish to make her smile.

A shutter descended over his expression. Tugging his hand from hers, he started to rise. "I'll get you a fork for the cake."

Rory closed her hand around his wrist. "I don't want the cake. Well. Not right *now*."

He hesitated, his shoulders tensing. She sensed him waging an internal war, as if he wanted to be on one side but needed to be on the other. Beneath her fingertips, his pulse beat heavily.

"Speaking of cowardly…" He paused and swallowed. "This isn't fair to you. I should never have asked you to lie for me. I'll tell my parents the truth tomorrow."

"And make things worse? What if they never forgive you?"

"I'll handle it."

"Grant, if you tell them the truth, then they'll certainly never come back to Bliss Cove again. At least now, you're moving in the right direction."

"With a lie." His mouth twisted. "A date is one thing, but I never intended for us to have a fake relationship."

"Then let's make it real."

His gaze crashed into hers so powerfully that her whole body surged with awareness. He took hold of her other hand and tugged her to her feet, his expression unreadable. A muscle ticked in his jaw. Standing, he was so much bigger than she was that her belly twisted with anxiety.

Hooking up with Grant the Tavern Owner was one thing. Hooking up with big, strong, sexy Grant the Hunk whose kisses made her toes curl was something else entirely.

No, wait. Those two men were one and the same. It had just taken her a long time to figure that out.

Rory pulled in a breath, her anxiety heightening at the thought that she'd just ruined things between them for good. "I meant—"

"I know what you meant." He brushed his thumb over her lower lip. Heat flickered in his eyes. "Do you know why I've never crossed that line with you before?"

She shook her head. A tremble ran through her blood.

"Because I'm not interested in long-term, or even short-term commitment. I don't want or need a relationship. The women I've been with understand that, though I've had a few tell me they wanted to change my mind. They failed."

He touched the hollow of her throat. "But whenever I've thought about it, when I've imagined the only woman in the world who *could* change my mind...you're the one I see."

For the first time in her life, Rory went weak in the knees. Pleasure swirled through her. She grabbed hold of Grant's T-shirt to steady herself.

He slipped his arms around her waist, pulling their lower bodies together. The hard ridge of his erection pressed against her belly. A rippling shock of arousal jolted her.

"Does..." She flicked her tongue out to lick her dry lips. "Does that mean you're going to cross the line now?"

He searched her face, his green eyes penetrating. "Only if you say *yes*."

"I think you've always been my *yes*."

He smiled. He moved his hands to the sides of her neck and lowered his head to kiss her. Bliss exploded through her along with another emotion...*relief*, as if a tight constraint had finally snapped, releasing them both.

He tilted her head, probing her mouth gently with his tongue. She curled her hands against his sides as he pressed one hand to her lower back and molded her body to his.

*God.* He was such a man—all hard muscles and tense physicality. While Rory had no doubt that Grant was capable of losing control, she sensed his self-restraint as if it were tangible. Not for anything would he push her too far. He wouldn't even go close to the edge unless she gave him her full consent.

"Yes." She drove one hand into his hair, tightening her fingers into the thick strands. She was starting to burn. *"Yes."*

Together, they moved toward the bed. He stopped just short of lowering her onto it to unzip her gray hoodie, which just so happened to be the only thing she was wearing. His eyes darkened as he slowly revealed her bare breasts. His hot gaze raking over her skin was enough to make Rory bite her lip on a moan.

"You are so damned beautiful." He lowered her onto the bed, easing his body between her legs as he planted both hands on either side of her head and kissed her again.

Rory squirmed. Hot currents of electricity streamed from the touch of his mouth all the way down to her toes. He spread his hand over her torso and into her pants. A low murmur of approval escaped him when he discovered she wasn't wearing any panties.

She couldn't speak past the heat rising to her throat. Her heart hammered as he slipped her pants off, and then she was naked while he was still fully clothed. Not that his pajama pants did a thing to hide his own considerable arousal. She reached for him.

"Wait." He closed his hand around her wrist. "I don't have a condom."

"It's okay. I'm protected, and…" A flush rose to her cheeks. "It's been a while."

He brushed his mouth against hers. "For me, too."

His admission dissolved any lingering questions, leaving her in no doubt that they had been converging toward this moment together. She gestured to his clothes. "Your turn."

He shucked off his shirt and dropped it to the floor, then moved away and stepped out of his pants. Rory's mouth went dry at the sight of his body, which was more gorgeous and powerful than she could have imagined. His sculpted pecs sloped down to a washboard abdomen whose ridges she wanted to trace with her tongue.

He put one knee on the bed. Their gazes met, hot and charged. Rory grabbed his forearms and pulled him on top of her, wrapping her legs around his thighs in a full-body *yes*.

His eyes blazed. She opened for him, so ready she ached. But he appeared to be in no hurry, as he skimmed his lips over her shoulder and lower to her breasts.

A hot thread of tension uncoiled inside her. Never before had a man made love to her with such thorough attention, as if her pleasure overshadowed his. She rose to her elbows as he kissed and stroked his way down her body, every inch of contact eliciting sparks of arousal.

Had she even known she was capable of this kind of physical response? Or maybe it was him—the way he sensed exactly where she liked to be touched, the control winding through his strong body, his low murmurs vibrating against her skin. Every part of her felt alive, sensitized to his callused touch and the press of his beautiful mouth.

Finally, she reached down to twist her fingers into his hair. "Grant, please."

Positioning himself between her legs, he locked his gaze to hers. Sweat trickled down his temple. He eased inside her. Rory gasped. Fire shot across her nerves. A groan shook his chest, the deep echo vibrating through her.

Curling her fingers into his biceps, she arched her hips just as he thrust forward. She paused, dragging a breath into her burning lungs, letting him set the pace of their union.

Then they were rocking forward and back together, a slow

gentle rhythm increasing in speed as their urgency grew. She drove her hands into his hair as he brought his mouth down on hers again, his kiss hot and greedy.

Her need mounted in agonizingly delicious increments until she couldn't contain it any longer. Murmuring sexy words of encouragement, Grant slipped his hand between their bodies and stimulated her to completion. She bucked up against him and dug her fingers into his arms. A cry of pleasure tore from her throat as sensations consumed her.

Like the anchor he was, he steadied her and let her cling to him as she rose and fell through the wave. Only when her pleasure began to ebb did he loosen the reins of his control. He sank deep inside her with a rough shout, his muscles locking and tensing beautifully as he surrendered to his own release.

He rolled beside her on the bed, his chest heaving. Rory fell back against the pillows and struggled to catch her breath. Though her body still trembled with lingering sensations, an incredible lightness filled her, as if she were made of fine-spun cotton candy.

She turned her head to find Grant watching her, a flush cresting his cheekbones and his skin damp with sweat. A hint of wariness darkened his eyes.

Rory brought her hand up to touch his stubbly face. She traced the hard line of his jaw, rubbed his nose, ran her finger over his beautifully shaped mouth.

"Do you want to know why I love computer programming?" she asked.

"Not the post-sex talk I was hoping for, but sure." He stroked his hand over her torso to her breasts.

"It's so logical. When you write a program, you're

creating something out of nothing, but with order. You can rewrite code endlessly until you get the results you want. You find solutions to problems. When I'm in a programming zone, everything is clear and structured. Being in that world makes it easier to deal with the rest of life, which is always messy and unpredictable."

"And computers are easier to handle than people, right?"

"Sometimes. At least they always do what I tell them to do." She shifted and leaned on his chest, propping her chin on her folded arms. "My point is that I start writing a program knowing exactly what my end goal is and how I plan to get there. But real life is obviously very different, and I've never started a relationship thinking there's an end goal."

Grant lifted his head, his eyes narrowing slightly. "You don't need to use a technology metaphor to tell me you've never dreamed of fairy tales and happily ever after."

Rory's face heated. "I know you haven't either. I just didn't want you to think I was expecting something beyond a good time."

"Why, because I said you were the one woman who could change my mind about relationships?" He frowned, his muscles tensing underneath her arms. "This is about a hell of a lot more than a *good time*. I get why you can't admit that, but you're forgetting that I know you. Yeah, you're a computer nerd who wants everyone to think you live on binary codes and JavaScript, but you also have a heart bigger than the sun and a soul made up of kindness and loyalty. Letting other people see that doesn't make you weak or vulnerable. It makes you *you*."

Swallowing past a flood of emotion, Rory rested her forehead on his chest. If her heart really was "bigger than the sun," then he was becoming the flame right in the very center.

"I still don't dream of fairy tales," she mumbled.

A laugh vibrated through his chest. "Neither do I."

She wasn't convinced about *happily ever after* either. But she was beginning to think that Grant was the only man in the world who could change her mind.

# CHAPTER 13

Rory woke with darkness still pressing against the windows, and Grant's arm and leg pinning her to the mattress. She breathed in his scent, kissed his shoulder, and poked him in the abs.

"Hey, Rock, let me up. I need to pee."

He grunted in his sleep and shifted, pulling her closer. Rory's eyes widened as his erection pushed against her thigh. Apparently he had his own needs. Which she would be more than happy to meet...just not right this second.

She shoved at his arm and wiggled her way out from underneath his muscular bulk. He must work out regularly because a man didn't get biceps like that from chopping tomatoes.

Pulling on a T-shirt, she padded into the bathroom and used the toilet, pausing at the sink to study herself in the mirror. Her hair was a tousled mess, her cheeks were flushed, and her eyes gleamed with a deep, womanly satisfaction that she still felt clear down to her bones.

*Fold up that feeling and put it in a little box, Rory*

*Prescott. You'll want to remember it when you're back staring at a computer screen in your claustrophobic office cubicle, jacked up on Sour Patch Kids and getting your thrills by making a program work.*

*In that moment, you'll remember Grant. His touch. His breath on your neck. Your response to the flick of his tongue. Warm, solid muscles and taut skin. Him inside you. How alive he is.*

She shivered. She'd known she would miss his presence in her life. His being *right over there*. But deep inside, she suspected that now she would miss him in ways she couldn't even fully comprehend.

A knock thumped on the bathroom door.

"You in there?" His voice was gruff and scowly.

"Nope."

"Too bad." The doorknob rattled. "Because I'm coming in, and I have dirty intentions."

"Oh. Well, in that case, I'm definitely in here."

She turned as the door opened, her heart jumping at the sight of him—sleep-rumpled, messy hair falling over his forehead, and a feral gleam in his eyes. Not to mention…still more than ready. Though less than five feet of space separated them, he stalked toward her in a thrillingly sexy, purposeful approach.

"Next time…" He grabbed her hips and tugged her toward him. "I want to wake up with you there."

"Yeah, I noticed you could've used me right away." Her blood heated as she brushed her fingers across his erection.

"Not *used*." He slid one hand to the back of her neck. "I could have loved you right away."

Rory's breath caught in her throat. Grant brought his mouth down on hers.

"Instead, I'll do it right now," he murmured against her lips.

A thousand colors burst through her heart, like fireworks and spiraling rainbows. He eased her back up against the counter, edging one powerful thigh between her legs. She wound her arms around his neck as their kiss deepened and the air grew thick with heat. He lifted her onto the counter, sliding his hands up her thighs and underneath her T-shirt.

She shivered, no longer surprised by how quickly she responded to him. She'd always kept her attraction to him carefully concealed, even from herself, and it was an enormous relief to unlock those feelings and set them free.

Despite his obvious arousal, he was once again in no hurry to rush things. He slowed the pace of their kiss, stroking his hands up and down her thighs until she was panting and wrapping her legs around him in invitation. He eased away from her only long enough to turn on the shower before picking her up and stepping under the spray with her.

It was like being in a shoebox with a bull. Rory laughed as he lowered her to her feet, letting her body slide against his. "No way can we do anything fun in here. I can barely move."

"You don't have to." He licked a drop of water from her nose. "I'll do all the moving."

She let him figure out the puzzle of fitting them together. After indulging in more of his slow kissing and caresses that brought her right to the delicious edge, he turned her to face the wall and took her from behind.

The combination of the hot water and his heavy thrusts

pushed Rory's urgency higher every second. She had nothing to grasp to hold herself upright, but she didn't fear falling because Grant's grip on her was so tight and secure that she knew on some primal level that he would never let go.

When the waves crashed over her again, he pulled her back against him and used his fingers to ease the final sensations from her body. But this time, before he could give in to his own release, she turned and went down on her knees.

Urging him to completion, watching his gorgeous body tense and contract with pleasure, gave Rory a rich feeling of both power and yielding. As if she was affirming that she could take care of him, when he had always taken care of her.

Even if she hadn't known that was what he was doing.

When the shower water began to cool, Grant wrapped her in a towel so big and fluffy it felt like a cloud.

"I had no idea you were into luxury bath towels." She rubbed the thick cotton over her legs.

"I got those for you after you asked to move into the cottage."

"Really?"

"Yeah, when I was getting the place cleaned up." He hitched on his pajama pants and returned to the main room.

Rory followed, oddly pleased by the idea of him buying towels for her. She didn't even buy towels for herself. As far as she could remember, she'd been using Callie's old hand-me-downs.

Since it was still dark, they tumbled back into bed. Grant wrapped himself around her again, his body a striking combination of solid muscle and a warm haven. Ignoring the persistent feeling that she could get used to this, Rory tucked herself against him.

"So now do we pretend like we're pretending that we're real?" she murmured.

"I don't know about you…" He pressed his lips to the top of her head. "But I'm not pretending anymore."

"Good." She slipped her arm around his waist and fitted her body to his. "Neither am I."

~

GRANT WOKE JUST AS DAWN BEGAN TO STREAK ACROSS THE horizon. He was pushed to the edge of the bed with Rory half-sprawled over him in a tumble of soft skin and silky hair.

He breathed her in and tightened his hold. Her revelation of what she'd endured at some of her past jobs, and what she might be returning to, had forged a white-hot ball of rage right in the middle of his chest.

He knew she didn't talk about that often, if at all. She'd locked it behind her armor so she wouldn't seem vulnerable.

While he'd never pretend to understand what she'd gone through, he did know how it felt to be considered less. That was just one of the reasons he'd constructed his own life. It sounded like she'd tried to do that once, too, with the MedCure software system before that fucker venture capitalist had destroyed her opportunities.

Rory shifted, her black hair sliding across his chest, her bare leg slipping between his. She spread her hand over his abdomen and opened her eyes. Blue like the sea. He stroked his finger against her full lower lip. Already his body was stirring with lust again.

"Morning." He edged his hand under her T-shirt and rubbed her perfect ass.

"Morning." She leaned in to kiss his chin. "I'm hungry."

"Me too." He slipped his fingers between her thighs.

She caught her breath, but bucked to dislodge his explorations. "Hand me that bag of gummy worms, and then we can get busy again."

With a groan, Grant reluctantly detached himself from her soft heat. "No way are you eating gummy worms for breakfast."

He hitched on a pair of track pants and a T-shirt, pushing his feet into his tennis shoes. "Any requests?"

"Your cooking."

"Give me twenty minutes." He picked up the tavern keys and started toward the door.

"Actually, I really like cinnamon French toast." Rory pushed up on to her elbows. Her hair tumbled around her shoulders, and the sheet barely covered her incredible breasts.

Grant's heart thumped. She was so damned beautiful. "Okay."

"And bacon." Rory pursed her lips. "Coffee, of course. Oh, a cheese omelet would be great. Maybe some fruit, too. Do you know how to cut a strawberry into the shape of a flower?"

He didn't, but for her he'd figure it out.

In the tavern kitchen, he started a pot of coffee, collected ingredients, and began whipping up a batch of French toast. As the cinnamon toast slices sizzled in a pan, he cracked eggs into a bowl.

Behind him, the door opened.

"You'd better not be eating a gummy worm," he remarked.

"There is no earthly reason why I would be," his father

replied.

Grant turned, his spine tensing. His father strode into the kitchen, dressed in jeans and a button-down shirt. Even in casual clothes, Edward Taylor had a formidable presence.

"Sorry. Thought you were Rory."

"I figured. Your mother is still sleeping, but I woke early and was making a few calls. Is there coffee?"

"Help yourself." Grant tilted his head toward the pot. "Mugs are on the shelf over there."

His father poured a cup, eyeing the array of food spread over the counter. "You don't serve breakfast here, do you?"

"No. This is for Rory." Grant flipped the French toast and dropped a pat of butter into the omelet pan. Aware of his father's scrutiny, he started chopping chives.

"Your mother says we're going fishing today." Edward leaned back against the counter and sipped his coffee.

"Sure, if you want to."

Edward shrugged. Grant dumped the chives into a bowl.

"You making an omelet?" his father asked.

"Yeah."

"You need to turn the heat up." Edward turned the knob on the gas burner. "Put the filling in while the eggs are cooking."

"I know how to make an omelet, Dad."

"I would hope so. Not many people realize there's a technique."

Grant set the bowl down. "*You* know how to make an omelet?"

"Damn right I do."

Grant held out the spatula in a silent challenge. His father took it and adjusted the burner flame again.

"I was a short-order diner cook after college." Edward made a disparaging *harrumph* in his throat as he salted the eggs. "Shittiest job I ever had. Long hours, low pay. The place was a dive, too. Probably could have made a book out of the health-code violations. Manager was an asshole. I kept the job because it was the only one that worked with my schedule. Finally, your mother said she was going to walk out on me if I didn't quit."

Grant couldn't remember the last time his father had ever said so much to him all at once. He cut into a brick of cheese and began grating it. "Did you?"

"Turned in my notice the next day. Hated doing it, though. I never wanted to be unemployed."

Grant paused. "Was that when you started Intellix?"

Edward nodded. He added more butter to the pan and swirled it around. "I had an idea for how to improve relational databases, and I contacted a former professor for advice. I worked on it in our apartment living room for a year before I looked for funding. Your mother didn't complain once that we were scraping by on her paycheck. You got any mushrooms? Ham?"

"In the fridge." Setting his knife down, Grant went to the walk-in.

"Get some spinach, too."

After retrieving the items, Grant returned to the counter to find his father starting a bowl of filling. He set the ingredients down and focused on the French toast and bacon. Strange as it was to be cooking beside his father, it was a hell of a lot better than cold silence.

"The eggs should set immediately at the edges." Edward poured the eggs into the hot pan. "Then you push the uncooked part toward the center. I made so many goddamn omelets, I didn't eat eggs for a year after I quit."

"Is that diner still open?"

"No, they shut down a while back." Edward studied the cooking eggs. "Good riddance."

Grant slid the toast onto a plate and dusted it with powdered sugar. After adding slices of bacon, he started paring down a large strawberry.

His father set an impressive omelet, golden-brown and stuffed with a hearty mixture of ham, spinach, mushrooms, and cheese, onto another plate.

"What the hell are you doing to that strawberry?" Edward pulled his heavy eyebrows together and picked up his mug.

Grant frowned at the mangled berry on the cutting board. "Rory asked if I knew how to make a strawberry flower."

"You couldn't just tell her no?"

The kitchen door opened. "I had to eat an apple gummy worm as an appetizer."

Rory entered, a disheveled beauty in slouchy sweatpants and a T-shirt that said *Back That Thing Up*. Under any other circumstances, Grant would have crossed the room to kiss her, but with his father here, everything inside him locked down.

"Oh, morning, Edward." She paused and gave him a little wave. "Didn't realize you were here."

"Didn't realize gummy worms were a suitable food first thing in the morning." He took another sip of coffee. "Or ever."

"They're not." Grant set the plates on the counter and gestured for Rory to sit down. "Which is why she's had to supplement them with nutritional paste."

"Only in times of need." She hitched herself onto a stool and picked up a fork. "This looks amazing."

"My father made the omelet." Grant added two sugars to a cup of coffee and set it in front of her. "A hidden talent."

"I have a few." Edward picked up a knife and plucked a large strawberry from the box. With a few flicks of the blade, he turned the strawberry into a perfect little rose.

"I'll be damned." Grant shook his head in amused surprise. "Did you learn how to do that at the diner?"

"No." Edward presented the rose to Rory, who took it with a smile. "Since your mother was supporting us after I quit working there, I made breakfast every day. Roses were always Joanna's favorite flower, but for years we couldn't afford them. So I learned how to make them out of strawberries."

"That is very sweet." Rory gave Edward an *"I'd never have guessed"* look. "No wonder you've been married for so long."

"I'd be nothing without her." Edward glanced at the wall clock and poured another cup of coffee. "I'll go see if she's up. Leave the food out. I'll make her breakfast this morning."

After he'd left the kitchen, Rory hooked her leg around Grant's thighs and pulled him closer. He bent his head to kiss her. His blood heated.

"Was that progress?" She rubbed his chest.

"I don't know." He ran his hand through her hair. Something loosened inside him, though he knew that had more to do with Rory than his father.

Still, a week ago, he'd never have imagined his father setting foot in the tavern kitchen, much less cooking here. If that was progress, then Grant would take it.

# CHAPTER 14

"Well, that should be interesting." Joanna shaded her eyes with her hand as she and Rory watched Grant and Edward trudge toward Grant's truck with a tackle box, a net, and two fishing rods. "Those two have spent more time together in the past few days than they have in the past three years."

"It sounds to me like your husband is angry over how this whole rift has affected you." Rory closed the cottage door, and she and Joanna started walking toward downtown. "That makes it surprising that he criticizes Grant so often and so publicly. He has to know how much that upsets you."

"Yes, but he's a bit of a bear, as you've noticed." Joanna slipped on her large sunglasses and sighed. "He lets his anger get the better of him. He also just doesn't understand it. Why would his eldest son walk away from everything we've provided for him? Why would he want to run a restaurant, of all professions? Edward hated being a cook so much. He finds it untenable that Grant *chose* that work. He sees it as

Grant turning his back on the legacy he intends to leave to both his family and the world."

*Grant sees it as both you and Edward trying to force him into a life he doesn't want.*

Rory bit her tongue on the remark. Sleeping with Grant didn't give her the right to interfere in his relationship with his parents. It didn't give her any rights at all, in fact. It didn't give him any, either. She'd overstayed her time in Bliss Cove, and now that she had a job waiting for her, she wasn't going to give it up. Not even for him.

"Look at this place." Joanna stopped in front of Naked. "Handmade organic skincare. Heavens, you can smell the florals all the way out here. Let's go in."

"I really don't…" Rory groaned inwardly as Joanna pulled open the door and swept into the fragrant interior. She followed reluctantly, hoping Madeline wasn't working.

"Good morning!" Madeline, stunning in a white sweater dress and perfect makeup—how did she do that smoky thing with eyeshadow?—came out from the backroom. "May I help you?"

"Good morning. I'm visiting from San Francisco, and I was passing by." Joanna peered at the colorful array of bar soaps. "Everything here is organic?"

"Absolutely. Pesticide-free, handmade, ethically sourced, and vegetarian. Oh, hello, Rory. I didn't see you lurking about back there." A smile curved her bow-shaped red mouth.

"Morning, Madeline." Rory picked up a bottle of facial mister and pretended to scrutinize the label.

"How are the Natural Beauty products working out for you?"

"Just fine, thanks."

"Oh!" Joanna lifted her forefinger as if she'd just had an epiphany. She turned to a shelf of Natural Beauty products. "I thought the labels looked familiar. Rory, is this the lotion you have in the bathroom?"

Madeline blinked. Dread began to pool in Rory's stomach.

"Uh, I think so."

"I'm sorry." Madeline shook her head, as if she couldn't imagine what association the elegant woman with the Hermès scarf and Prada bag would have with torn-jeans-and-sweat-shirt Rory Prescott. "Are you together?"

"I'm Grant Taylor's mother." Joanna beamed and set her bag on the front counter. "We're staying at his house, and I sampled some of the lotion and body wash Rory has in the bathroom. I'd been meaning to ask her where she got them."

Madeline's smile turned tight. "Why, Rory. I had no idea you kept your lotions in Grant's bathroom."

Rory scratched her head. For the life of her, she couldn't come up with a single logical explanation for why she would have girly products in the bathroom of one of the most sought-after bachelors in town. The real reason was entirely illogical. And she certainly couldn't refute the obvious reason in front of Joanna.

She and Grant were no longer pretending with each other, but they hadn't discussed actually going public. It wasn't as if they were in a relationship, and Rory didn't want her mother or sisters to question what the heck she was doing hooking up with Grant for a couple of months. She didn't want to question herself either.

"There was a cream that contained almond oil and a hint of orange, I believe." Joanna plucked the cap off a bottle of essential oil and sniffed. "It was nice and light. Do you recall the name?"

"That was our Fresh Skin hydration cream." Madeline walked to a shelf, her heels clicking, and extended a small pot to Joanna. "We also have it in a shower gel, bath bar, and body conditioner. Would you like some free samples?"

"No need, dear. I've already tried them." Joanna examined the bottles. "I'll take them all. Can you hold them for pick-up later? Rory and I have more shopping to do."

"Of course." Madeline carried the products to the front counter. "I'm so glad Rory has introduced you to our little establishment here."

As Joanna searched for her credit card, Madeline swept her gaze to Rory. "Grant might be interested in our line of men's skin care products. You should bring him in sometime."

"Good to know." Rory forced a responding smile, deciding that the less she said, the better.

Joanna seemed to take forever paying for her purchases and asking questions about how, exactly, to apply the facial cream. When they finally left Naked, Rory took a deep breath of fresh air and sent up a silent prayer that Madeline would keep this little visit to herself.

Her hope lasted until lunchtime. After an uneventful and rather pleasant few hours shopping, she and Joanna ate at a soup-and-salad restaurant.

When Joanna went to use the restroom, Rory checked her phone. A text from Aria appeared that was the virtual equivalent of a screech. *YOU AND GRANT?! I KNEW something was going on. Why wouldn't you tell me?*

Rory closed her eyes briefly. She wanted to avoid having

to tell her family anything about what was going on with Grant, but now should she lie or tell them the truth? What *was* the truth, anyway? They were pretending, but last night had been *so not pretend*.

Telling Aria the whole story could come back to bite Rory on the ass—her sister could keep a secret, but if Rory started saying one thing, and Grant another...and with the way gossip spread in this town, any number of variations could get back to Edward and Joanna.

Then what?

She finally responded with: *What are you talking about?*

PESKY LITTLE SISTER: Oh, please. Brooke saw Madeline when she was helping with the Harvest Festival prep, and Madeline dropped the bomb about your stuff in Grant's bathroom or something and you guys living together?!
RORY: In case you forgot, I'm moving away right after Thanksgiving.
PLS: Way to avoid the issue. What is going on?
RORY: I'm staying in Grant's cottage until I move. That's all you need to know.
PLS: Srsly? You won't even throw me a bone?

Rory shoved her phone back into her pocket as Joanna approached. Owing to his lack of connectivity, Grant was likely oblivious to the fact that they were now the hottest topic of gossip in town. He wouldn't like it, either. As much a part of Bliss Cove as he'd become, everyone knew he fiercely guarded his privacy. Pretend or real.

"Edward says they're back at the tavern." Joanna slipped her purse over her shoulder. "Let's go there, and then I'm sure you and Grant have work to do. We'll meet you later for the festival."

"Sounds good. Be sure to check the schedule of events so you won't miss anything you want to see."

They returned to the Mousehole, which was in the midst of the post-lunch lull. A few patrons still sat at the tables finishing their meals, and Grant and his father were at the bar. From the look of things, they weren't being all buddy-buddy, but they weren't at each other's throats either.

"Hello, you two," Joanna trilled, leaning in to kiss her husband's cheek. "How was fishing?"

"Excellent." Edward sipped his beer. He looked sunburned and tired, both of which gave him somewhat relaxed air that Rory hadn't seen before now. Good fishing probably had something to do with that. Maybe so had making a strawberry rose and cooking breakfast for his wife again.

She glanced at Grant, who was working behind the bar. He met her gaze, his eyes crinkling with warmth. A pleasurable shiver rained down her spine.

She returned his smile with a quick, private one of her own. She wanted desperately to kiss him, to smell his windy, outdoors scent, but she didn't know what the rules were about that kind of public display.

"Rory, Grant mentioned you're researching software about urban planning and restoration." Edward swiveled on the barstool to face her. "Tell me more."

Though Rory hadn't wanted to seem as if she were taking advantage of her relationship with Grant by seeking his father's input, she figured it was okay if he offered. She explained about the redevelopment of Mariposa Street and showed Edward the list of functions Hunter and Studio Twenty-Five were looking for.

"Planning grids, 3D visualization, project history, document linking, and all this other stuff. They use several different programs, but want to find something more comprehensive."

Edward studied the email. "Forward this to me, and I'll look into it. Orion has a team working on a real estate app, so they might have a lead."

"I'd appreciate that, thanks."

As Edward turned back to Joanna, Rory slipped behind the bar to give Grant a squeeze around the waist.

"You hungry?" He patted her hip.

Considering she'd eaten a cup of broccoli soup and a garden salad for lunch, she was starving, but she shook her head. "Your mother and I just ate. But…er, actually, if you have a second, I wanted to go over the weekend plans with you."

"Sure." He glanced at his parents, who were sitting and talking together. Edward had his hand over Joanna's. "Let's go in the back."

Rory followed him through the kitchen to the back door. As soon as they stepped outside, he hauled her close and kissed her. Sunlight burst through her veins at the hard press of his mouth, the possessive grip of his hands on her hips.

After kissing her so thoroughly that her whole body went soft, he lifted his head. Heat turned his green eyes molten.

"You want the bad news first or the good?" he asked.

"Ugh." She toyed with the hair at the nape of his neck. "I don't want any bad news, but you might as well give it to me fast. And hard. And—"

"Careful." He pinched her ass. "I'm only giving you the good stuff fast and hard. The bad news is that my father wants to go deep-sea fishing, which means I have to spend a whole day on a boat with him."

"Okay, that sucks, but the silver lining is that he obviously enjoyed fishing with you today. That's why he wants an upgrade."

"But *that* means you'll have to entertain my mother while we're off hooking salmon."

She shrugged. "Still not devastating news. We had a good time shopping this morning. Did you know she owned a consignment store after she and your father graduated from college? She'd been a nanny for this wealthy San Francisco family, and when she said she was going to open a shop, the wife gave her a bunch of expensive stuff she was going to throw away. So your mother's shop gained a reputation for high-end goods, and that was where she started learning about things like antique china and collectibles."

"Wow." Grant lifted his eyebrows. "You two get along better than I'd hoped."

"Underneath her manipulative streak, I think she does mean well." Rory patted his chest. "I'm sure that what she really wants is for all of you to mend this rift. She just had to find a way to do it that involved a lot of subterfuge."

"Yeah." Guilt flashed across his features. "I know something about that."

"You're doing everything right." Rory's heart twisted, and she stood on tiptoe to kiss him again. "What's the good news?"

"That to make up for a day of fishing, my father wants to spend the weekend alone with my mother." He pulled her lower body against his. "And you know what that means for us..."

Rory lifted her hand to stop him from kissing her. "Grant."

His forehead creased. "What's wrong?"

"Kind of a long story, but it's getting around that you and I are an...um, item. Madeline figured it out, and she told Brooke, who told Aria, which means...well, everyone else in town will find out sooner rather than later."

"So?"

She blinked. "You're okay with that?"

"Why wouldn't I be?" He slipped his hands down to cup her ass. "It's no one's business, but we're not trying to hide anything." He paused, consternation darkening his expression. "Are we?"

"No, but I know you guard your privacy." She bit her lip. "I'm not really sure how to explain this to my mother and sisters. Obviously, I'm an adult and can do whatever I want, but I don't want to give them reason to think..."

Her voice trailed off.

"That you intend to stay," Grant finished.

"God." She shook her head with a hollow laugh. "I'm sorry. One night together...okay, one night and one morning...and I'm worried my mother will think you and I are serious about each other."

"Aren't we?" He curled a lock of her hair around his finger.

Rory's heart thumped. "Um...I don't know?"

"Rory." He cupped her neck, lifting her face to look at him. His eyes were serious but tender. "What I said about you being the only woman who could change my mind about relationships…I meant it. But not for a second do I expect or want you to give up your new job and stay in Bliss Cove because of me. I'd guess that your family wouldn't expect that either. You're headstrong, loyal, stubborn as hell, and you do what you say you're going to do."

He pressed his lips against her forehead. "Those are just some of the reasons I've always liked you. And you don't need to tie your brilliant mind into knots over this. We're going to get through the rest of my parents' visit, and we're not going to worry about gossip or what anyone else thinks. Because this is about you and me…and sort of Bob, but we'll deal with him later."

Rory smiled, the tension easing from her shoulders. "That sounds easy enough."

"It is easy." The late-afternoon sunlight glinted gold in his eyes. Rory wanted to lose herself in them. Maybe she already had.

As they returned to the tavern, she remembered something her mother had once said in response to a question from Aria.

"Before you married Dad, how did you know he was The One?" Aria had asked.

"It was easy," Eleanor had replied matter-of-factly. "If it's right, it's easy."

So if it was easy…then it must also be right.

CHAPTER 15

*R*ory zipped up her jacket against the cold evening air and walked along Starfish Avenue. She was meeting Joanna at six for the Harvest Festival, and it was now five-thirty. That gave her enough time for a quick meeting with Hunter about the restoration software.

Downtown Bliss Cove had gone all out for the festival—orange, gold, and white lights twinkled around the town gazebo and the trees lining the street. Hay bales surrounded the square, and food and arts-and-crafts booths were set up on the stretch of lawn around the gazebo. People wandered among the booths, danced to the folk music of the six-piece band, or stood around eating popcorn and drinking hot apple cider.

In one corner of the square, a few local police officers were corralling a line of both adults and kids who were waiting for their chance to interact with the strikingly handsome action-movie star Jake Ryan.

Last spring, Jake had left a glittering life in Hollywood to come and live with Callie in Bliss Cove. Since he'd been out of the spotlight and living a small-town "normal" life, the paparazzi no longer bothered him—though Bliss Cove residents were exceedingly protective of him and his privacy.

The only times both Jake and the town officially acknowledged his movie-star status were for fundraisers and local charities. Now, a banner proclaiming *Meet Blaze Ripley! All donations go to the Bliss Cove Children's Hospital!* stretched between two trees.

Jake, as his iconic *Fatal Glory* character, was taking pictures, signing autographs, talking with fans, and teaching kids some choreographed fight moves. Callie staffed a booth nearby, collecting donations and giving out information on the new wing of the children's hospital.

Catching her sister's eye, Rory gave her a quick wave but didn't approach the booth. No doubt Callie would have questions about Grant, too.

She rounded the corner of Dandelion Street, where lights blazed from Sugar Joy and spilled into the courtyard in front of the bakery. Inside, Eleanor and Linda were busy helping a few customers, though since everyone was at the square, Hunter was the only person seated at a table.

"Hey, Rory." He pulled out a chair for her. "Thanks for your help with this. I hadn't expected to have such a hard time finding the right program."

"I'm guessing that's because your project is quite unique." Rory waved at her mother and sat beside Hunter. "There's not much software development for historic preservation, but when you combine that with new construction and planning, you'll likely have to use several different programs. There's that program where you can get 3D geographic information systems, but if you can combine that with architectural modeling and property management software, you'd have a much more comprehensive program. What would be really cool is if you could write a code to include the dimension of *time* to show how historic sites have changed and will potentially evolve in the future."

"That would have a big impact on the site planning." With a frown, Hunter leaned back in his chair and crossed his arms. "I was thinking about how interesting it would be to have 3D models of all the historic buildings on Mariposa. That would be a huge help with the restoration, but it could also be a cool interactive tool for visitors. Like a merging of history and technology."

"Which we could even use now before the restoration work begins." Aria set a plate of cookies on the table and sat down on Hunter's other side. "If we can give people an interesting experience when they visit Mariposa now, they'll be all the more likely to donate to the preservation fund."

They talked for a few more minutes about all the possible innovations before Eleanor came to the table.

"Would you like some coffee or cocoa, Rory?" she asked.

"No, thanks, Mom." Rory glanced at her watch. "I need to get going."

"Meeting someone?" Aria arched an eyebrow. Hunter shot Rory a look of amusement that told her Aria had filled him in on the gossip.

Rory sighed. She grabbed one of the cookies. Best to tell it like it was rather than leave the door open for more speculation.

"Okay, look." She picked a chocolate chip out of the cookie and ate it. "Grant Taylor and I are casually dating, but that's it. His parents are in town, and I'm staying with him because my apartment lease expired. I'm not turning down the Digicore job offer, and I'm not staying in Bliss Cove. We're just, um…seeing each other."

A flush heated her cheeks. Aria grinned an *I knew it* grin.

"It seems to me," Eleanor placed her hand on Rory's shoulder, "that you and Grant Taylor have been *seeing* each other for quite some time. I would hope that by now you're actually hooking up."

Rory blinked. Hunter and Aria both laughed.

"He's a really good guy," Aria said, her eyes twinkling.

"And he makes a killer burger," Hunter added.

"I think we all just have one question." Eleanor patted Rory's shoulder. "What took you both so long?"

"This is so much fun." Joanna sipped the hot apple cider and gazed at the bustle around the town square. "You know, Edward and I used to go to street fairs and arts shows all the time when we were first married. We had so little money, and it was a perfect way to get out and enjoy good music for free. I'd almost forgotten how much we loved them."

A wistful look crossed her face. Rory again experienced a surge of admiration for this woman who'd been such a force in her husband's success—which was also Joanna's success. It was hardly a wonder that she wanted her family to reflect the strength of what they had built together, even if she hadn't always gone about her ambitions in the best of ways.

"Oh, that must be Edward." Joanna pulled her phone out of her bag and checked the text. "He's going back to the house to shower and change, and then he and Grant will meet us here. Edward says they caught a nine-pound salmon, which Grant is going to use for the tavern menu."

"Sounds like they might be getting along," Rory suggested as they continued walking and looking at the arts-and-crafts booths.

"Considering neither one of them ended up overboard, I'd say that's the best we can hope for." Joanna shrugged. "Obviously, you can't mend wounds overnight, but maybe fishing is a good start."

"Or a visit to Bliss Cove."

Joanna smiled. "It's been lovely getting to know you, Rory. Thank you for putting up with us. Grant is lucky to have you."

Rory returned her smile, ignoring a rustle of lingering guilt. Different as she and Joanna were, she'd enjoyed the older woman's company. They'd visited the old Mariposa district, had ice cream on the boardwalk, and toured the historical museum. Joanna had been gratifyingly complimentary about everything. Rory didn't think she'd ever seen Bliss Cove through the eyes of someone who'd never been there before.

"Aren't these lovely?" Joanna paused at the Moonbeams booth to examine a display of jewelry. "Are they handmade?"

"Indeed." Destiny Rose stood from a chair behind the counter, resplendent in a silver caftan and dangling gold earrings. "They each contain a crystal with healing powers for the mind, body, and soul. Which crystal you choose depends on which aspect of your life needs a little boost."

"Goodness." Joanna raised her eyebrows. "Is there an all-purpose healing crystal?"

"Oh, yes." Destiny picked up a silver chain dangling with a pendant. "Clear quartz is considered to be the master healer. It balances your energies and simulates your immune system."

"Hey, Rory." The deep male voice filtered over the noise of the band and the crowd.

Rory turned to find Max Weatherford approaching. Though he was golden-boy handsome with his striking smile and dimples, her stomach tensed.

Fixing on a smile, she edged away from the Moonbeams booth to greet him. "How are you, Max?"

"Good. You?"

"Fine." She glanced back at Joanna, who was holding the quartz up to the light. "Are you working tonight?"

"Not officially, but I'm always on call in case of emergencies." He glanced toward the Moonbeams booth. "Getting an Oracle card reading?"

"No, just here with a friend."

"I've been meaning to get in touch with you," he said. "I enjoyed our date the other day. I have tickets to the Rolling Thunder music festival in San Jose next weekend, if you'd like to go."

Shock bolted through her. She opened and closed her mouth. "You enjoyed having lunch with me?"

"Sure." A faint puzzlement appeared in his eyes. "Why do you look so surprised?"

"It's just...um, I thought I was boring you silly with all that talk about veterinary software."

He laughed, a warm, rich sound. "Not at all. I'm kind of a computer geek myself. But don't tell anyone I said that."

"I can keep a secret."

"Good. So...the music festival?"

"Oh." *Oh!* God, for a smart girl, she could be awfully slow about this dating thing. "Max, I'm so sorry. I mean, I...I had a nice time, too, but I'm afraid I—"

"What do you think?" Joanna appeared at her side, the pendant around her neck. "It's beautiful, isn't it?"

Rory forced another smile. "Beautiful. Joanna, this is Max Weatherford, Bliss Cove's resident veterinarian. Max, Joanna is Grant's mother."

"Pleasure." Max extended his hand. "Are you visiting?"

"Just for a week." She smiled, though her eyes narrowed. "Did I overhear you say you're going to San Jose? We're from the Bay Area. Nob Hill, to be precise."

"Yes, there's a music festival at Shoreline. I was just telling Rory that—"

"Oh, look, there's Edward and Grant." Rory waved enthusiastically in the general direction of the gazebo and took hold of Joanna's arm. "We should go. Max, it was great to see you again. I'll...um, I'll be in touch, okay?"

"Sure." He stepped back, confusion crossing his features for an instant before he shrugged and turned away.

"He's an old friend." Rory hustled Joanna toward the gazebo. "We were in the same graduating class."

"Rory." Joanna came to a halt and pulled her arm away. She lifted her chin, her features tightening. "Do you know how old I am?"

Rory shook her head. Her heart began a slow, sick descent.

"I'm sixty-one." Joanna hitched her bag higher on her shoulder. A hard glint appeared in her eyes. "I have spent the last thirty-five years dabbling in my own work, but mostly I have spent it learning how to best support my husband. I've socialized with senators and foreign dignitaries. I can host a dinner party that would put the Duchess of Windsor to shame. Everyone who is anyone in the technology industry knows my name. They all want invitations to my parties. I know how terroir affects wine, what the nuances are of Louis the thirteen, fourteenth, fifteenth, *and* sixteenth antiques, and at any given moment, I can tell you the top players in the NBA, the NFL, the NHL, and the MLB. In other words, my dear, I did not just fall off the turnip truck."

Hot shame rose in Rory's chest along with a flicker of panic. "I know you didn't."

"Yet you *do* seem to think I'm oblivious to what's going on here." Joanna fisted her hands on her hips. "You're in love with my son."

The earth tilted under Rory's feet. "Excuse me?"

"You're in love with my son, and you haven't told him yet." Joanna spread her arms out as if that explained everything. "Well, you needn't worry because clearly he's in love with you, too."

A wave of dizziness swept over her. "I...Joanna, I'm not...I mean, I...Grant and I are *together*, but we..."

"I know, I know." Joanna shook her head dismissively. "You've been circling each other for months, trying to keep it casual, and you decided to experiment with seeing other people, but of course such ridiculousness isn't going to work for either one of you, given that you are *in love with each other*."

She enunciated each word with such clarity that they pinged off Rory like shiny little pebbles. "Joanna, I—"

"Edward, over here!" Joanna waved gaily toward her husband as he and Grant maneuvered through the crowd.

She lowered her hand and edged closer to Rory. "I realize there are all sorts of options for you young people today with these dating apps and whatnot, but if I may offer you a bit of advice. Put down your phone and pay attention to the notifications popping up in your heart and your head. If you don't, you might miss something important. Hello, my two gentlemen! How were the salmon treating you today?"

She stepped into Edward's arms and lifted her face for his kiss. Rory couldn't even look at Grant. Her heart was racing wildly. She almost couldn't breathe.

*What the hell had just happened?*

"Hey." He curled his strong hand around her wrist, concern darkening his eyes. "You okay?"

"Yes, I just…" She pulled air into her lungs and exhaled slowly. "I'm just hungry, I guess. A nine-pound salmon, huh?"

She stood on tiptoe, tugging him down to whisper in his ear. "I think your mother is a witch."

"Hmm. Not the word most people would use, but you got the rhyme right."

# CHAPTER 16

*R*ory wouldn't have classified the Taylors' visit to Bliss Cove as *uneventful*—in fact, the course of events had been more earth-shattering and mind-boggling than anything else she'd experienced in recent months—but there was no shocking revelation of her and Grant's "once pretend" relationship. She cleared things up privately with Max, who wished her the best and was nicer than he probably should have been about the whole thing.

Joanna stocked up on Naked products to bring as gifts for her friends, they enjoyed all the activities on Rory's itinerary, and Edward eased up on criticism of his son's profession. Rory introduced Edward to Hunter, and over coffee and Chaos Cookies at Sugar Joy, the three of them talked about urban planning and property development technology.

When the morning of the Taylors' departure arrived, Rory concluded that the visit had been a success all around, especially since Nathan and Alice were still enjoying their Indonesian honeymoon alone. They said their goodbyes, Grant and his father shaking hands stoically but not unpleasantly, and the Taylors headed back to the Bay Area.

For the next few days, Grant spent most of his time at the tavern catching up on all he'd missed and giving his employees time off. Rory set up her computer in the bedroom of his house and began fortifying her knowledge of Digi-core's recent projects and structures.

She tried very hard not to think about Joanna's comment —or her advice—but the words *in love* popped around her mind like corn in a sizzling pan. But even if her heart had been leading her in that direction for a long time, *love* wasn't a feeling she could indulge in right now.

Since she'd missed last week's get-together, she joined Aria and her friends on Friday night at the Mousehole for dinner and drinks.

"He really is a hottie." Aria sipped her mojito as she eyed Grant behind the bar. "Madeline must be gnashing her teeth with jealousy."

"Most single women are, from what I hear, not to mention a few married ones." Brooke, reporter for *The Bliss Cove Gazette*, followed her gaze. "Though a lot of people are amused by the fact that Rory Prescott is the one who finally cracked the Grant Taylor code."

Rory was amused by that herself. "If we were newsworthy, that would make a great headline."

"I just can't believe I missed it." Destiny shook her head mournfully and ate a bite of artichoke soup. "The Oracle cards are never *that* wrong. You and Max? What was I thinking? What was I *divining*?"

She looked so distressed that Rory patted her arm in consolation. "It's okay, Destiny."

"What are you, a Scorpio?" Destiny squinted at her, gold eyeshadow glittering in the light of the table lantern. "And Grant is a Taurus. Of *course*! You're both fixed-quality signs of deep physical pleasure combined with the intensity of earth and water, and the sexual energy of Mars and Venus…well, I just need to turn in my intuitive card right now because I am *horrified* at how badly I missed the mark."

"You didn't miss the mark." Grant stopped by the table with a plate of pan-fried salmon, roasted asparagus, and crispy potatoes. "If you hadn't sent Rory out with Max, she'd never have ricocheted off the date and landed right in my arms."

He winked at Destiny, who grabbed her cloth napkin and began fanning herself. Aria and Brooke emitted simultaneous *"awws."*

"As far as I'm concerned, it all worked out perfectly." Grant set the plate in front of Rory, his gaze warm.

For the sake of maintaining her image, Rory started to roll her eyes. Then she gave up and smiled at him…because, really, there was no longer a point in pretending *anything*.

"Well." Destiny watched Grant as he walked back to the kitchen. "I still can't believe I didn't see it when you first came back to town, Rory."

Rory turned her attention to her food, ignoring a rustle of discomfort. Part of her wished the same thing—that she and Grant had given in sooner so they'd have had many months together—but she also knew that life, fate, timing, luck, and even a bit of mysticism had all conspired to create this wild, tender leap into becoming…*them*.

Not that she would ever tell Destiny that.

"Hey, what's going on with the Vitaphone?" Ready to turn

the subject to something else, Rory glanced at Aria. "When is it going to be reopened for movies?"

"Christmas." Her sister took out her phone and pulled up a calendar. "The Mortimers are planning a holiday movie series to celebrate the grand re-opening. Check your phone. I just emailed you the dates."

"I'll check later. I don't have my phone." Rory cut into the flaky, perfectly cooked salmon.

Silence fell. She glanced up. "What?"

Aria leaned forward, her mouth open. "You. Don't. Have. Your. Phone."

"No, I left it back at the house." She frowned. "Why are you all staring at me like that?"

*"Rory Prescott Forgets Phone."* Brooke spread her hands out as if she were framing the words. "Now that's a headline."

"Here's another." Eyes twinkling, Destiny lifted her wine-glass. *"Rory Prescott is Besotted."*

"And hungry." With a scowl, she turned her attention back to her dinner.

Though Destiny was right, there was no way Rory would admit it.

At least, not out loud.

MID-OCTOBER BROUGHT COOLER, FOGGY DAYS AND CRISP, salt-scented evenings to Bliss Cove. For the first time in her life, Rory experienced what it felt like to be part of an almost domestic couple. She'd never lived with a man before, or even been in a relationship that was decidedly *real*.

Given their schedules, her and Grant's combined life was

also quirky and uniquely theirs. He ended most of his work-days close to midnight, which was often when Rory was just getting started.

Neither of them was ever too tired or too busy for love-making, and as time progressed, their intimacy became even more nuanced—adventurous, tender, wild, gentle, sweet, and dirty in varying degrees and frequently all at the same time.

Then while Rory educated herself on Digicore, and researched and tested urban planning software systems for Hunter, Grant caught a few hours' sleep. When he woke, they went out for an early morning jog, which often involved him sandbagging his pace so he could watch her run in front of him.

After returning to the house, their sweaty exertion leading to endorphin-fueled sex either in bed or in the shower, Grant made breakfast while Rory pestered and teased him by patting his ass, squeezing his biceps, and remarking on the size of his sausage.

After parting ways, she went to Sugar Joy to see if her mother needed any help, and he returned to the Mousehole. They connected again when she stopped by the tavern for lunch and dinner. Grant took breaks to both cook for her—always delicious, hearty meals, including the promised burrito that Rory admitted ruined her for all other burritos—and eat with her before they returned to their tasks.

It was as close to perfect as Rory could have imagined a relationship to be. Not until now had she known that a life with the right man could make her so happy. Mind-blowing sex and incredible cooking aside, Grant knew exactly how to treat her—just as he'd known how to kiss her that first time.

He touched her often in quiet, private ways that were less about possession and more about assuring her he was there. He gave her space when she was immersed in debugging a program for a friend who'd asked for her help. He included a vast array of autumn fruits and vegetables in their meals, and he left packages of gummy worms and Twizzlers next to her computer.

He wrapped her in his arms after every sexual interlude, whether hot and fast or slow and easy, but he moved to the other side of the bed at night because he knew she needed the space to sleep and stay cool. He understood that sometimes she needed to be alone to think or listen to music.

Every time he kissed her, he got it exactly right.

The time Rory spent on her own made every minute with Grant burst at the seams with pleasure, laughter, and the intensifying feeling that she didn't want to end what was happening between them.

She chose to ignore that feeling by focusing on the fact that they had over a month left before she started work at Digicore, and they were making the absolute most of their time together.

Two weeks into their sexy, tasty, and tender life, Rory left a message on the Mousehole voicemail for Grant *not* to bring dinner home. When he came back a little after ten, she was in the kitchen with one of his bandanas wrapped around her forehead, an apron tied around her waist, and about a thousand ingredients strewn on the counters.

"Can I help you in here?" He leaned his shoulder on the doorjamb as he surveyed both her and the mess.

"Yes." Rory wiped a trickle of sweat from her temple. "Shower, get a drink, pour the wine, whatever. Just go away.

I'm making dinner tonight, and it's going to be…well, edible. Maybe. Jacques and Julia are helping me out."

She nodded to the open cookbook beside the stove.

"You're cooking for me?" Grant's eyes crinkled with amusement and warmth.

"Shrimp cocktail, beef bourguignon…which, oh my god, takes a million years to cook…and potatoes called…hold on a sec." Rory wiped her hands on her apron and flipped a few pages of the cookbook. "*Pommes de Terre Mont d'Or*. Anyway, I'm supposed to have everything timed, and I totally don't think I do."

"Sweetie, you didn't have to—"

"Go, go." She shooed him out of the kitchen with a dishrag and got back to work.

She was a hot, sweaty, greasy mess. She'd been cooking for hours and had vastly overestimated the ease of Jacques and Julia's recipes. Not to mention her own culinary know-how. A software engineer who lived on fast-food burritos and Sour Patch Kids probably should have stuck with *Quick and Easy 30-Minute Recipes* instead of a cookbook written by the most renowned chefs in history.

Well. Lesson learned.

She checked pots, peered at the bubbling beef, chopped parsley, and tasted one of the croutons.

"Are you ready?" she yelled.

"Born ready, baby."

"I mean, for my *cooking*."

"Bring it."

Rory carted two dishes of shrimp cocktail with horse-radish sauce and lemon to the table. Grant was already seated and had poured the wine.

At least she'd had the wherewithal to set the table nicely with candles and cloth napkins, which Aria had brought over earlier—after she'd squealed like a baby goat over the fact that Rory was planning to cook dinner.

Grant picked up a shrimp, which dangled like a sad little comma from his fork.

"I had to clean and devein them." Rory poked at the shrimp in her dish. "It was pretty gross. How the hell you do this all day is beyond me."

"You did a great job." He peered at the shrimp and popped it into his mouth. "Delicious. How did you cook them?"

"In something called a *court bouillon*." She ate one of the shrimp, which was tough but not inedible.

"Really? That's a classic broth for poaching."

"That's what Jacques and Julia told me. I've discovered that *classic* means *it will take you forever and you'll burn yourself twice*."

He grinned and nudged her wineglass toward her. "Relax. Presentation is a major part of cooking. Act like everything came out exactly the way you intended."

Rory let out her breath and forced herself to calm down. Grant would love whatever she cooked, even if it was frozen pizza. He wasn't necessarily easy to please out in the world— like her, he was too guarded—but it was easy for her to please him.

In fact, pleasing him might have been the easiest thing she'd ever done.

He proclaimed the rest of the meal excellent, though it wasn't. The beef was overcooked, the potatoes undercooked, and the sauce was too salty, but it didn't turn out to be the disaster Rory was expecting. Grant ate every bite and scraped up the extra sauce with a buttered roll.

"I was going to make crepes Suzette for dessert, but I was afraid I might set the whole place on fire." She picked up their plates and brought them back to the kitchen. "So I made Julia's dessert crepes. She said it was okay to make them ahead of time."

She warmed up the crepes and arranged them on plates with berries and whipped cream. The dish turned out to be the best one of the night, and after they were done, Grant leaned across the table to kiss her.

"Thank you. I can't remember the last time someone cooked for me. I couldn't be happier that it was you. Go take a break. I'll clean up."

"You've been working at the restaurant all day." Rory put her hand on his chest to urge him to sit back down. "You're not cleaning the kitchen when you get home. Drink your coffee. I'll throw everything in the dishwasher."

"Come on. We'll do it together." He picked up more dishes and headed into the kitchen.

*Together* was the way they seemed to do things the best, and within half an hour, they'd cleaned up the kitchen— including the splatters on the ceiling—and stretched out on the sofa with Rory's feet in Grant's lap.

"Really." She leaned her head against the cushion and closed her eyes. "You've skyrocketed in my esteem like you wouldn't believe. Cooking is hard."

"Depends on what you're cooking." He rubbed the soles of her feet. "I could give you some lessons."

She opened her eyes. "Cooking lessons?"

"Sure." He wiggled her big toe gently back and forth.

"Just basics like roasted chicken, and mac and cheese. Maybe a frittata or fried rice."

Much as Rory liked the idea of Grant teaching her to cook, a touch of unease diluted her pleasure. Six weeks from now, she'd be living alone again, without him to serve her gourmet meals as if he'd conjured them up out of thin air. If she hoped to live on something besides candy and preservatives, she'd need to know how to cook a chicken or a frittata.

Whatever a *frittata* was.

"That would be great." She nudged his leg with her foot. "I'd like to take lessons from you. I'm a really good student."

"I know you are." The hint of a smile tugged at his mouth. "Straight A, right?"

"Mmm. I'm very eager to do extra credit, too." She slid her toes up the length of his thigh back to his lap.

"I'll have plenty for you." He stroked his hand underneath the leg of her yoga pants. "In fact, you might be the teacher's pet."

"*Might* be?" She arched an eyebrow.

"Gotta prove yourself first." He edged his fingers higher to her calf. "Raise your hand a lot. Sit in the front row. Ask to stay after class and review the lecture notes."

"I'll do all of that." She sat up and touched his whiskered jaw. "I might even do some kissing up."

"Well, then." He slipped his hand around her nape, heat brewing in his eyes. "Class is in session, Miss Prescott."

"I'm present and accounted for, Mr. Taylor."

Their lips met in a lovely kiss that tasted like berries and that felt both familiar and thrillingly new. He eased her back against the sofa cushions, his lips still locked to hers.

Winding her arms around his neck, she stretched out

underneath him and hooked her legs around his. She loved the way their bodies fit together, all her curves yielding to the hard planes of his chest and abdomen.

He deepened the kiss, his body tensing. Emotions flooded her, a riotous combination of desire, happiness, and the urgency of knowing that their time together was limited. She parted her lips under his and pulled at his T-shirt with a murmur of impatience.

He eased away from her to shuck off the shirt. His muscles gleamed beautifully in the dim light as he hooked his fingers into the waistband of her pants and slowly stripped them off her.

Rory had never before been so comfortable, so open, with a man. She knew her level of freedom had everything to do with the way Grant looked at her and touched her as if she were the most incredible person he'd ever encountered. As if he almost couldn't believe she was real.

When they were both naked, he took his time pleasuring her—skimming his hands over her breasts, trailing his tongue down her body, kissing her from her lips to her bellybutton. She slipped easily under his erotic spell, little gasps and moans breaking from her throat, her hips arching upward with increasing need for him.

Sensations flamed through her blood. She was on the verge of begging when he slipped his hands between her thighs and positioned himself between them. Rory dug her fingers into his biceps, crying out when he sank deep inside her. Every time, their union stunned her with both its power and utter ease, as if they'd been made for each other.

They moved in a slow, rocking rhythm that Rory wanted

to last forever. Grant kissed her, licked the hollow of her throat, stroked her breasts and hips. Each touch and thrust pushed her closer and closer to the blissful edge. Gripping him tightly, she convulsed again, gasping his name. He groaned, his muscles flexing as his own body shuddered with release.

Breathing hard, he pressed his forehead to hers. Their eyes locked. Tenderness and an emotion more intense than Rory could articulate passed between them. Her heart beat heavily against his chest. They'd been together for less than a month, and yet she knew she would never have this kind of life with another man. Ever.

He eased to the side, pulling her back against his chest on the narrow sofa. Rory nestled herself against him and closed her eyes. His breath stirred her hair. He circled his arm around her waist and cupped her breast in his hand. His body was a solid wall of heat and muscle behind her.

She had the striking sense that she could do anything —*anything*—with his strength backing her up.

Her phone buzzed unpleasantly. Grant clamped his arm tighter around her waist. "Do not answer that."

"What if it's for you?" She nudged him with her ass and reached for her phone on the coffee table. "People are starting to text me with messages for you. Don't you think that's perhaps an indication that it's really time for you to get a phone?"

"No. I don't want people to be able to reach me all the time. Tell them to stop bugging you and to call me on my landline like they always have before. Leave a message if I don't pick up." He nuzzled her shoulder. "I could be busy, you know."

"Oh, I know." She swiped the screen to check the notifications. Her heart stuttered.

Grant stilled. "What's wrong?"

"Email from the Digicore CEO." Rory pulled up the full message.

*Rory, we got funding in place for the cloud solutions project earlier than expected. Deadline now moved up. Your start date is next Monday. Apartment available in nearby building.*

She tossed the phone aside and sat up, her breath escaping in a hard rush. Monday was four days from now.

With a frown, Grant picked up her phone and read the message. "Monday, huh?"

"I knew there was a chance my start date could shift." She rubbed her chest, where an ache was starting to form. "I told them that was fine, since I was finishing up my contract work, and Mom had already hired Linda to help at the bakery. I figured I'd just be spinning my wheels here until Thanksgiving. But that was before…"

Her voice trailed off. Straightening, Grant slipped his arm around her and pulled her closer. "That was before I knocked your wheels loose and sent you careening off the road."

Rory smiled, even as sorrow collected in her throat. "Hardly. I think it's more like you set me rolling on a path I didn't know existed."

"Hey." He pressed his lips to her temple. "You're moving less than two hours away. I don't think even the guidebooks consider that *long distance*. I'll come up every chance I get."

"Really?"

"Of course. Gotta make sure you're not subsisting on tube

goo and gummy worms. Though now that you have Jacques and Julia on your side, I might not have to worry about that too much. I'll take a day off and help you move."

"You don't have to. I can do it by myself."

"I know you *can*. I'm saying you don't have to."

Rory shifted to look at him and put her hand against the side of his face. Warmth, tenderness, and a hint of regret darkened his green eyes. She traced the edges of his sharp cheekbones. She ran her fingertips over his well-shaped mouth, his dark eyebrows, the strong, stubbly line of his jaw.

Yes, she wished they'd crossed the line sooner so that they would have had more time together in Bliss Cove, but at least she wouldn't be moving away without knowing just how much Grant Taylor meant to her.

"So we're still...you know." She moved her hand down to his chest. "You and me?"

He captured her wrist. "You once told me you've never thought of an end goal in a relationship."

She rested her palm over his heart and shook her head.

"That means you haven't thought of an end goal with us, either." He rubbed the inside of her wrist right against her pulse. "And that means you haven't thought of an *end*."

A smile started from somewhere deep inside her. "I guess I haven't."

"Good." He kissed her. "To answer your question, yes. We're still you and me. No end in sight."

# CHAPTER 17

"*I* know you won't be far, but it feels like you're moving across the country." Eleanor Prescott wiped a tear from her eye before hugging Rory close. "Henry and I are already hoping to come up next weekend. I can help you decorate."

"You mean you can't wait to decorate for me." Rory tightened her arms around her mother, battling back her own emotions. "Just please don't bring me any houseplants."

"Okay, but I'm definitely bringing framed family photos, and at least one wooden sign painted with a positive-thinking quote." Eleanor released her and stepped back, squeezing her hands. "Something like *Never Give Up*."

"Mom, she'll just hang that in the bathroom." Callie shook her head in amusement and embraced Rory. "Don't take any crap. Don't back down. And call us if you need anything."

"These are for the trip." Eleanor handed Rory a bakery box containing enough Sugar Joy cookies to last a week. "Let me know as soon as you arrive."

"I will. Thanks, Mom." Before she started getting choked up, Rory left the bakery and returned to the Mousehole, where, under Aria's direction, Grant and Hunter were loading her boxes into the back of the truck.

"There's room here for more." Hunter tightened the bungee cord and nodded to an empty space.

"That's everything." Grant hefted his duffel bag into the truck and dusted off his hands. "Rory doesn't have much stuff."

"She's a minimalist," Aria corrected.

"Good spin." Rory hugged her little sister. "Be good, okay? I'll keep an eye out for anyone who looks like they could use a cat companion."

"Like you?" Aria tightened her arms around Rory, her words clogging with tears. "Make sure you see some sunlight at least twice a day. We're going to video chat every other day so we can talk face-to-face instead of through texts. Here's some stuff you might need for your new place. I'll put it in your car."

She picked up a floral box with a lid and set it in the backseat of Rory's car.

"Thanks." Rory turned to hug Hunter. "I'll keep you posted if I find anything more about the software."

"I'll do the same. Good luck to you, Rory. Thanks for everything."

A few minutes later, she was in her car, following Grant as he headed north on the coastal highway toward the Bay Area. She almost couldn't believe it had been less than a month ago when they'd traveled this exact route on the way to Nathan and Alice's wedding. Then, Grant had been her contentious but ever-present friend, the man she counted on to be there all the time.

Not once had he let her down.

Before long, they were pulling into the parking lot of a beige stucco apartment building. After getting the keys from the manager, they hauled her boxes up to the third-floor apartment—one room with a window overlooking the back alley.

It actually wasn't all that different from her Bliss Cove apartment, though there she'd had a view of the park behind the building, but it couldn't compare to the Mousehole cottage with its wood-burning fireplace and bed just big enough for the two of them. Or to Grant's house, which had felt so much like *home*.

He stayed with her for the afternoon, helping her shop for actual furniture and making several trips to transport it all back in his truck. They ordered out for pizza and ate it at her new little kitchen table, where she lit a tapered candle she'd found in Aria's box. The box also contained a number of other items that Rory would never have bought for herself— cat figurines, decorative bookends, flower vases, throw pillows, and a "healing crystal."

After putting the leftover pizza in the fridge, Grant turned to face her. Though he smiled, regret darkened his eyes. "Even though it's not long distance, I'll still miss you."

"Even if we hadn't...you know, *this*..." Rory gestured between them and swallowed past the tightness in her throat. "I'd still miss you, too."

"Come here."

She closed the distance between them, tucking her head under his chin. He tightened his arms around her. The heavy thump of his heart echoed through her. Constant and steady.

"You can stay the night." She rubbed her cheek against his chest.

"If I stay the night, I might not leave."

"That wouldn't be a bad thing."

"It would be a great thing, if we both didn't have to work." He pressed his lips to her forehead. "With tomorrow being your first day, you don't need any distractions. I do have something for you, though."

He eased away from her and unzipped his duffel bag. He pulled out Bob the Singing Fish and handed it to her. Rory took the mounted monstrosity with a laugh.

"You don't have to give him to me."

"I'm not. You earned him." Grant pushed the button on the plaque, and "Love Me Tender" warbled out. "Now you can do with him as you please."

"Hmm." She ran her fingers down the front of his T-shirt and set the fish on the counter. "Can I do the same with you?"

"Always." He tugged a lock of her hair. "As for the three meals a day, since I did promise to make them until Thanksgiving, you'll have to claim the rest on visits. It could take a while to get through all the meals I owe you."

"I can wait." She slipped her hand under his shirt and stroked his warm abdomen.

Sadness and warmth shimmered in the air between them. He cupped her face and slanted his mouth over hers again, his kiss so thorough and compelling that for the first time in her life, Rory understood what it felt like to be *claimed*.

"Work hard." He lifted his head and tweaked her nose. "If any shit comes your way, you call me. The Taylor name carries a lot of weight, and I'll use it if I have to. But first I'll beat any guy up for you."

"My hero." She took a breath, trying to smother her fear of being alone again. "I'll see you soon."

"You sure will." He kissed her again and started for the door. As he pulled his keys from his pocket, he turned back to face her. "I've always wondered…exactly *why* do you hate the singing fish so much?"

Rory skated her gaze from him.

"When I…" She touched the plastic fish as memories rushed swiftly back to the surface. "You know I came back to Bliss Cove when my father died. Two weeks after we buried him, I spent the day helping my mother sort through his things, and then I went out for a walk. It was December fifteenth, and the whole town was decorated with all these bright lights and Christmas trees that seemed so *wrong* to me. I ended up at the Mousehole, and you brought me tomato soup and a grilled cheese sandwich. It was the first time we met."

"I remember." Tenderness darkened his eyes. "I thought I knew everyone in Bliss Cove. Then I looked up and saw this stunning woman with long black hair sitting at the bar, and my heart almost went into a freefall."

Her breath caught. "Really?"

"How could it not? But then I noticed that you looked so sad. Hollowed out, like you had nothing left inside you."

"You started Bob singing and said you hoped it'd make me smile."

"And you did." His eyes crinkled at the corners, and he pressed a hand to his chest. "Your smile hit me right here. Then my heart did go into a freefall."

Rory managed a smile, wiping her eyes. "When I went back to the Mousehole a couple of weeks later, I was…well, I was *anticipating* seeing you again because you'd made me feel good. Sally Gaines was at the bar and she must have asked you to start the singing fish because you did. And she got all giggly and flirty, and I..."

She shrugged, her face heating. "I got a little jealous. I guess I had some silly idea that you only wanted to make me smile, and then there you were playing the fish for Sally Gaines. Oh my god, I can't believe I just said that out loud."

Grant blinked, a faintly stunned look rising to his eyes. Rory's embarrassment deepened.

Suddenly he laughed, a warm rich chuckle that settled somewhere deep inside her. Before she could move, he pulled her against him again, securing his grip so tightly that she never wanted to leave the circle of his arms.

"I may have played the fish for Sally Gaines and any number of other women," he murmured against her hair, "but you're the only one I love, Rory Prescott."

"Oh, you *cannot* do this to me now." Tears spilled down her cheeks as her heart overflowed.

"I sure can." He eased back to look at her, wiping her cheeks with his thumbs. "I only wish I'd done it sooner. Then maybe I'd still have Bob."

She gave a watery laugh. "He's mine now. But you can have me instead."

"Best trade of my life." He kissed her again. "Take care of yourself for me, okay?"

"I will. I promise."

She watched him leave, waiting until the taillights of his truck had turned the corner and disappeared from sight before she closed the door.

# CHAPTER 18

"*M*edium rare." Winslow punched his finger at the order ticket. "That's, like, *burned*, man. What's the matter with you? Since when do you fuck up a steak order?"

*Since Rory left.*

"I'll get another going." Grant wiped his forehead with the back of his hand. "Tell the customer we'll comp his dinner."

Winslow looked as if he was about to say something else, but then he turned and walked back to the dining room.

Grant tossed a raw steak on the grill. Fire and steam flared up around the meat.

In the week since Rory's departure, he couldn't get his brain to work right. Couldn't seem to focus.

All he wanted was a few minutes' break so he could call and talk to her, but he couldn't bug her during the day at her new job, and at night she sounded so tired that they spoke for ten minutes before he ended the call so she could get some sleep.

Despite his promise to visit her, he couldn't even pin down a date when he'd have time to drive up to San Jose. His employees had taken up a lot of slack when his parents had been in town, and he didn't want to ask them to do it again. Not to mention, several were due for vacations and time off. Much as he wanted to be with Rory, the tavern and his employees had to be his first responsibility.

But not being able to see her, much less talk to her nearly as much as he wanted…he was almost tempted to go out a buy a damned phone so they could exchange shorthand texts with no punctuation and stupid emojis. At least that would be *something*.

He got through all the dinner orders without a disaster, and they closed everything down at eleven. Grant locked the door after the last employee left. He poured himself a whiskey and brought it back to his house.

Before he'd set the glass down, he called Rory on his landline. Her voicemail picked up.

He started to speak, then stopped and set the receiver down. She'd know it was him, and what could he say, anyway?

*I miss you. I love you. Why does a hundred miles feel like a thousand?*

He wanted to drive up this weekend, but a server and a chef were both out, and he'd be working from open to close both days. If he left right at midnight, he'd get a few hours with her before he'd have to be back in Bliss Cove by nine.

He'd do it, too, if he didn't know that his showing up at her door at two in the morning would screw up Rory's schedule. She'd probably be working, anyway. Not for anything would he interfere in her new job.

His phone rang, and he grabbed it like a man in a desert diving for a bottle of water. "Rory?"

"Hi. Sorry I missed your call. I was driving back."

"From work?"

"Yes."

"They're making you work this late during your first week?"

"They're not *making* me. I just am. We don't have set hours, and I need to stay on top of things. So I come in early and leave late."

Grant smothered the urge to warn her about burnout. "You're not eating tube goo, are you?"

"Not yet." A faint smile lit her voice.

"You like it there so far?"

"I think so. I love getting back into the work. I have to get accustomed to working with a team again, though. Oh, I meant to tell you your father and I have exchanged a few emails about the software for Mariposa Street. He's sending a test version of a program to Hunter and the design team."

"That's great."

"I thought it was good of him to follow through, especially given that he wasn't all that thrilled about Bliss Cove in the first place." She paused. "Have you talked to him at all?"

"No. We don't have a lot to talk about."

"You did okay when you were fishing, and when he came into the kitchen that one time."

"One time." Grant expelled a sigh. "I'm glad the visit went well, and I'm staying in touch with my mother, but my father and I aren't suddenly going to become best friends. Or friends at all."

"Maybe when you come up to visit me, we could take a quick trip to see them."

"If you want to, sure."

She hesitated, then said, "I want *you* to want to."

"Rory." Despite his instinctive resistance, his heart ached for her. She probably didn't even realize that the undercurrent of her words revealed how much she missed her own father. Moving away from her mother and sisters must have brought her grief and loneliness sharply back to the surface.

All the more reason for him to bend time itself in order to be with her again.

"Maybe you and your father both need to try a little harder," she urged. "For your mother's sake, if nothing else. I mean, you and I have been apart for a week, and I miss you like crazy. I can't imagine what your mother feels like with you having been so far away for *years*. You have this tendency to grow on people, you know. If you left Bliss Cove, the town wouldn't know what to do with itself."

A mixture of guilt and tenderness stirred through him. "If I can swing a visit for longer than a day, then yes, we'll stop and see my parents. Did I tell you I love you?"

She laughed, and the warm sound settled right underneath his heart. "You're still not getting Bob back."

"You haven't thrown him away yet?"

"He's hanging on the wall. He might be growing on me, too."

"Does he still make you smile?"

"Not really, but he doesn't make me frown either."

"Well, that's a start."

They stayed on the phone for another hour, eventually veering off into dirty talk that left them both panting and a little sweaty. Grant caught a few hours' sleep before waking to finish the payroll and inventory.

Close to nine, he went for a jog and ended up on the historic Mariposa Street, which Aria and Hunter had turned into a major project for both themselves and Bliss Cove. Hunter's company, Monarch Enterprises, had spent the past six months consulting and partnering with architects, construction firms, historians, and structural engineers to assess every building in the district before they created a building and reconstruction plan.

"Morning, hon." Destiny waved from the doorway of Moonbeams, her jewelry twinkling in the sunlight. "Joe brought me one of your pumpkin pies the other day, and it was scrumptious. If you don't mind me saying so, it also proved to be something of an aphrodisiac."

Grant grinned. "Good to know. I might have to put that in my advertising."

"If you need a quote, just let me know." She wiggled her fingers at him.

He lifted his hand and started back to Sunshine Road. A pure white cat blinked at him from the window of the Meow and Then Cat Café. He walked up the porch steps and went inside. Aria was standing on a stepladder, writing a list of bakery items on the chalkboard menu.

"Hi, Grant." Dusting off her hands, she descended the ladder. "Did you run out of coffee?"

"No, but I'll take one. Large, please." He dug into his pocket for cash. "Nice not to have to make it myself."

An image of Rory bringing him a cup of coffee appeared in his head. He put a ten on the counter. "A blueberry muffin, too."

He shook his head at her attempt to give him change, and in response she added a croissant to the plate.

"Go have a seat in the Cat Lounge, and I'll bring your food in after heating up the croissant." She handed him a mug of coffee. "Hunter's in there working. Don't take his glower personally."

Opening the door of the adjoining room, Grant blocked a tabby cat's attempt to escape. About a dozen cats lolled on the sofas and chairs, stalked around the tables, and slept in the hideaways.

Hunter was sprawled on the sofa, his sock feet on the coffee table and a laptop balanced on one knee. An old, one-eyed orange cat with a fanged tooth and torn ear was stretched out beside him, his head resting on Hunter's other knee.

"Hey, man." Hunter lifted his chin in greeting. "What're you doing here?"

"Just went for a jog." Grant sank into an easy chair. "Are you looking at the software Rory sent you?"

"Yeah. She said your dad helped her out. Thanks for that." Hunter frowned at his laptop screen and punched a few buttons. "It's a pain in the ass, though, because I don't know what a program is missing until I try and do something with it. Then I find out I can't, and I have to email Rory to see if there's a way to add it, or if there's another program with that exact function."

"My father didn't come up with anything more innovative?"

"His recommendations were great, but not as comprehensive as I want." Hunter closed the laptop and ran a hand through his hair. "I don't know if what I want even exists. I hate bugging Rory all the time, but she knows so damned much, and she always gets what I'm trying to explain, you know?"

"Yeah." Grant swallowed some coffee, not sure if he should ask his next question but taking the plunge anyway. "You ever think of hiring her to work for Monarch?"

Hunter chuckled. "She was the first person I wanted to hire, but I can't afford to pay her what she's worth. At least, not long-term. She already did a crapload of work for free on the Mariposa Street database. Even if I could eventually pay her well, I don't think she'd be interested in working with us."

"Why not?" A spindly kitten butted its head against Grant's leg. He bent to pick it up, and it promptly hooked its claws into his shirt.

"I asked her about the possibility, but she said historic restoration and development aren't her areas of expertise." Hunter scratched Fang behind the ears. "It's a limited scope, too."

Grant glanced through the adjoining window at the front room. "What has Aria said about it?"

"She's all over the idea. She worships Rory." Hunter pulled his feet off the coffee table and stretched. "But she also thinks Rory needs a variety of projects to keep her interested and to make the most of her skills. Anyway, it's enough that she's helping us find the right software. Again without pay."

Aria came in with the muffin and croissant, which she set on a table beside Grant. She nudged Hunter's arm and indicated the wall clock. "Meeting at ten. Don't forget."

"No, ma'am." He stood and grabbed her hand, tugging her closer for a quick kiss.

After Hunter left, Grant finished his coffee and food with the kitten pawing at his shirt and crawling over his lap.

"That's Button." Aria stopped in again to refill his coffee. "She'd been adopted, but the family returned her to the Rescue House because they said she didn't get along with their dog. So she's looking for her forever home."

"Her what?"

"The home where she can stay forever with a family who loves and wants her. She's really friendly and curious. She'd be a great companion."

Grant couldn't help laughing. "Not afraid of the hard sell, are you?"

"Not when it comes to cats." She straightened and smiled. "My sales pitch is truthful, though. And you'd be a great pet owner because you practically work from home. You'd be able to check on Button regularly to make sure she's not lonely."

"Much as I appreciate your cause, I'm not looking for a pet." Grant plucked the weightless kitten from his shirt and set her back on the floor. She let out a little mew of protest. "I doubt you'll have any trouble getting Button adopted."

"Okay, but if you find yourself thinking about her a lot, you'll know that she's meant to be yours." Aria picked up the plate and mug.

Grant thanked her again and left the café. If only that theory also applied to Rory.

# CHAPTER 19

"*D*id you hear?" Douglas, one of the architects on the Systems Development Team, scooted his roller chair closer to Rory's desk. Which was all of two inches, considering the office desks were crammed together like Legos in order to promote "collaborative ideation."

"Hear what?" Rory kept her gaze on the computer screen.

Almost two weeks into her new job, the work was progressing well. She cautiously liked her other team members—Winkey-Face jerk aside, a mid-twenties guy named John who thankfully was working on a different project. For now.

Douglas seemed like a reasonably good guy, but Rory was keeping her guard firmly in place. He was one of six other people working on the cloud-based system that Rory had also been assigned.

"The C-suite approved a research team dedicated to developing cloud applications with built-in AI systems." His voice lowered to a conspiratorial whisper. "They haven't picked a project manager or a technical lead yet."

Rory suppressed a surge of hope. "Well, neither one will be me. I just started working here."

"Rumor has it you might've been hired with the Principal Engineer position in mind." Douglas rubbed his scraggly goatee. "Obviously, we won't know until it's a done deal, but you're being watched."

He nodded toward Brenda Davis, one of the few women in the company and the supervisor of the Systems Development Team. "Brenda's in line for the manager slot. Stay alert."

"Thanks for the tip."

"Can I have one of those?" Douglas indicated the open bag of Sour Patch Kids on her desk.

"Help yourself."

He shook a few pieces of the candy into his palm and rolled back to his desk. Rory pulled on her noise-cancelling headphones, which was the only way she could disassociate herself from the surrounding activity.

Desks, chairs, and computers cluttered the open space of the Digicore office, which had been nicknamed The Hive. It was larger than an airplane hangar with concrete walls, exposed pipes, and only a narrow row of high windows. The ceilings created an echo from the hundreds of conversations zinging around.

Rory's desk was smack dab in the middle of the chaos. She'd gotten accustomed to working in the silence of her own apartment in Bliss Cove, so it was jarring to be immersed in constant noise and activity—keyboard clicking, people talking, papers rustling, chairs squeaking, phones buzzing nonstop. Her headphones only went so far, as none of her new colleagues were above tapping her on the shoulder or nudging into her peripheral vision to get her attention.

She'd get used to it, she kept telling herself. The work itself was the most energizing part of her new environment—a hotbed of ideas about artificial intelligence, platforms and integrations, and endless possibilities for innovation.

If only she could somehow share this life with Grant. Their conversations at night were warm, but short-lived. His talk about the Mousehole and Bliss Cove created an ache of longing in her chest, and she frequently cut him short to avoid feeling lonelier than she already was.

Her responses to his queries about her life—had she found a favorite restaurant yet, visited the museums, gone to a show at the performing arts center—were always *"not yet."* And recounting her workday was an exercise in sheer boredom.

The really pathetic part was that she had nothing else to talk about. Grant understood much of the minutiae of her work and never seemed bored when she discussed it, but he'd turned his back on technology long ago. Why would he be interested in listening to details about neuromorphic chips and GPUs?

"One of my coworkers told me they're looking for someone to lead a new AI cloud project," she told him during their call that night. She rested her head back on the pillows and looked at Bob the Fish, who was hanging on the opposite wall. "He said I was in the running, but I'm not so sure."

"Why wouldn't you be?"

"They're not going to assign the new kid as the lead."

"The new kid in question is Rory Prescott. No one deserves to lead a team more than you."

Rory let out her breath slowly. Did he miss her as much as she missed him?

She'd gotten accustomed to her solitary, work-centric life-style over the past couple of years, but in Bliss Cove she'd had her mother, her sisters, her friends. She'd had the bakery, the boardwalk, the crash and roll of the ocean, the achingly familiar sea air. She'd had Grant, as dependable as the tides.

"So what else is going on in town?" she asked.

"At the town meeting last night, Mayor Bowers announced that we need a pie shop either downtown or on Mariposa Street. She's planning to try and convince your mother to open a branch of Sugar Joy called Sugar Pie."

Rory laughed. "Mom didn't tell me that."

"She might not know yet. She was over at the high school last night helping with the bake sale fundraiser for the orchestra."

"Well, she might be convinced. Even though we don't sell pie at Sugar Joy, everyone knows that my mom makes the best apple pie in town."

"Those are fighting words." A frown entered his voice. "You haven't tried my apple pie yet."

"You know how to make apple pie?"

"Sure. Three varieties of apples. It's amazing."

"Why isn't it on the menu at the Mousehole?"

"It's on a special seasonal menu only in the fall."

"Really? Why didn't I know that?"

"Because you just order cheese curds and fried onions. Speaking of which, what'd you have for dinner?"

"Huh. No wonder I'm hungry."

"Listen." The word held a stern note of command. "There's an Indian restaurant called Maharaja three blocks from your apartment building. Walk down there and order vegetable pakora, chicken curry, and palak paneer. They'll bring you rice and a basket of naan. Get a beer or a glass of wine while you're at it. The food is excellent."

"How do you know?"

"I've been there, but I've also researched all the restaurants in your neighborhood so you don't end up at Fast-Food Heaven every night. Go. And text me a picture of the curry so I know you're actually there."

"That does sound...*text you* a picture?"

"Don't tell anyone." He sounded as if he were scowling. "I got a cell phone intended only for you. It's top secret, like the Bat Phone."

"Grant Taylor. I think that's the most romantic thing anyone has ever done for me."

"Baby, if a cell phone is your definition of romantic, then I have serious work to do. I'll text you my number." He sighed. "I can't believe I just said that."

"Neither can I. Say it again."

"I'll text you my number."

"I'm getting so turned on right now."

He laughed. "Hold that thought for later. Go eat."

Rory was still smiling after they'd said goodbye. She pushed up from the bed and searched for her shoes. On the "romantic gesture" scale of *hold open a door* to *sell his soul to the devil*, she knew that *buy a cell phone* was pretty low on the list.

But still. Grant's rejection of technology went deeper than

a mere dislike of chargers and blinking apps. And if he'd specifically gotten a phone just because she'd moved away, there was no telling what else he would do for her.

# CHAPTER 20

*R*ory got through the rest of her second week of work fortified by care packages from her mother, video chats with Aria, emails from friends, and a visit from Callie, who was on her way to a symposium at Cal Berkeley. None of it was the same as being immersed in Bliss Cove life again, but it all strengthened both her spine and her positive outlook.

Throughout the day, she exchanged multiple texts and quick calls with Grant, who was struggling to find a solid window of time to visit her around his employees' vacations, sick leave, and two unexpected departures.

She also received a phone message from Joanna Taylor, who said to please let her know when Rory might be free for lunch or dinner. *"I know you're terribly busy, but I want to take you to this extraordinary Japanese restaurant in Los Gatos, and I would love to catch up. Text me as soon as you have a minute!"*

Rory texted immediately, and they set up a lunch date for the week after next. She hadn't yet gotten together with anyone socially, and she was already looking forward to a couple of hours with chatty Joanna.

Though Rory spent most of her time at the office, she knew Grant wouldn't like the idea of her sitting at her desk for fifteen hours straight, so she made an effort to take breaks and eat lunch. Also remembering her promise that she'd take care of herself, she bought spinach salad or a fruit cup along with whatever main course looked good in the company cafeteria—usually lasagna or pizza.

In the middle of her third week with Digicore, she was seated at a table by the window, eating her salad and leafing through the Jacques and Julia cookbook that Grant had insisted she take with her.

Her phone buzzed with an email from Hunter, providing a link to an article about 3D digital scanning technology. *Thought you'd be interested in this—great tool for historic buildings.*

Rory skimmed the article, which detailed the creation of 3D models both for design purposes and to enhance the visitor experience. She hit the reply button. *Very interesting—would be even more so if they were 4D. I'll look into it.*

"May I?"

Rory looked up at Brenda, the supervisor of her team, and set her phone down. "Sure."

Brenda pulled out a chair and sat across from her. In her mid-forties with a sleek, geometric haircut and no-nonsense business suits, she'd been with Digicore for several years. Rory had heard a lot of buzz about the other woman, as Brenda was known for her sharp business sense and strategic initiatives.

"How do you like it here so far?" Brenda leaned forward, eyeing Rory from behind her glasses.

"It's been great. The work is challenging, and I'm looking forward to learning more about what's coming up in the future."

"That's what I want to talk to you about." Brenda tapped her finger on the table, slanting her gaze toward the other employees seated around the cafeteria. "I'm aware that there have been rumors about the AI project we're planning to launch. I've just been asked to form and manage the new team. Nothing is official yet, but I want you to know I'm pushing for you to be named the Principal Engineer."

Rory's heart jumped. "Really?"

"On paper, you're the most qualified. Some of the others have more recent practical experience, but I've been impressed with your tech writing. Between that, all the courses you've taken in the last two years, and your contract work, you're up to date on all new developments. From what I've seen these past few weeks, you're committed, hard-working, and persistent about getting things right and fixing problems. I like that about you."

"Thank you."

"Considering the number of hours you've already put in here, you also appear to have no life whatsoever." Brenda's mouth twisted with a little smirk. "That might be the number one quality we're looking for in a lead."

Rory attempted to smile, even as a rock fell into the pit of her stomach. Brenda's remark didn't really bother her—truth was truth, after all—but Bliss Cove had proven that she didn't want to have "no life." She didn't just want any old life, either. She wanted to do the work she loved while living a full, happy life like the brief one she'd had with Grant back at home.

"Thanks for considering me for the position," she told Brenda. "I'm honored."

Brenda studied her for a moment. A flinty hardness appeared in her eyes.

"I know you can go head-to-head with any male engineer, Rory. I also know you'd probably win. You're very good, and you're very smart. On a technical level, at least. Unfortunately, that's not enough. You need to be smart on an emotional level, and you need to have a dragon-thick skin. Keep that in mind."

She stood and gave a short nod before walking away. Rory watched her leave, not quite sure what to make of that remark. She'd grown that thick skin over her ten years of working in tech, and she knew how to deal with uncomfortable situations.

Yes, she still experienced pangs of vulnerability and unease, but she was keeping her guard firmly in place while going above and beyond her duties.

Later that night, she flopped down on her bed for her usual eleven-thirty p.m. call with Grant. They'd gotten into the habit of talking just after he finished the closing shift at the Mousehole.

When he didn't answer her call, she texted.

RORY: You home yet?
GRANT: Almost.
RORY: Call me when you are.
GRANT: Did you eat dinner?

RORY: I had a gummy worm casserole with a side of Twizzlers.

GRANT: I have a jerk chicken platter, rice and beans, fried plantains, and Jamaican cornmeal bread.

RORY: Can I have some?

GRANT: Sure. Open the door.


Rory caught her breath. Her heart cartwheeled. Tossing her phone down, she leapt off the bed and ran to unlock the door.

*Oh my god.* Everything inside her lit up like a thousand Christmas trees.

Grant smiled, his green eyes crinkling in the way that she loved so much. He looked wonderful, his hair rumpled and his strong, handsome features vibrant with anticipation. He set down several paper bags and extended his arms. With a laugh of sheer happiness, she flung herself at him, hugging him tightly and wrapping her legs around his waist.

"I can't believe it." She buried her face in his shoulder and inhaled his familiar scent, feeling as if it had been years rather than a few weeks since she'd seen him. "I *missed* you."

"I missed you." He kissed her forehead, his arms tight around her. "Can I come in?"

She laughed again. "Yes, sorry. Don't forget the food."

"Never."

He brought the food inside and set it on the kitchen counter before pulling her close and giving her a hot, greedy kiss that weakened her knees and fired up her lust. Within seconds, they were tugging at each other's clothes, their hands seeking naked skin, their lips locked.

Already the hard evidence of Grant's arousal pushed

against the fly of his jeans, and a throbbing ache expanded through Rory's lower body. Urgency swept over them both like a wave, engulfing them in the dizzying reminder of what they were together.

He lowered her to the bed and took her in the way she both needed and desperately wanted—swift, fast, and hard. He gripped her wrists, pinning them to the mattress, his emerald gaze burning right to her soul. She clutched his shoulders, pleaded for more, and cried out his name when a pent-up orgasm shattered her into a million exquisite pieces.

He covered her mouth, drinking her moans as his self-control stretched tight and broke. He thrust deep inside her with a rough shout, and another flood of sensations suffused Rory.

When Grant stilled, his breathing raw, he started to roll off her.

Rory tightened her hold on him. "Don't go."

"I'm crushing you."

"In the best possible way." She kissed his shoulder and stroked her hands over his slick, muscular back. "How long can you stay?"

"I have to be back by nine tomorrow morning. Ten, at the latest." He shifted and pulled her into his arms. "I kept waiting for a time when I could stay longer, but finally I couldn't take it anymore. If the only time I can see you is for a few hours on a Friday night, I'll have to live with that."

*For how long?*

Swallowing the question, Rory ignored a stab of unease. Two hours apart might be sustainable for some couples, but with their jobs and crazy hours...*okay, stop.* Grant was here now, and that was what mattered.

She stroked his chest and kissed his cheek before easing away to pull on a T-shirt. "That food smells amazing."

"It's from a Caribbean restaurant I read about a while ago." He hitched on his jeans and joined her in the kitchen. "Much as I love cooking for you, I didn't want to waste time doing that tonight."

"Good call." She nudged his hip with hers. "We have plenty of other ways to spend our time."

Sitting at her kitchen table, they devoured the food straight from the containers, mostly using their hands and only a couple of napkins. Rory told him about her conversation with Brenda and the potential of the Principal Engineer position.

He gave her a smile of pride. "I'm not surprised they already want to give you a promotion."

"It'll be more work, but definitely an advancement." She picked up the half-empty containers, sensing his questions about *more work*. "Hey, you should get some rest."

"I'm rested." He slipped his arms around her from behind and nibbled her ear.

"You need to sleep a little before driving back." She set the leftovers in the fridge and led him back to bed. An enormous relief filled her as she nestled against his side, as if it were the place she was meant to be.

"Oh, did I tell you I contacted two women I met at a conference awhile back?" She rubbed her cheek on his shoulder. "We're getting together for lunch next week. I realized that I've always spent so much time working that I never really tried to make friends with women who are also working in tech. And I miss my Bliss Cove friends, so I decided to try and make some up here."

"That's great." He pressed his lips to her temple. "You need a tribe."

"I'm also having lunch with your mother the week after next."

"Joanna Taylor may have her faults, but she probably knows every tribe in the Bay Area. She'll be thrilled to take charge of your social life."

"I just might let her."

Silence fell. Rory pulled up the comforter. She had a code review on Monday and needed to work as much as she could, but not for anything would she give up a few hours of sleep with Grant.

"You good here?" He stroked his hand over her arm, though a faint tension rippled through his body.

She nodded, understanding his unspoken question. "Brenda is my supervisor, but I'm the only woman on the development team. That's always the case, though. I'm used to it."

"Any problems?"

She hesitated, not wanting to lie but not wanting to give him reason to worry. "I've learned how to pick and choose my battles, so whatever problems I've had, I can deal with."

"What does that mean?" He shifted to face her, his expression darkening.

"What I said." She put her hand on his chest. "Grant, it's okay. The fact is that I'm a woman in a male-dominated field not known for being inclusive, but I choose to stay because I love the industry, the potential for innovation, and the work. Do I love the culture? Not always. Will it change? Maybe one day. But until then, I can deal with it."

"What exactly is *it* you're dealing with?"

"Look." She sat up, dropping her hand away from him. "It's nothing that would or should surprise you or anyone else. And is this really how you want to spend your few hours here?"

"You mean finding out what you haven't told me?" Irritation edged his voice.

"There's nothing to tell." Rory shoved off the bed. Frustration swelled in her chest. "No one's put his hand on my ass or propositioned me for sex or asked me to go to a strip club. One guy did make a bumbling attempt to ask me out for a drink, but he was clueless rather than predatory, and believe me, I know the difference. I'm documenting and broadcasting all my work because I know if anyone is going to be the victim of theft, it'll be me. There's the usual locker-room talk that I choose to ignore, and every day I challenge coworkers who try to ignore me, interrupt me, or talk over me. Can it be exhausting? Yes, but I refuse to be invisible."

Grant's mouth tightened. "You shouldn't be treated as if you are."

"I know, but it's not going to change if women *like me* don't challenge it."

He dragged a hand down his face, and a heavy sigh rasped from his chest. "Why should you have to endure that crap to challenge the status quo? Why not shake it up another way, from another angle?"

"What angle, Grant?" Rory paced across the room, her throat tightening. "I already tried to start my own project, and look how that ended up."

"You have way too much to offer to let one asshole venture capitalist stifle all your other ideas."

"Did you come here to fight?" She whirled around and spread her arms out. "Is that what this visit is about?"

"No." He pushed off the bed, his eyes dark. "I'm here because I miss you, and I fucking hate the idea of you being in any kind of environment where you feel even *slightly* unsafe or diminished."

Rory smothered an intense, aching wave of emotion. "You've known from the beginning what my career is, Grant. You know far better than most what this industry can be like. As much as I appreciate your concern, you have no right to question my choice of work."

"I'm just telling you that you deserve better."

"Did you hear what I said?" Rory snapped. "I told you weeks ago that this is a great job with excellent benefits and potential for advancement. Even if I'm not offered the Principal Engineer position, I'm already on the radar."

He held up his hands in a gesture of surrender. "I'm not questioning you. You're right, I do know what this industry can be like, which is only one of the reasons I didn't want to be part of it."

"Well, I am part of it." She swallowed a rising tide of tears. "Even if I wanted to leave, which I don't, I have no idea what else I could or even would do."

"Rory, you can do *anything*."

He spoke with such conviction that something inside her broke, as if all the beliefs she'd held about herself suddenly gave way to the possibility of new ones. Her tears spilled over.

Grant closed the distance between them in three strides. The instant his arms went around her, all the anger and tension drained from her.

"I'm not telling you to leave the tech industry." He stroked his hand down her back. "God knows it needs you. But don't you dare think that this is all you are."

She pressed her face to his chest and let out a shuddering sigh.

"By the way," she mumbled. "I love you, too."

A soft laugh escaped him. His breath brushed against her hair.

"Don't worry." He tightened his grip on her. "I won't tell anyone."

Rory let herself sink into the warm, protective circle of his arms. Much as she wanted her work, Grant, her family, Bliss Cove, and a fulfilling, happy, fun life all wrapped up in one pretty package, she'd learned long ago that she couldn't have everything.

But she could have *enough*.

# CHAPTER 21

*R*ory settled into a routine as mid-November approached, due a great deal to Grant's regularly scheduled weekend visits. After his manager returned from vacation, Grant was able to turn the Mousehole over to him and stay with Rory through Saturday morning and afternoon. She made a point of not even turning on her computer when he visited, and together they explored more of the neighborhood and surrounding enclaves.

When he wasn't there, she still worked constantly. No one at Digicore had set hours, but most of the others didn't get to the office until nine or ten, so Rory arrived by six and worked in relative quiet. She answered emails, checked code reviews and log files, studied debugging reports, and worked on her own code.

Her supervisor Brenda didn't mention the AI cloud project again, and since Rory had plenty of experience with unfounded rumors and unfulfilled promises, she didn't take the radio silence personally.

In an effort to establish her tribe, she had lunch with

Joanna Taylor and several other women who worked for different tech companies, and she attended a networking conference in San Francisco.

Her mother and sisters all drove up for visits, she kept updated on Hunter and Aria's plans for Mariposa Street, and she made plans for a Thanksgiving trip back to Bliss Cove.

All in all, it was working out as best as she could have hoped for.

She learned to tolerate the open space of The Hive, deflecting coworkers who suddenly came up behind her to remark on her code or tell her she was doing it wrong. She established mutually respectful working relationships with several colleagues and gained a great sense of accomplishment when the project neared its final stages.

"You're out." Douglas held up the empty bag of gummy bears from her desk.

"I know. I can't believe I let that happen." Rory leaned back in her chair, eyeing the code that wasn't working. "I have to stop at the gas station during lunch, so I'll pick up a new supply."

"Can you get me some Starbursts?"

"Sure." She stood and stretched her lower back, then zipped up her hoodie. "I've got a bug somewhere, but I can't find it. I'm going to take a break."

She secured her computer and maneuvered through all the desks and chairs to one of the breakrooms. Her phone buzzed with a text from Joanna confirming their one o'clock lunch date and adding, *I need to make a stop at an antique store not far from your office, so I'll pick you up.*

Figuring she could fill her gas tank on the way home,

Rory texted back: *That would be great. I'll wait for you outside.*

She took a mug from the breakroom cupboard and picked up the coffeepot. The coffee had a sharp, bitter scent and looked like mud—probably because it had been sitting there for hours. She dumped it out and scrounged around for filters and coffee grinds, which always ended up in different places.

Opening a lower cupboard, she found a package of filters and started to shut the door.

Cold slithered down her spine. A large, messy sheet of paper was taped to the inside of the cupboard door, bearing a crude drawing of a large-breasted woman with long dark hair.

Rory pulled the paper off and straightened. The woman in the drawing wore a skimpy bikini that concealed little, and her face was a caricature made up of exaggerated bow-shaped lips and fluttering eyelashes. A lengthy column on the left side contained cryptic scrawls in various handwritings—*JTD, 1x, Nov. 7, DTK, 3x, Oct. 20, 25, Nov. 2, MPL, 2x, Nov. 5 &10.*

Her breath shortened. The cold intensified, hardening into a tight ball in the middle of her chest.

"You want me to take a look at your code?"

Rory jerked her head up at the sound of the male voice. Douglas stood in the doorway, a mug in his hands. His gaze went from her to the paper and back again. Two spots of red appeared on his cheeks.

Rory crumpled the paper in her fist and held it up. "What the fuck is this?"

"Nothing." He shrugged, his color deepening. "Just some harmless fun."

"It looks neither harmless nor fun to me." She tried to keep her voice even. "What is it, Douglas?"

He averted his gaze and scratched his head.

"Are you going to tell me, or should I take this straight to HR?"

"John started it." A faint, childish whine infused his voice.

Rory almost choked on a humorless laugh. "What *is* it?"

"It's just a game, okay?" He scowled in defensiveness. "To see who…you know."

"I don't know." She gritted her teeth. "But it's pretty clear this is supposed to be me. What's the game, Douglas?"

"There's a…um, code." He rubbed his neck and looked at the floor. "We've just been keeping track of…well, stuff about you."

The cold inside Rory spread to her blood and bones. "What kind of stuff?"

"Just guy stuff, that's all. Like how many times one of us got close enough to touch you, or who could look down the front of your shirt. Honestly, it was harmless."

Rory stared at the paper. The column contained at least half-a-dozen initials, all of which she now recognized as the members of her team, plus another project manager.

She pointed a shaking finger at all the numbers. "What do these mean?"

A dull flush rose to his face. "Uh, that first one is the total number of points. Whoever earned the most by the end of the year would, uh, be the first to try and…you know."

*"What?"*

"Get in your pan…um, sleep with you."

Nausea roiled in the pit of her stomach. "And the others?"

Douglas squinted at the paper. "Those are related to

touching you or catching a mistake in your code. The blue one is when you…uh, bent over, and the orange one is…we just kind of made up some fantasies about you and rated them on a scale of one to ten for hotness. Mine was rated a ten. That letter H in red next to John's name…well, I told him not to do that, but he did."

"What?"

"He said he was going to cut off a piece of your hair and keep it." Douglas winced and took a step back. "I'm sorry about that. I thought it was kind of creepy and told him not to."

Rory used every ounce of strength to control her rising panic. "He cut my hair?"

"When he was passing behind your chair one day. I guess a couple of weeks ago? He had a pair of scissors, and your hair is always hanging over the back of your chair, and he just…snipped off a piece. You didn't even notice."

No, she hadn't. She scoured her brain for a memory of the violation, but couldn't pinpoint anything. The open office space meant people were constantly walking behind her. She'd learned to ignore the nonstop movement, and if she'd had her headphones on, it was entirely possible that she'd not have noticed John slithering behind her chair and slicing off a piece of her hair.

The sick feeling intensified. She grabbed her ponytail and tugged it around to peer at the ends. Sure enough, a strip of about four inches was gone from the thickest part. She hadn't even noticed it was missing. She hadn't been looking.

"We really didn't mean anything by it." Douglas twisted his coffee mug around in his hands. "We taped it to the cabinet just so all the players would have access to it."

*Players?* "I can't fucking believe this."

"It's not, like, personal." He tugged at his earlobe. "Um, it's just that you're the first girl who's been hired in a while and, you know, you're hot and all, so it was meant to be fun."

"Fun for *you*." Alongside her bitter disgust and anger, a deep, black sorrow began to flood Rory's heart. No, she hadn't been buddies with her team members and, yes, she'd kept her guard up, but…this? *Fun?*

"Excuse me." Still gripping the paper, she gestured sharply for Douglas to get out of her way.

"Come on, Rory. Can't you take a joke?"

Suppressing the urge to slam her fist into his nose, she stalked past him and headed for the elevators.

Though she was sorely tempted to storm into the office and publicly confront her team members head-on with the disgusting paper, the rational part of her knew exactly how that would be perceived. She could almost hear the laughter and condescending remarks that she needed to "calm down."

After stepping into the elevator, she punched the second-floor button. She hadn't always had the best experiences with HR, but there was no way they could deny the evidence of this sick little "game."

As the elevator descended to the next floor, she pulled in a gulping breath and tried to calm the racing of her heart. The doors opened again, and Brenda stepped into the elevator.

"Is something wrong?" Her sharp gaze pierced through Rory.

"I…I need to talk to Human Resources." Rory struggled to keep her voice even. "I found out that my team members have been using me as the subject of a demeaning game. I'm going to report them and file complaints."

Brenda's eyes narrowed. She stepped out at the second floor and nodded toward the corridor. "Come with me."

Rory followed her to the women's restroom, where Brenda closed and locked the door behind them. She snapped her fingers and extended her hand.

After giving her the paper, Rory managed to explain the details of the "game" and the code.

Brenda's lip curled. "So they stared at your tits and tried to touch your ass."

Rory swallowed hard. "They made a game of it. John even cut off a piece of my hair."

"Can you prove that?"

"There's a four-inch piece of my hair missing."

"How do I know you didn't cut it yourself?"

Tension gripped Rory's stomach. "I'm telling HR about this."

"No, you are not." Brenda tore the paper in half. She crumpled the pieces into a ball and threw them in the trash. "If you want even a hope of getting the Principal Engineer position, you're not going to file silly complaints about your team members. You've been here for, what, a little over a month? And now you're going to whine to HR that the boys are pulling your pigtails and chasing you on the playground?"

"That..." Rory's hand shook as she pointed at the trash. "That is harassment and a personal violation. I won't pretend like they were just having *fun*."

"You don't have to pretend anything." Brenda put her fists on her hips, her features hardening. "I'll tell you what you're going to do. You're going to go back to your desk and get to work, and you're going to forget you ever saw that stupid paper. Every single person on your team is a high performer, and I will not have this project jeopardized because poor little Rory couldn't take a juvenile joke."

Brenda stepped closer. "I told you that you need a thick skin to survive here. You start filing complaints now, and not only will you get yourself a reputation as a whiner, you'll kill any possibility of becoming Principal Engineer *ever*. In fact, you'll be conveniently transferred off any development team and get stuck reviewing code and doing maintenance until you get so bored you quit. And chances are high that a number of men in this company will do whatever they can to *make* you quit. I guarantee it won't be pleasant."

She unlocked the door and yanked it open, tossing Rory a hard look over her shoulder. "Get back to work. We have a project update meeting at four."

She strode out, letting the door swing shut behind her.

Rory turned on the sink faucet and splashed cold water on her face. Her heart thumped a heavy beat, like a drum warning her of some horrible consequence.

She grabbed the torn, crushed paper from the trash and left the bathroom. It was close enough to lunch that she ignored Brenda's command and headed outside to wait for Joanna. She needed a few minutes to compose herself before facing Grant's mother.

*Grant.*

She ached to call him, if only to hear his deep voice reminding her that she was valued. But God only knew what he'd do in retaliation on her behalf. She needed to figure out how to handle this alone.

"Hello, Rory!" Joanna's cheerful voice came from the parking lot. "Beautiful day, isn't it? Have you been to Bird Dog before? They have a seasonal menu, but the last time I was there they had this most wonderful trout that reminded me of Grant's…my dear, are you all right?"

Rory blinked. She couldn't seem to form a coherent thought.

"You're quite pale." Joanna stopped and peered at her over the tops of her sunglasses. "What on earth is the matter?"

"N-nothing." Rory waved a hand in front of her face. "It's just warmer here in the sun than I was expecting. Did you have trouble parking?"

"No. I'm just over…" Joanna's gaze skirted to the crumpled ball of paper that Rory was clenching and unclenching in her fist. "What are you doing with that?"

"Nothing." Rory shoved the paper into the side pocket of her bag and forced a smile. "Shall we go?"

She walked toward the parking lot, feeling Joanna's frown like a burn.

# CHAPTER 22

*A*fter reading Rory's text, Grant tried to call her three times. Each time, her voicemail picked up. He glowered again at the text.

*Turns out I'll be really busy this weekend, so it's not a great time for you to visit. I'm coming home for Thanksgiving anyway, so I'll see you then. xo*

He wasn't about to wait until Thanksgiving to see her. While he knew she was putting in far more hours than she should, not for a second did he believe she was using work as a legitimate excuse to keep him away.

Something was wrong.

On Friday evening, he left his manager in charge of the tavern and drove up to San Jose without letting Rory know he was on his way. She wasn't at home when he arrived at her apartment, and he let himself in with the key she'd given him.

Setting his duffel on the floor, he called her cell. Voicemail picked up. He ended the call without leaving a message and paced from one end of the small room to the other. Close to nine, a key turned in the lock. Rory walked in.

"I saw your truck outside." She dropped her bag onto her computer chair, her eyes narrowing slightly. "Didn't you get my text?"

"I got your text." He curled his hands at his sides, resisting the urge to grab her up into his arms. She looked exhausted, dark circles under her eyes and skin paler than usual. "Looks like you're home early."

"There's a company party going on at a bar near the office." She shrugged out of her jacket and tossed it over the chair. "I didn't feel like going. Plus, as I told you, I have a busy weekend and need to be up early."

"For what?"

"Work."

"Tomorrow is Saturday."

"That doesn't change my deadline."

"What's going on?" Grant folded his arms. "Is this about the lead position you were up for?"

"No." Rory averted her gaze and took a glass from the kitchen cupboard. "Just a deadline. Nothing more."

"You think I believe that?" He flexed his hands, hating the tension flooding through him. "Something happened between last Saturday and now. Tell me what it is."

"Don't order me around." She twisted the faucet knob with an abrupt movement and filled the glass with water. "If I don't want to tell you something, I don't have to. A few weeks together doesn't give you the right to every part of my life."

"What will, then?"

She looked up sharply. "What does that mean?"

"It means..." he stepped closer to her, his heart thumping, "...that I *want* the right to every part of your life. What do I need to do to earn it?"

"You..." Rory stared at him. Her breath hitched. "You never needed to *earn* it, Grant. I'm not keeping you out because I don't trust you. There are just things I can handle alone."

"I know you *can*." He clenched his jaw so tightly it ached. "I'm saying you don't have to."

Her eyes glittered. She wiped a drop of water from the outside of her glass. Her hands were shaking.

It took everything he had to keep his distance from her. She was brittle, fragile, exactly the way she'd been the first time he saw her sitting at the bar in the Mousehole.

Only then, even though he'd never seen her before, he'd known what he could do to try and make her feel better.

Now? He knew Rory more intimately, more completely, than he'd ever known anyone and yet he had no idea how to fix this. He didn't know what the fuck *it* was.

He paced to the window, dragging a hand through his hair. He hated being helpless.

"Rory." He turned to face her, clenching his fists against a bolt of fury. "Who was the fucker, and what did he do?"

She pressed her lips together. Her face drained of color. "You can't fix this for me."

*"Tell me."*

She set her glass down and walked to her desk, pulling open a file drawer. She took out a wrinkled, torn piece of paper that had been taped back together and handed it to him.

One look at the crude drawing, and Grant's anger went nuclear. "What the fuck—"

"They said it was a game. Those are the initials of five of the men on my team. I'm pretty sure it was started by John, the asshole who called me *hot stuff* right after I'd been hired. Apparently, the others thought it was great fun."

Grant stared at the paper, his blood scorched. "I'm going to fucking *kill* those—"

*"You cannot fix this."* Rory stepped closer. Her eyes sparked. "You can't go to HR, to your father, to the police, to anyone. My supervisor, one of the few women in the entire company, warned me not to file a complaint because it'd backlash on me, and even worse is the fact that she was right. Another coworker knew I'd found that paper…he was the one who told me I'd been the subject of an interoffice game…and he told our other team members. You can guess how well that went over. Now they're all thinking I have it out for them, and they want me to either quit or get fired, which means I'm taking a lot of crap. Stop."

He kicked the desk chair backward until it hit the wall. His blood was molten with rage, every muscle locked for battle. "You are not staying there. No fucking way."

She pulled in a heavy breath. "I'm trying to find a way to get out that won't destroy my next job prospect or even my career. I already have a reputation for *drama* because I've fought back, and a shitload of good that did me."

"Rory, quit the fucking job!" Grant flung his arms out, his breathing rapid. "To hell with anyone who won't hire you because you stood up for yourself. Turn in your notice now. Get all your documentation together. I'll call my lawyer, and we'll hit those bastards with a heavy and very public lawsuit. By the time we're done with them, there won't be a Digicore left."

"No." She shook her head in defiance. "It's not that easy. I know too many cases of women getting tied up in expensive legal battles for years before they end up losing anyway. Suing your former company is a career death sentence."

"The tech industry is not the only place where you can use your talent and skills." Frustration gripped him like a fist. "There are hundreds of other companies that would kill to have you on their payroll and who would value and respect you instead of treating you like garbage. Why would you *want* to stay?"

Rory stepped back. Silence fell like an anvil. His pulse hammered.

"Why do you stay at the Mousehole?" A cold note infused her voice.

"What?"

"Why would you *want* to stay?" She shrugged and held up her hands. "As a matter of fact, why would you want to stay in the restaurant world at all? It's hard work, uncertain, unpredictable. It screwed up your relationship with your family. The hours are crazy. You can't even get away long enough to see your girlfriend for more than ten hours a week. As a chef, you're on your feet all day. You get burned constantly—stove, grill, boiling water, hot oil. It's dangerous and physically tough. You have to deal with complaints from customers, vendors, suppliers. It's lonely and the pay probably sucks. So why don't you just quit, Grant? Go work at a bookstore or write about food for a magazine. Why do you stay?"

He couldn't even form a response. His chest was so tight it hurt.

"When I..." Rory paused, pushing a lock of hair away

from her forehead. "When I first learned to code, I thought it was like a magic spell. I could use it to create amazing and wonderful things. Technology was changing the world in so many different ways. Science, medicine, engineering, education. Everything. I wanted to be part of it. I wanted to change the world."

She walked to the kitchen, her spine rigid. "Whenever one of my sisters, friends, or even my parents was working on something, I'd think about how to design a program or app to help. Like a better way for Aria to target customers when she was selling macramé art, or a system to pair her stray animals with the right families. Or I'd dream up a game that Callie could use to teach Greek mythology or a way for my mother to network with other bakers. It was *exciting*, the idea that I had the knowledge and creativity to actually turn those ideas into reality.

"That's the reason I went to school. Why I worked so hard. Why I wrote letters to women who'd made it to the upper echelons of the tech industry and asked for their advice. It's why I made both friends and enemies, and it's why I've always wanted to work for the companies that were creating the most interesting and innovative programs.

"I looked to Callie and the way she charted her own path to becoming a tenured professor. I could see myself doing the same thing. I wanted to prove myself as a lead, as a manager, and eventually as an executive who could really make a difference, like the maverick women who've blazed the trail before me. I thought one day I could even run my own company."

She spun to face him, her eyes suddenly flashing. "And every time I quit a job or asked for a transfer or filed a complaint or ignored a nasty comment, it was like getting another chip knocked out of this vision I'd had since I was a kid. You know that game *Chutes and Ladders* where you can end up sliding right back down to the bottom with one spin of the wheel? That's what it was like. I'd end up right back at the bottom again, if not literally, then in the eyes of the people in power, which was even worse.

"But when I was working with good companies and good people, it was like being in the eye of a hurricane where everything is calm and perfect. Where we could all just do what we did best and work together. Where I remembered what it *could* be like. Twice, I thought I'd found it, the company I'd never leave, but the first one was a start-up that went under, and the second was sold and had a reorganization that pushed many of us out. I could see it, though, the way I wanted to work and be treated. I still can."

She shook her head and compressed her mouth. "And then something like *this* happens, and I'm reminded that it can be so fucking hard and, yes, I want to flip all those bastards off and walk out and never look back because, really, is it worth it? Why am I putting myself through this?

"Then I remember *I'm* not the one at fault, that no one has the right to treat anyone like they're inferior, to demean, bully, and violate them. It's not okay for anyone to make me the subject of a game, and why the fuck should I let them destroy me and everything I've worked for and wanted? So to answer your question, Grant, *that's* why I want to stay."

She was breathing hard, her eyes hot with blue fire, her fists clenched.

Every part of him weakened—his bones, his soul, his

heart. He could live a thousand years and never love a woman as much as he loved her.

"I'm sorry." He didn't know what else to say. There were no words. "I'm a fucking idiot, Rory. I'm so sorry."

"You stay because you love it." Her expression softened a little, and she took a step toward him. "Because you want to make people feel good. I stay because I love it. Because while I no longer think I can change the entire world, I still believe I can change a corner of the world. Maybe even two corners."

"What…" Something stuck in his throat. He swallowed hard and tried again. "What do you need me to do? What do you want me to do? Anything. I'll do anything for you."

She looked at him for a long moment before a faint smile curved her mouth. "You can do what you've been doing for two years, Grant. You can just be *right over there*."

He crossed the room in three strides and hauled her against him, tightening his arms so hard around her that he was probably crushing her. He couldn't let go, couldn't loosen his grip.

"I'm not over there." His voice was rough. "I'm right here."

He pressed his face into her hair and struggled to calm the fire raging inside him, the black fury that anyone would dare to hurt her, the urge for violent revenge.

He pulled in a heavy breath. He'd be here for her always. But it wasn't enough, not for him. He couldn't just stand on the sidelines while she went into battle. He had to take action, to do something. He'd fought for the life he wanted, and with everything he had, he would fight for hers. Her war was his war.

# CHAPTER 23

To Rory's complete lack of surprise, almost a week after she'd found the "game" scoresheet, her supervisor Brenda informed her after a meeting that she hadn't been chosen as the Principal Engineer on the AI cloud project.

"It turns out you weren't what we were looking for." Brenda pushed her glasses up the bridge of her nose and gave a little *too bad* shrug.

"Imagine that." Rory turned away, not bothering to thank the other woman as she headed back to The Hive.

Her enthusiasm for the possibility of the lead position had nosedived considerably over the past week, though part of her had been hoping for the chance at professional vindication. Being transferred to another division would also have bought her some time to look for another job. She could still request a transfer, but given her label as a "troublemaker," she had little doubt it would be blocked.

As she entered the open office space, the Digicore CEO Brad Dawson, a youngish man with glasses and wheat-colored hair, came out of a conference room. He stepped in front of her to block her path. "Rory."

Her spine tensed. "Hello, Brad."

"I've been hearing rumors about a little office...dust-up." His eyes narrowed. "Your name has been mentioned. Given that we don't tolerate distractions here at Digicore, I wanted to warn you that it appears you're becoming one."

She clenched her teeth. "Digicore doesn't tolerate *distractions*? Great. In case you didn't know, harassment and bullying are serious *distractions*. I'm not the one who needs a warning."

She shoved past him and stalked through the maze of desks back to her workstation. Suppressing her anger out of longstanding habit, she sat and pulled up the program she was working on. All of her recent code reviews had come back with extensive change lists, most of which were either nitpicky or unnecessary and some of which were legitimate. She made the changes and sent them back for another round.

Three more days, and she could return to Bliss Cove for Thanksgiving. She and Grant were spending Thanksgiving Day with her family, then they were driving to San Francisco on Friday for a dinner with his parents.

The holiday couldn't come fast enough. Rory ached to see her mother and sisters, to be around the people who loved her. Her emotions had been ricocheting through her like bullets. She was at constant war with herself—her self-preserving urge to walk out of the office *right now* battling her determination not to let the assholes win.

The long weekend would give her a chance to regroup and figure out her next step. She had no intention of staying in her current situation, but she wasn't going to leave without a plan in place. That plan would likely come without any form of punishment for the men involved, but she'd been through that before. She was hardly the only woman who had.

"Got any candy?" Douglas turned his chair toward her, his eyebrows rising hopefully.

Rory smothered the urge to slap him. He'd been trying, and failing, to act like everything was back to "normal."

She shook her head, angling her chair so he was out of her peripheral vision. If only they at least had cubicles.

As she was fixing an inconsistency in her code, a noticeable hush settled over the room. Rory looked up. Everyone's attention was shifting toward the elevators, where a group of six people had just exited. Four Digicore senior executives and CEO Brad followed Edward and Nathan Taylor into the office.

Rory's heart stuttered. Some of her coworkers were openly looking at Edward, while others cast him surreptitious glances. Most people outside of the insular Silicon Valley tech world didn't know the Intellix founder on sight, but everyone in the Digicore office certainly did. Brad spoke to him and indicated the open office space, as if he were explaining the company's operations.

Rory turned back to her computer, her insides twisting. It looked as if Edward and Nathan might be having a high-level meeting with the Digicore C-suite. But why?

They started walking around The Hive, pausing at desks and asking questions. She tried to focus on her work, but it was impossible to ignore them the closer they got.

"I heard he's here to talk about a possible collaboration on AI solutions." Douglas's bitter coffee-breath wafted to Rory's nose as he leaned closer. "Especially in the hybrid cloud space. That'd be pretty cool, huh? Intellix is doing some amazing stuff with AI."

Rory edged her chair away from him and didn't respond. Edward, Nathan, and the execs were getting closer to her workstation. Anxiety gripped her.

Not for a second did she think the execs would deign to discuss the harassment at a meeting—if they all even knew about it—but she'd never imagined what she'd do if her work life intersected negatively with that of the Taylors.

"Hey, Rory." Nathan's friendly voice carried over the sound of her heart hammering. "I was hoping we'd see you here."

"We expected we would," Edward announced.

Aware of her coworkers going silent with surprise—how, after all, would Rory Prescott know Edward and Nathan Taylor?—she rose to her feet.

"Just a worker bee in The Hive." She smiled and extended her hand to Edward, then Nathan. "Good to see you both, though I have to say I hadn't expected it."

"Kind of an impromptu meeting, or we'd have let you know we were coming." Nathan smiled.

Edward indicated her workstation. "You work okay here?"

"It's fine."

He made a *harrumph* noise. "We have closed office spaces at Intellix. Less distractions. More privacy. Never been a fan of this open space concept."

"It takes some getting used to," Rory allowed, acutely aware of the stares from all angles, especially the Digicore executives.

"How do you like working here?" Edward pulled his eyebrows together.

From over his shoulder, Brad glared at Rory, as if warning her to watch her response.

"It's challenging and…interesting." That was somewhat true, at least. "Well, I'll let you continue your tour. Pleasure seeing you again."

"Do you have my number?" Nathan took out his phone. "I assume Grant didn't give it to you since he doesn't even know what it is."

Rory unlocked her phone and quickly exchanged numbers with Nathan. After they'd said goodbye and continued walking, she sat back down.

Whispers rose around her. She didn't want to know what they were saying.

"Dude. How'd you know them?" Douglas asked. "Are you, like, dating him?"

"Shut up, you disgusting little toad."

"Whoa. Harsh." He held up his hands and rolled back to his workstation.

After the Taylors had left the office, a message from Edward popped up on her phone. *Join me for lunch. Italian restaurant over on Fourth Street. One o'clock.*

Though she appreciated the invitation, she hesitated. She didn't want him to know the first thing about the hostile atmosphere surrounding her. She couldn't risk him stepping in on her behalf, and if things got really convoluted and it ended up affecting whatever business prospects Digicore had with Intellix… God. She'd be totally vilified, like Yoko Ono breaking up the Beatles.

Then again, she was a small cog in a vast wheel. The

unpleasantness affected every part of her work and life, but the reverberations wouldn't impact Digicore's upper management. Certainly no one at Intellix had reason to get involved.

She agreed to the invitation and returned to work.

Close to one, she drove to the Italian restaurant and found Edward seated at a quiet table beside a window. He rose when she approached and pulled out her chair for her.

"Thank you." She looped her purse over the back of the chair and sat down. "Where's Nathan?"

"Back at the office." Edward sat across from her. "He tends to come in early and leave early so he can get back home to Alice."

Rory ignored a faint pang at the idea of *getting back home* to one's love.

She and Edward placed their drink and food orders and talked about the weather and local happenings. Edward had purchased tickets for him and Joanna to a Bay Area music festival, which reminded Rory of Joanna's remark about how much she and her husband had loved watching music shows when they were first married. It was nice to think that perhaps Joanna's wish for a "second honeymoon" had taken root in Bliss Cove and was continuing to flourish.

The server brought their plates over and refilled their water glasses before departing.

"So, my wife tells me you're still in a relationship with Grant." Edward took a swallow of his gin-and-tonic and studied Rory.

She nodded and draped her napkin in her lap. "It's working long distance." *More or less.*

"She hoped that you living here would bring Grant home

more often." He shrugged, his forehead creasing. "Hasn't happened."

"I know. Honestly, I don't get to see him as much as I'd like to, either." She took a bite of chicken piccata. "I haven't managed to get back to Bliss Cove at all, and Grant is so busy running the Mousehole that he can only come up for a few hours at a time."

"You haven't convinced him to quit?"

"I don't want to. I would never ask him to quit doing what he loves. His dedication to the tavern, to his customers, is just one of the many, *many* reasons your son is so well-regarded in Bliss Cove."

He frowned and sliced into his filet mignon. "I didn't raise either of my sons to be a chef."

"But that's what Grant is." If Edward had asked her to lunch in order to gripe about Grant, then the least she could do was defend him with everything she had. "He's an incredible chef and a restaurant owner. Though it's none of my business, you can't raise your children to be what *you* want them to be. If they want the same thing, great. Win win. But if they want to be and do something else, especially if they're willing to walk away from you to do it, then you might want to consider shifting the old perspective there. Recode the algorithm."

He barked out a laugh. "Never expected him to end up with a software engineer, either. Joanna seems to think you two *work well together*, whatever that means."

Gratitude toward Joanna filled her. "Your wife is right."

"You're staying in the Bay Area, huh?" He swallowed another gulp of liquor.

Deflecting a pang of sorrow, Rory nodded.

"Well, it's not up to me to figure out the logistics." Edward set his hand on the table as if he were calling a meeting to order. "I wanted to talk to you about your work."

Her stomach tightened. "At Digicore or overall?"

"I know about your career and expertise." Edward took a bite of steak and leaned back in his chair. "You applied for a position at Intellix a few years ago."

She smiled faintly. "I didn't get the job."

"Sounds like that might have been our mistake. We still have your resume on file." He sliced off another piece of steak. "You've garnered more experience since then, and I want you to know we now have an open role at Intellix for which you would be well suited, should you ever decide to branch out."

Shock bolted through her. "You're offering me a job?"

"I'm telling you there's an open role at Intellix for which you would be well suited," Edward corrected, eyeing her from underneath his thick eyebrows. "Systems Development software engineer. You'd be part of a team under Nathan's management."

Rory couldn't speak. The sudden, striking beauty of that image crashed right up against the hard wall of reality.

"I'm not trying to poach you away from Digicore." Edward set his fork down and reached for his drink. "If you're intent on staying there, I respect that. Just be aware you have options."

"I…I don't know what to say."

"In answer to the question you don't want to ask, yes. I'm making this offer because I know you through Grant." He swirled the liquor around in the glass. "However, your relationship with him only brought you to my attention. On an objective level, I'd have hired you based on your credentials and experience alone. I would never make a business or a hiring decision based on *sentiment*."

Rory put down her fork and knife. Her chest was tight. Edward was giving her an out. All she had to do was turn in her notice, and she could start work at Intellix. The company was known for being inclusive and hiring strong, smart women—several of whom now held top-level positions. Edward hadn't always treated his son right, but Rory didn't doubt he ran a tight ship at his company. Harassment of any kind would never be tolerated or swept under the rug at Intellix.

This was also no coincidence.

"Don't make a decision yet," Edward said. "Think about it. Pay is either commensurate with or more than what you're making at Digicore. Full benefits, vacation, the works. We can be flexible with a start date, but Nathan is starting to work on ways to scale AI learning models and increase computational power. Wouldn't be a bad idea for you to get in on the ground floor."

"I'm…" Her hand shaking, she picked up her water glass and took a sip. "I appreciate the offer very much. Thank you."

"Let me know." Edward patted his beard with his napkin. "If you want to leave or stay."

*Why would you want to stay?*

Grant's question ricocheted through her.

Later that evening, she didn't wait around for his usual call. Instead, she left a message at Digicore that she wouldn't be in the following day. Then she grabbed her keys and drove to Bliss Cove.

~

"HE OFFERED YOU A JOB?" GRANT SHOOK HIS HEAD. HE hadn't heard that right. His father wanted to hire Rory? On an intellectual level, it made perfect sense—who wouldn't want to hire her?—but on every other level, it made no sense.

"You didn't know." Her voice was flat. She was standing by the fireplace in his living room, tension lacing her shoulders.

"No, I didn't fucking know. When did this happen?"

"This afternoon. It's a software engineer job with a team in Nathan's division." She folded her arms tightly over her chest. "I asked you not to tell him. Not to tell anyone or to try and fix this for me."

Grant stared at her in disbelief. "Rory, I didn't ask my father to hire you."

"Then this is one hell of a strange coincidence." She lowered her arms, her hands fisting. "Maybe we'd better call Destiny and find out if Mars is in retrograde or whatever because clearly something is totally out of whack."

"You *told me not to tell anyone*." His jaw tightened. "I *wanted* to tell everyone—the cops, *The New York Times*, the managers, the senior execs, the CEO, and, yeah, even my father. But I didn't because you asked me not to. Do you think I'm lying?"

"Why would he suddenly offer to hire me now, Grant?" Rory flung her arms out to her sides, her face flushing with anger. "Right after those fuckwads in my office thought it would be funny to mess with me? I haven't gone to HR and certainly none of my coworkers have access to anyone close to your father's caliber, so it's not as if he'd have heard any random gossip. I don't even think any of the senior managers at Digicore know or care what's going on, and if they did, they sure as hell would make sure Edward Taylor didn't hear about it. So how else could the founder and CEO of the Intellix Corporation have learned that low-level Rory Prescott is getting harassed and bullied?"

Grant dragged his hands over his face. There was no question his father *knew* stuff, owing to his standard practice of working alongside everyone from Intellix executives to programmers.

Had Edward been keeping an eye on Rory? Spying on her? Or had he just made a few inquiries and found out the sordid truth?

Or was it Nathan? No. His brother would have talked to him before asking their father to hire Rory.

"Wait." He turned to face her. "My mother."

"She doesn't know, Grant." Rory pressed her hands to her temples. "I had lunch with her the day I found the scoresheet. I didn't tell her anything about it."

Grant strode into the bedroom and grabbed his duffel. He tossed a few clothes into it and picked up his keys. "Come on."

"Where are we going?"

"To talk to my parents."

"I just drove down here."

"I'm driving us back."

# CHAPTER 24

*G*rant gripped the steering wheel so tightly his knuckles were white the entire drive to San Francisco. He punched in the code at the security gate and drove toward the circular driveway in front of the spot-lit mansion. Rory had barely said a word on the drive back up, but he sensed her withdrawing as if she were retreating into a shell.

She was reaching her breaking point. There was nothing more he wanted to do than pull her into his arms and let her retreat into *him*. He wanted to destroy everyone who had ever hurt her, and he wanted to build a world where she could do everything she wanted and be everything she was.

"Do they know we're here?" Rory closed the car door, sweeping her gaze over the façade of the house.

"No. The element of surprise is the best approach sometimes. That's partly how I got my mother to admit that she was involved in the set-up with Vivian."

He took her arm as they climbed the porch steps and rang

the doorbell. The massive door opened to reveal a sour-looking maid. "May I help you?"

"Grant Taylor and Rory Prescott."

Her eyes widened slightly. "Please come in, Mr. Taylor. Can I take your—"

"We're fine." Pressing his hand to Rory's lower back, he urged her into the plush, antique-filled living room. "Please tell my parents we're here."

"Of course, sir."

She hurried off. Grant took Rory's jacket and draped it along with his over the back of the sofa. He went to the sidebar and splashed whiskey into two glasses. After handing her one, he took a long swallow. The alcohol was a welcome burn through his cold veins.

"Grant?" Joanna hurried down the sweeping staircase in a bathrobe and slippers, her eyes wide. "What on earth are you doing here? Is everything all right?"

"Everything's fine, Mom. But we need to talk to you and Dad."

"Your father is in his study." She closed her eyes and pressed a hand to her chest. "I almost had a heart attack when Wilma said you were here. What time is it?"

"Close to midnight." Grant set his glass down. "I'll get Dad."

"No, no. I'll get him." Joanna waved him to sit down and hurried over to embrace Rory. "Lovely to see you again, dear, but my goodness. Text or call in advance next time, would you? I'd at least have a chance to tell Wilma to prepare refreshments."

She crossed the marble foyer to a heavy, closed door and entered after a swift knock. A moment later, she emerged with a rumpled Edward, who looked as if he'd been sleeping.

"What are you doing here?" With a scowl, he pulled his glasses from his breast pocket and set them on his nose. "What's wrong?"

"They need to *talk* to us." Joana nudged her husband in the side, her eyes suddenly brightening. "It must be very important if you need to talk to us so urgently in the middle of the night. Edward, pour us a drink."

With a mumble of irritation, he shuffled to the sidebar to mix a couple of drinks. Joanna perched on the edge of a chair, her eyes slanting surreptitiously to Rory's left hand.

"So." She gave a happy little shrug. "What do you need to talk to us about?"

"Did you know that Dad was planning to offer Rory a job at Intellix?" Grant asked.

His mother blinked. Guilt flashed in her eyes for less than a second before she gave him a wide, innocent smile. "Well, isn't that wonderful? Edward, what a marvelous idea. Rory is a perfect fit for Intellix."

Grant rubbed the back of his neck. "You didn't answer the question, Mom."

"Your father has always trusted me with the details of the business, Grant." She clasped her hands on her lap and pursed her lips. "Since Rory is your girlfriend, of course I knew that he was hoping to recruit her. Nathan's division is doing more and more work with cloud platforms and AI, and I know that's one of Rory's interests. It's an excellent idea."

Grant shifted his gaze to his father. Edward handed Joanna a drink and took a gulp from his own glass.

"When and where did you get the idea, Dad?"

"Ideas come out of everywhere, don't they?" Joanna lifted her hands and pantomimed plucking ideas from the air. "I wouldn't be surprised if your father thought of hiring Rory when we first met her at the wedding. He's no fool, you know. He can spot talent and dedication a mile away."

"In other words..." Edward arched an eyebrow at his wife. "Your mother suggested it."

"Why did you do that, Joanna?" Rory gripped her hands together, looking as if she were sensing the approach of a terrible storm. "I mean, I appreciate it, of course, but I don't understand why *now*, of all times."

"Well, why not now?" Joanna furrowed her brow. "Obviously, it wouldn't have been prudent to have offered you a job when we didn't know if your and Grant's relationship would survive your move, but since you two seem committed to each other, I—"

"Mom." Grant curled his hands into fists. "If you're trying to hook Rory into the company because you think she can get me to move back to the Bay Area, then she and I are walking out of here and not coming back. I will not stand for you manipulating her the way you did me."

"Don't you dare accuse your mother of being manipulative," Edward snapped. "All she has ever wanted is for you to be loyal to this family the way your brother is."

"Right, and to do that, she has to constantly—" Grant stopped and shook his head, forcing down old latent anger. "This is about Rory. What's going on, Mom?"

"Do you know what happened at Digicore?" Rory leaned forward, her eyes dark. "How?"

Joanna pressed her lips together. She picked up her glass and walked to the sidebar. "I would like you both to know that I had no manipulative or nefarious intentions whatsoever. I was simply concerned. As it turned out, I had good reason to be."

His expression darkening, Edward poured her a fresh drink.

"What did you do?" Rory rubbed her hands on her thighs. "How did you find out?"

"That day I came to pick you up for lunch." Joanna took the glass from her husband and turned to face Rory. "You looked as if you were about to be sick. You looked as if you *were* sick."

Grant's heart started beating too fast. That must have been the day Rory found the fucking scoresheet. It made him crazy to think of how horrified and shocked she must have been... and that he hadn't been there for her. She'd been alone.

"You had this crumpled piece of paper in your hands, and you kept twisting it around and wadding it up...it was very strange to see you like that, Rory." Joanna shook her head as Edward put his hand on her shoulder. "It wasn't like you at all, and the only thing I could think of was that something had happened with Grant. But, of course, I didn't want to *pry*, so off we went to lunch. You'd put the crumpled paper in the side pocket of your handbag."

She shifted her gaze to the opposite wall and took a sip of her drink. "I noticed it when you went to use the ladies' room."

"Mom." Grant grated the word out past the anger collecting in his throat. "You did *not* take that paper out of Rory's bag."

"Grant, I was terribly worried!" Joanna lifted her hand as if that explained everything. "I just wanted to take a quick peek. I thought maybe it had something to do with you, and when I saw what it was... Well, it was quite clear that someone was being very cruel at Rory's expense, and that was the reason she was so upset."

Rory lowered her head, her breath escaping in a hard rush. Every muscle in Grant's body locked in defense of her. He forced himself not to cross the room, or he'd grab her hand and walk out the door without looking back. Maybe he still would.

"That was a complete violation of her privacy and her trust in you." He turned to his mother, his anger boiling over. "You had no right to do that. None! I don't care what you were worried about or why you think you can justify it. This is the kind of shit I can't fucking stand, when you—"

"Stop." Edward held up a hand. His voice boomed, but he sounded loud rather than angry. "I will agree that your mother overstepped her bounds, but I won't have you shouting at her."

"Overstepped her bounds?" Grant stared at his father. "She took Rory's property because she has to be in the fucking center of everything and interfere every chance she gets."

"Grant, please." Rory stood swiftly and crossed to him, putting her hand on his lower back. Though her expression was calm, he could feel her shaking. "I don't want to be the reason you're fighting again."

"Rory, I am so sorry." Joanna dabbed at her eyes with a cocktail napkin. "I really didn't mean to snoop. Well, I *did*, obviously, so I suppose in some way I did mean to, but it wasn't premeditated. I just saw a corner of the paper sticking out of your bag and impulsively wanted to see what it was."

"Why didn't you ask me?"

"I did ask you when I was picking you up. You said it was nothing when it was clearly *something*." Joanna crumpled the napkin in her hand. "Then I couldn't upset you further by telling you I'd seen that horrible drawing. So, later that day, I made some calls and did a bit of investigating."

"Christ." Grant sank into a chair, wishing he could disbelieve what he was hearing. Unfortunately, mucking around in other people's lives was one of the things his mother did best.

"Your mother knows several women whose husbands work at Digicore." Edward swirled the liquor around in his glass. "They were all too eager to gossip about what was going on in *The Hive*, as they call it. Though we didn't know the details, it wasn't difficult to piece together the situation. Rory had become the target of inter-office bullying and harassment, and neither HR nor management appeared to be interested in doing anything about it."

"You may think I'm just an extravagant housewife who hosts dinner parties and spends time at my women's club." Joanna lifted her chin, eyeing Grant with a sudden hard glint in her expression. "But since the day your father founded Intellix, I've made it my mission to be educated about technology. I wanted to be able to talk to anyone, from programmers to vice-presidents, about software development, research, virtual reality, even game design. You'd better believe I know the business profiles of all the top players in the industry *and* all the rumors surrounding them."

She spread her hands out. "When I discovered that Rory was in a bad situation, I also guessed that she would have a difficult time extracting herself from it without ruining her other job prospects and possibly even her career. I've heard plenty of revolting stories about the way some companies treat women, and I couldn't stand the idea of Rory being one of them. So, I approached your father."

And, of course, Edward Taylor would do whatever his wife asked. Grant shook his head, his insides knotted.

"The situation instigated the job offer." Edward studied Rory, a deep crease between his eyebrows. "But I wouldn't have made the offer if I didn't know you'd be a valuable asset to the company."

"I appreciate that," Rory said. "But surely you can see how it looks, given my relationship with Grant and with both of you. Even with Nathan. This is not a normal hiring practice."

"Why should it be?" Joanna shrugged. "People do favors for others all the time. It was easy enough for Edward and Nathan to create a role that would suit you."

Rory paled. "You *created* the position just for me?"

His parents didn't respond. Grant got to his feet and paced to the other side of the room, his hands flexing. "Mom, none of this excuses what you did."

"I didn't do it to be excused." Joanna flung her hand toward Rory. "I did it to help get Rory out of a terrible situation and into a safe one. Do you think for one second that she would be exposed to that kind of treatment *anywhere* at Intellix?"

"No, of course not." Grant pulled a heavy breath into his lungs. "But if Rory had wanted your help or my help, she'd have asked for it. She's been in this business for over ten years on her own, and she doesn't need you interfering. No one does."

"One would think that *you* would be appreciative as

well." Edward pierced Grant with a glare. "You couldn't do anything about Rory's situation, could you? If you'd been working for me and knew what the hell was—"

"Dad, don't you get it?" Grant spun to confront his father. "If I'd been working for you, I'd never have met Rory. I wouldn't have the life I want. I wouldn't have the woman I love. Did it fucking kill me that I couldn't do anything to help her? Yeah, but you know what? She's smart. Hell, she's brilliant. She's strong. Even if you hadn't made the offer, she'd have figured out what *she* was going to do. And I guarantee it wouldn't have involved her coming to you."

"Well, then, it's a good thing I stepped in, isn't it?" Joanna lifted her chin in defiance. "Your father is giving Rory an excellent opportunity, and while I acknowledge I could have handled the situation differently, I won't apologize for taking action."

"It wasn't your situation to handle," Grant snapped.

"You've never wanted our help." Edward set his glass on a table with a hard thunk. "That was one of the reasons you moved away, isn't it? Now, you can't stand that your mother and I can rectify a problem where you have no power whatsoever."

"Excuse me." Rory stood, her hands fisting at her sides. "My issues at Digicore have nothing to do with your relationship with your son. I meant it when I said I appreciate the offer and your efforts to help, but I have to say no."

"No?" Joanna looked as if she'd never heard that word before. "No to what?"

"To working at Intellix." Rory turned to Edward. "I'm not diminishing the extent of what you're doing to try and help me, but I can't justify working for Intellix under these circumstances. I can't pretend that I earned the position legitimately when I didn't. And not for anything will I cause more trouble between you and Grant."

Her eyes glittered. "Grant is the *best* man I know. The best man all of Bliss Cove knows. Even if he doesn't want people to recognize it, he's smart, talented, loyal to a fault, and *so* incredibly kind. He knows how to treat people the way they deserve to be treated. He would do anything for anyone. He doesn't even realize how much power he has."

Grant's heart hammered so hard he could hear it in his head. His mother opened and closed her mouth.

Edward cleared his throat. "I will admit, Rory, that Grant is right in saying he wouldn't have met you if he hadn't made the choices he did. And it has become abundantly clear that he couldn't have made a better choice than you."

A tight part of Grant unlocked, like a door opening a crack to let in fresh air and light. Rory wiped her eyes with the back of her hand.

"Thank you," she told his father. "I chose him, too."

She picked up her handbag and looked at Joanna. "I know you did what you thought was right, but I really wish you'd talked to me about it first."

Joanna pressed her lips together, her eyes shiny. "I'm sorry, Rory."

Rory hesitated for a second before she turned and hurried out the door. Grant started after her.

"Grant, I was just trying to help." A plea colored his mother's voice.

"I know, Mom." He dragged his hands over his face. "But you can't keep doing this. When you go too far, you push people away. Now you might end up losing Rory. If you lose her...you'll lose me, too."

He left the room and went outside, where Rory was halfway down the porch steps. He caught up with her at the bottom of the steps and reached for her hand. She stopped to face him, but pulled away from his touch.

Unease cut through him. The spotlights cast an eerie glow on her face. She zipped up her coat. Her hand trembled slightly.

"I love you." His voice came out rough. "Don't turn the job down because of me."

"He offered me the job because of you." She twisted the strap of her handbag around her fingers. "But that's not the only reason I'm turning it down. I didn't earn the job legitimately, and I meant it when I said I won't pretend anymore."

"You wouldn't be. You've already proven yourself a thousand times over."

"And you? You'd be okay with me working for your father?"

The word *yes* pushed up into his throat and stopped. He would be okay with it because he knew she would be respected at Intellix. But—

"I once told you that you can do anything." He reached out to tuck a lock of hair behind her ear. "That you can *be* anything. I'll always believe that. I want you to believe it, too."

Her eyes clouded. She paced a few feet away, her spine rigid. She spun back around and extended her hands.

"It's so fucking *embarrassing*, Grant. This harassment crap is what everyone is going to remember when they look at me, not the programs I designed or the articles I've written.

Your father probably doesn't even know about my ideas for merging artificial intelligence with virtual and augmented reality. How can I be *anything* when I'm dragging around all this garbage? I don't even know how to get rid of it."

"You don't have to." Pain cracked through him, along with a sudden sense that everything was about to change. "Just like you don't have to be stuck in a job where you're either invisible or humiliated. No one should be."

"So, the alternatives are to work at Intellix at a job I didn't earn or to quit tech altogether." Her mouth tightened. "Maybe it is time for me to leave. I've tried and failed to get to where I'd always hoped I would be, so…"

"You're not going to quit. It's not in you to quit."

"But this time, I'm out of options." She held up her hand when he stepped toward her. "Look, I…I'm going to need some time to think."

"Okay. We'll go back to your place and—"

"No." She shook her head and skidded her gaze away from him. "I need to be alone, Grant."

The edge to her voice sliced right through him. He stepped back.

He knew her. From the moment they first met, he'd sensed what she'd needed. Over the years at the Mousehole, he'd learned when to give her space, when she wanted to talk, when her snarkiness was hiding something more. He knew exactly how crispy she liked fried cheese curds and that cherry gummy worms were her favorite.

Now, he also knew that she needed three pillows to sleep, that she liked mint-flavored dental floss, and where to kiss her to make her giggle. He knew that the crease between her eyebrows meant she was struggling with a design problem and that when she unconsciously licked her lower lip, she was thinking about sex.

He knew how to touch her. He knew how to love her.

But he didn't, for the life of him, know how to walk away from her.

"Take these." He handed her his car keys. "I'll borrow one of Nathan's cars to drive home."

After a brief hesitation, she got into his car. Seconds later, the taillights disappeared into the darkness.

# CHAPTER 25

"*I*sn't Grant joining us?" Eleanor stirred the mashed potatoes on the stove and glanced at the clock. "The turkey should be done in less than half an hour."

"He's...um, working." Rory leaned her elbows on the counter and fiddled with her phone.

"The Mousehole is open on Thanksgiving Day?" Henry, Eleanor's significant other, popped the cork of a wine bottle. "I didn't know that."

"No, Grant makes dinner over at the soup kitchen." Aria took a bunch of silverware from a drawer. "He's usually there cooking and serving all day."

"Rory said he was planning to leave a bit early today so he could be here." Eleanor set the spoon down, her brow furrowing as she looked at her middle daughter. "Did I get that wrong?"

"He's not coming, Mom." Rory reached for a piece of cheese from the appetizer platter. "He's busy."

Eleanor opened her mouth to speak, then closed it again

and turned to check on the turkey. Aria and Callie exchanged glances across the central island.

Rory hitched herself off the stool and went into the living room, where a football game blared from the TV. She flopped down in an easy chair and put her feet on the coffee table.

She'd been looking forward to the refuge of Thanksgiving for days, but now she felt like stone, as if her guard had somehow penetrated to her bones and her heart. Though she knew Grant would be *right over there* for as long as she needed, she had to navigate this new chaos without him at her side as her partner-in-crime, her support system, her kindred spirit. She also had no idea how she ever would.

Anyone would call her a fool for turning down the Intellix job. Maybe she was. On the surface, it would have been so easy—out with the old, in with the new.

Joanna was right. She'd have been valued and productive at Edward Taylor's company. Yes, she'd have had to get past Joanna's snooping, but that would have been a small price to pay.

Or not. If Grant had submitted to his mother's interference, he never would have carved his own path or created his own life.

She sighed and rested her head against the back of the chair. She wanted to do the same thing. She'd always known she was an exceptional programmer and tech expert. She could dream up and design innovative programs for many different spaces—medical, home, education—but she'd never believed she could do "anything." She was too practical for that. She worked, paid her bills, and was grateful for good health benefits.

What did "anything" mean, anyway? She didn't want to

be a different person—she liked being Rory Prescott—but had she kept her life too focused and narrow? Could she have looked beyond a full-time software engineering job to something bigger?

Maybe she'd done that once when she'd created the MedCure program in an effort to strike out on her own, but after the scumbag venture capitalist had shut her down and another company beat her to the market with their software, she'd retreated back into the relative stability of the corporate world.

"You okay?" Callie entered the room with a glass of wine, which she set on the table beside Rory. "You've been kind of quiet."

Rory shrugged. She hadn't wanted to burden her family with the sordid details of what was going down at Digicore, but she'd told them about the toxic culture and Edward's offer. "The job has just been more of a challenge than I was anticipating."

Callie sat on the arm of the sofa, her forehead creasing. "You've never backed away from a challenge."

Rory looked at her older sister, whose path in life had always seemed easy. She knew it hadn't been—Callie had worked her ass off to get a tenured professor position—but Rory had always admired her sister's confidence and commitment. In fact, she'd used Callie as an example for how to structure her own career. But the hallowed halls of academia were a lot different from the Wild West of the tech industry.

"The work is the best part," she finally said. "Unfortunately, the environment can be the worst."

Callie's mouth twisted. "All the assholes, huh?"

"Yeah." Rory plucked at a loose thread on the hem of her

T-shirt. "They've never made me dislike what I do, but they've made me doubt myself. Which I fucking hate."

"Is that why you stayed in Bliss Cove for so long?"

"Maybe. I don't know. I liked the contract work and being in charge of my own schedule. If I could have gotten benefits and a good, steady salary doing that, then I'd probably still be living here. But the only way I can make a reliable living and advance my career is to work for a corporation. Start-ups are exciting and a lot of fun, but so unpredictable. And stupid as it sounds, ageism hits in the tech industry before forty. I'm a thirty-year-old woman still trying to find the right fit."

She pushed to her feet in frustration. "So why the hell didn't I take the job Grant's father offered me?"

"Because it wasn't the right fit." Callie lifted her shoulders. "When I was first looking for jobs out of grad school, I had offers from several universities, including Skyline and Duke. Duke would have been a better career track, but I always knew I wanted to come back to Bliss Cove. So, for me, the right fit wasn't the more prestigious job."

Aria came into the room, munching on a raw carrot stick. "Last summer, I found this super cute dress with spaghetti straps on sale for, like, five bucks. First time I wore it, one of the straps broke. Half the bodice slipped down, and I flashed all of Mariposa Street before I managed to pull it back up. *So* not the right fit."

Rory and Callie both grinned.

"Remember how Dad used to call us Rock, Paper, and Scissors?" Callie stood and squeezed Rory's arm. "You're the sharp one who can slice through anything to create something new. So, maybe the reason you haven't found the right fit is because you shouldn't be looking for one. Maybe you need to cut your own pattern or material, or...um..."

"Make your own snowflake design out of construction paper," Aria suggested.

Rory smiled faintly. "I don't think I remember how."

"Well, if anyone can figure it out, you can." Aria started out of the room. "Come on, let's eat. I'm starving."

Rory followed her sisters into the kitchen as Jake and Hunter stomped in the front door, their hair tousled and faces flushed with cold. Hunter carried a jug of apple cider, and Jake was bearing three different kinds of pie.

"Parade clean-up completed." He set the pies on the counter and turned to plant a kiss on Callie. "Turkey Tom should last one more year, though his tail feathers are getting a little droopy."

"Better his than yours." Callie patted his rear.

"Mrs. Higgins says Happy Thanksgiving." Hunter put the cider in the fridge. "She wants everyone to stop by for cookies later. Damn, that turkey smells amazing." He pulled Aria in for a hug. "So do you."

"It's all ready." Eleanor waved them toward the dining room with a potholder. "Go sit down. Henry and I will bring everything in."

As the group started out of the kitchen, Rory tugged Hunter to a halt.

"Hey, do you have a minute later tonight?" she asked. "I want to talk to you about something."

"Sure. I'm planning on eating everything twice, so I'll be at the table for a few hours." He patted his flat stomach in anticipation. "What do you want to talk about?"

"I'm not sure yet." Rory walked beside him into the

dining room. "But it has something to do with scissors, a snowflake, and Aria flashing her boobs."

He laughed. "Well, then. I'm definitely in."

*GOING BACK TO SJ. WILL LYK WHEN I GET IN.*

Rory's text was followed by a little turkey emoji.

Without responding, Grant shoved his phone into his pocket and shut the car door. He hadn't seen her on Thanksgiving, and over the past few days, they'd been keeping in touch via text.

While he'd never liked texting, he'd been grateful for it as a way to quickly contact her. But now, the shorthand messages they exchanged were like bones stripped of meat. He avoided asking questions and struggled to respect her need to "be alone."

He hated forcing himself to back off. He hated that she wanted to keep him at a distance. After years of being accustomed to his own privacy, to not having anyone around, there was now a Rory-shaped hole in his life. He had no idea how, or *if*, it would be filled again.

He rang the bell of his parents' house, and his mother welcomed him with a smile that held a hint of nervousness. They hadn't spoken since the fight.

"Did Nathan tell you that Alice wants to visit Bliss Cove?" Joanna poured a scotch and handed it to him. "She was so intrigued by my descriptions that she's anxious to see the town for herself. Nathan is going to call you to work out the details."

"Good to know."

"So, how is everything?" Joanna smiled brightly. "Did you spend Thanksgiving with Rory's family?"

"No." He rubbed a hand over his hair. "I haven't seen her in a few days."

"Oh, dear." Dismay crinkled her forehead. "I really botched things up for you, didn't I?"

"Honestly, Rory wanted to handle the situation by herself before you...did what you did," he admitted, setting the glass on a table. "She'd never want anyone to rescue her."

Joanna lifted an eyebrow. "That must be hard on you."

"Yeah. But it's also one of the reasons I love her. She's so strong. Sometimes I have to do what she wants instead of what I want."

A shadow crossed his mother's face. She spread out her hand and studied her fingernails. "Sounds like a lesson I need to learn."

Grant's heart softened. "I know you have good intentions, Mom. But instead of your behind-the-scenes plotting, maybe straightforward talking would have better results."

"All right, then." She pressed her lips together and lifted her gaze to his. "I understand that you chose a different path in life, and I know you love being a chef and restaurant owner. After our visit, I can even appreciate it. I like your town, and clearly everyone there loves you. But even though you've said you didn't turn your back on this family, it took your brother's wedding to bring you back even for an overnight visit."

She held up a hand when he started to speak. "I know. Your father has often been cutting and cruel. There was no reason for you to subject yourself to that. But I've missed you. I've missed us being a family. If I promise to curb my meddling, will you *please* make an effort to visit us more? It's not as if you live across the country. Can you manage to have dinner with us once a month?"

"*Manage* isn't the right word." Grant crossed the room to pull his mother into his arms. "I would like that. If you want, I can even cook every now and then."

His mother smiled and hugged him. "I also promise to try and rein in your father, although he's only had good things to say about Bliss Cove. Grudging, but good. Speaking of him, can you please go outside and tell him lunch will be ready in an hour? He's trimming the hedges."

"Sure." Grant started toward the French doors leading to the backyard. A monthly dinner with his parents wouldn't heal all wounds, but maybe it was a start.

He found his father around the side of the house, with garden tools scattered nearby and a wheelbarrow half-full of clippings. After greeting him, Grant relayed the message about lunch and picked up a pair of shears.

"Is Rory here, too?" Edward glanced toward the house.

"No."

"You talked her right out of taking my job offer, didn't you?" Edward sheared off another branch and straightened. "You'd never want your girlfriend to work for Intellix."

"That's not true." Grant moved to another hedge and began trimming. "I've never hated Intellix. It's phenomenal company. I just wasn't cut out for IT work. And Intellix became this…I don't know, symbol for everything that was wrong. But it was never about the company."

His father frowned. "Intellix was the reason you had so many privileges and the life that you did."

"I had a lot because of Intellix, but it didn't give me all my privileges. I earned many of those."

Edward yanked a fistful of weeds from the dirt. "What about your trust fund?"

"It's still there."

"All of it?"

"Yeah. More of it now, with the interest."

Edward wiped his forehead with the back of his hand. "You didn't use any of the money to buy that tavern?"

"No." Grant picked up a few clippings and tossed them into the wheelbarrow. "I'd been saving for my own restaurant since I first started bussing tables. I was working at a restaurant up in Portland when I heard that the Mousehole was for sale. I'd been there a few times when I was traveling, so I made an offer. When the owners accepted it the next day, I knew it was the right fit. I moved to Bliss Cove the following week."

With a muttered, *"Huh,"* Edward returned to the trimming. So did Grant.

"What are you going to do next?" Edward asked. "Open a Mousehole in Santa Cruz or Los Angeles?"

"No. I might invest in a place for another chef one day, but I'm not moving. I have everything I need and want in Bliss Cove."

*Almost.*

"What about Rory?" Edward bent to pick up a stack of branches from the ground. "I assume she's not going to stay at Digicore, and she's not coming over to Intellix. You want her to move back to Bliss Cove and work in a bakery again? Waste her talent?"

"I want her to be happy." A sudden tightness constricted

his chest. "You know what it's like to want your girl to be happy, right? Rory has never had the chance to prove what she's really capable of, not even to herself. She's tried, but she's hit too many roadblocks. If you do what you're good at, what you want to do, how is that a waste of talent? Would you rather I was working at Intellix doing a shitty job because I don't know the difference between a bit and a byte?"

His father lifted an eyebrow. "A bit is part of a byte."

"A *small bite* is an appetizer that can be eaten all at once."

Edward slanted him a narrow glance. Amusement—faint, but there—glimmered in his expression. "That artichoke soup was something else. I'll give you that."

"Ancient secret recipe."

They finished cleaning up the branches and started back to the house.

"Your mother has mentioned wanting to visit Bliss Cove again." Edward's voice was gruff. "I wouldn't mind another bowl of that soup. Good fishing, too."

"I'll be there whenever you want to come back."

"Maybe after the new year." His father pulled open the door. "I'm taking your mother to Indonesia next spring for another second honeymoon. Which I guess makes it the third. Just the two of us this time. And believe it or not…no cell phones."

"Don't worry." Amused, Grant followed his father into the house. "I won't tell anyone."

# CHAPTER 26

*A*s much as Rory wanted to see Grant during the holiday weekend, she returned to San Jose without stopping at the Mousehole.

Throughout her life, she'd always had her parents and sisters, but she'd been the one with the independent, renegade streak. The one who didn't need anyone to take care of her. However, being with Grant was a whole other level of *care*, and she'd already told him that she was going to find her own way through this.

Just like he had.

She spent the rest of the weekend at her computer—testing and studying the various urban planning and architecture programs she'd sent to Hunter. She tracked down the designers and bombarded them with questions.

She contacted the chief of the architecture program at the National Center for Preservation Technology, the head of a forensic consulting and technology firm, and five historical preservationists. She scheduled meetings with the architects of the design firm and the engineers of the construction company Hunter had hired for the Mariposa Street expansion.

By the time she went to work on Monday morning, her mind was buzzing with ideas and her blood was zinging with excited energy. She didn't even mind walking into The Hive, and she didn't care what anyone was thinking when they looked at her.

"How was your weekend?" Douglas turned to her, scratching his goatee.

"Fine." Rory sat down and signed into her computer. "Yours?"

"Er...fine." Wariness flashed in his eyes, as if he didn't know what to make of her cordial response.

"Good." She pulled up the latest review files.

She worked until six, then left her Digicore code behind and went home to tackle more of her new project. She texted Grant a photo of her dinner—take-out chicken Pomodoro and a salad—and, in return, he texted her a photo of a fried onion blossom.

RORY: I want that.
GRANT: You'll have to come and get it this time.

Oh, she would. Soon.

Turning to her computer, she pulled all of her more questionable skills to the forefront and tracked down information on the five men who had been keeping score on her. She compiled her findings into separate folders and began printing things out—photos, emails, screenshots of various accounts, social media pages.

The next day, she did it all over again.

And again.

And again.

A week later, she scheduled a meeting with the Digicore CEO.

"What can I do for you?" Faintly impatient, Brad looked up at her from behind his desk.

"I quit." Rory put her resignation letter on his desk, narrowing her eyes on him. "Effective immediately. I won't work for a company that refuses to take action against or even acknowledge sexual harassment."

He opened and closed his mouth, his eyes widening. "What are you talking about?"

"Don't play dumb." Planting her hands on the desk, Rory looked him in the eye. "I know you discourage complaints to HR, not that HR would do anything about them, anyway, and that all of your policies and tactics contribute to a toxic atmosphere of pervasive discrimination and harassment. It will be interesting to see how your partnership with Intellix works out if they ever learn of Digicore's tolerance for reprehensible behavior. Starting with the CEO."

"Who the fuck are you to talk to me like that, you little bitch?" Brad bolted to his feet, his face flushing with anger.

"I'm a *distraction*, remember?" Rory pushed away from the desk and folded her arms. "Oh, did I mention I discovered your own record for groping and propositioning women, especially during interviews? You're lucky you didn't do that with me, or I'd have kicked you in the balls. Maybe I still will. Metaphorically, at least."

"What the—"

"Just a little warning, Brad." Rory swiveled on the heel of

her boot and walked to the door. "But don't let my threats *distract* you from your work."

Her spine straight, she strode out of the office. As she walked back to The Hive, her supervisor Brenda approached from the breakroom.

"Rory, we have a project meeting scheduled at three."

"I won't be there. I just quit."

Brenda's eyes widened. "You *quit*?"

"You were right about what you said to me." Rory looked the other woman in the eye. "Reporting harassment can destroy a woman's career in this industry. But it doesn't have to be like that. If you ever decide you're sick of playing their game, l know you can find a better place for yourself. I hear that Intellix has a much better environment. They could likely use a smart, experienced woman like you. Maybe you'll even learn that having a thick skin doesn't mean you need to compromise your integrity."

She brushed past Brenda and returned her workstation. She'd already cleared out her desk of a few personal items, and she grabbed the box and walked outside.

The second she stepped into the bright California sun, a combination of relief and fear flooded every part of her. Resigning and leaving The Hive didn't mean she was done with her former coworkers.

Not yet.

# CHAPTER 27

"*M*an, it was the *craziest* thing." Nathan grabbed the beer Grant set in front of him at the Mousehole bar. "Like one of those…what do you call it… domino effects. I've never seen legal and publicity departments move so fast to denounce discrimination and harassment. I swear, there must have been tweets from every company in the fucking Silicon Valley announcing that they were planning to review their hiring policies, and how they're so committed to inclusivity and diversity."

He took a swallow of beer and shook his head with a laugh. "With all the tech executives shaking in fear, the Bay Area almost had an earthquake."

"Good." Grant began wiping down the counter. "It's about time they took a serious hit."

How they'd taken the hit, he didn't know. Though Rory hadn't been mentioned in any of the reports over the past week, he knew she'd had something to do with the explosive news that Digicore had fired five male employees due to allegations of harassment.

Shortly afterward, Edward Taylor had issued a statement announcing that Intellix was cutting ties with Digicore on a developing partnership deal. The two stories had sent shock-waves through the tech industry, prompting a panicked slew of statements from all the major companies about their own policies.

It *was* an earthquake, in a sense. The execs were now scared that backlashes and allegations could fuck up their business deals.

Grant hoped they would, if that was what it took to insti-gate real change.

"Dad is sitting pretty because everyone's looking to Intellix as a model of an inclusive, respectful work environ-ment." Nathan hitched himself off the barstool and picked up his beer. "Mom is bursting with pride, of course."

He started back to the booth, where Alice was sitting with her mother and sister. Then he stopped and looked at Grant again.

"So, Rory's not working at Digicore anymore, huh?"

Grant shook his head. "She quit last week, I think. I haven't seen her since before Thanksgiving. She's still in San Jose."

"Because I know she...well, Mom said there were some..." Nathan stopped and shrugged. "Anyway, whatever went down, it sounds like she can do much better."

"She can."

His brother hesitated for a second longer before walking back to the booth to rejoin his wife. Grant finished wiping down the counter and tossed the dishrag aside. He mixed an old-fashioned for a customer, refilled the peanut bowls, and set clean glasses on the shelf.

After checking on a few other customers, he indicated for his manager to take over the bar and went back to the kitchen. As he seared steaks, made burgers, and roasted potatoes, he tried to ignore the unease that had been simmering under his skin for the past two weeks.

The feeling had been subsumed by elation over all the news reports and the knowledge that Rory had somehow taken down the men who'd messed with her. No question she was a force.

But there was still another question. *What happens next?*

After the Mousehole closed for the night, he and the crew cleaned up. He unlocked the front door, and his employees headed out to their cars.

When everyone was gone, he went into the back and cashed out the registers. Taking his order forms, he returned to the dining room to inventory the liquor.

His heart almost stopped. Rory sat at the bar, her long hair loose around her shoulders and her pale skin glowing in the dim lights.

"Fried onion, please." She smiled at him, though uncertainty filled her eyes. "With a side of cheese curds."

For a second, he couldn't move. Then his pulse bumped into life again. He fought the urge to leap over the bar and haul her into his arms.

"Kitchen's closed." He took a package of gummy worms from a box underneath the bar and set it in front of her. "I've got these, though."

"My favorite." She tore open the bag and chewed on one of the rubbery things.

"What are you…" He paused and cleared his throat. "What are you doing here?"

"Well, you told me I had to come and get the fried onion this time." She shrugged, her blue eyes as bright as stars. "But what I really came to get is *you*."

He reached across the bar and grabbed the front of her T-shirt, pulling her closer until their faces were inches apart. His chest knotted.

"You have no idea what it cost me to back off and wait for you." He fisted his hand in her shirt, his blood heating as her cherry-scented breath brushed against his lips. "To leave you alone. It's like there was a part of me missing. And that pissed me off because my life was supposed to be complete. I didn't want anyone around, remember?"

"I remember." She lowered her gaze to his mouth and then back up to his eyes. "But you always thought I could be the one to change your mind."

"Changing my mind is one thing." He dragged her even closer. "Carving a piece out of my heart is something else entirely."

"Good thing you have plenty of heart to spare." She slipped her warm hand around the back of his neck and rested her forehead against his. "I love you, Grant. I might have loved you from the minute you brought me tomato soup and a grilled cheese sandwich just because you wanted to make me feel better. I know I've loved you for much longer than I even realize. And, yes, that statement would start Destiny off on a lecture about fates, stars, and the Milky Way, but this time, I would actually believe her."

With one more tug, he crushed his mouth against hers. Heat exploded through him. Rory tightened her hand on the back of his neck and parted her lips. He drove his other hand into her hair, deepening the kiss, his greed for her intensifying with every second. A moan escaped her and spilled into him. A thousand feelings surged through his body—love, lust, need.

She broke the kiss first, her eyes darkening. "Can we continue this somewhere else? The edge of the bar is squishing my waist."

Less than a minute later, they were back at his house and tumbling onto the bed together, lips locked hot and deep. He climbed on top of her, fisting his hands in her hair, unable to get enough of her. She wrapped her legs around his waist, arching to rub herself against the growing hardness in his trousers.

All the desire he'd kept pent-up over the past two weeks bolted through him, setting his blood on fire. He devoured her mouth and trailed his lips over her cheek to the soft warmth of her neck. He bit down gently on her collarbone while tugging impatiently at her T-shirt.

With a laugh, Rory hitched the shirt over her head and took off her bra. The sight of her bare breasts sent his lust into a tailspin. He was already so hard it hurt.

"Your turn." Rory yanked at the zipper on his trousers and pushed them off, her breath catching as she curved her hand around his erection.

Grant managed to get the rest of their clothes off, throwing everything to the floor before descending on her again. Any lingering unease dissolved into the sweet, hot crush of her body against his and the little murmurs emerging from her throat. He slid his lips over her breasts and down her torso, pausing to dip his tongue into her belly-button. She let out a husky laugh and swept her hand through his hair.

The scent of her filled his head. He urged her thighs apart and continued the downward trek until he found her core.

"Grant." A gasp stuck in her throat.

Steadying her with his hands on her hips, he pleasured her with his mouth and tongue until she was writhing and moaning beneath him. Using every ounce of self-restraint not to move upward and plunge into her welcoming heat, he kept going until her body began to tense with need.

"Oh my god." She tightened her hand in his hair and bucked up against him. *"Grant."*

"Come on, sweetie."

One more stroke, and a high, keening cry broke from her. He planted his hands on her belly and soothed her with his tongue as she crested the wave and began to descend. He rose, clambering up her sweat-slick body to kiss her. She reached down to guide him inside her, and he sank into her with a groan of pleasure that shook him to his bones.

Pure desire and instinct took over. He thrust deep at the same instant that she arched up to meet him, their bodies falling into a push-and-pull rhythm that drenched the air with urgency and heat. He never wanted it to end, could have stayed buried inside her forever, but the drive for release took over, and he started moving faster.

With another cry, Rory convulsed around him a second time, her inner vibrations so intense that his own control snapped. He plunged into her and let go with a rough shout, pleasure ripping through him fast and hard. He dropped his head on to her shoulder as the sensations waned, his breath rasping against her damp skin.

"For the record," she kissed his ear, "I'm really glad you decided to keep me around."

With a hoarse laugh, he rolled off her and on to his back. "I'm not sure I had a choice. You have a way of sticking around."

Rory chuckled and turned to curl up against his side. "Well, it's a good thing I...what the hell is that?"

She sat up, staring in astonishment as a fluffy orange kitten pounced onto the bed and began making its way over the rumpled covers toward Grant.

He frowned. The kitten blinked its big green eyes.

"That's Button," he muttered.

"*Button?*" Rory shook her head with a laugh. "Are you kidding me? Aria talked you into adopting a kitten?"

"No, she didn't talk me into it." He threw her a scowl as Button pawed at his leg. "I was at the café one morning, and she gave me a sob story about this kitten who was looking for her forever home."

"Ah. The *forever home* pitch is hard to resist."

"When I went by the café again later, Button still hadn't been adopted. I figured cats aren't that much work, so I brought her home."

"She's adorable." Rory reached for the little fluff-ball.

Button hissed, the fur on her back standing up in little spikes.

"Whoa." Rory drew back. "She's territorial, too."

"I've only had her for a week." Grant lifted the kitten onto his chest and scratched her ears. "She's still adjusting."

He felt Rory grinning at him. "What?"

"It's just cute, that's all." She tweaked his ear. "Big, scowly Grant Taylor with the bulging muscles who burns meat with fire...has a pet kitten named Button."

"Yeah, well, don't tell anyone."

"It'll be our secret." She kissed his shoulder. "Are you hungry?"

"I guess that means you are." Setting the kitten down, he reached for his boxer briefs. "What'd you want?"

"I'll go with you."

After they were both dressed, they returned to the Mousehole kitchen. Grant set a pot of water on the stove to boil and drizzled a pan with olive oil before getting a few containers from the walk-in.

"What are you making?" Rory perched on a stool near the stove.

"Shrimp and scallops with linguine and roasted vegetables." He slanted her a glance as he started unwrapping the green beans. "Before I feed you, tell me how you managed to take down your tormentors and put a massive crack right through the entire tech industry."

"That was good, wasn't it?" Even as she smiled, a shadow passed over her lovely features. "All five of the men had big digital footprints. Social media, accounts with a ton of services, many different emails, articles, everything you can think of. It didn't take much work to dig up a bunch of dirt."

She shook her head, her expression darkening. "Three of them are married and one has a fiancée, but I found a profile on a dating website specifically for men seeking affairs, and another had uploaded stuff to revenge porn sites. They all had lots of porn accounts, some with legally questionable content. One of them had sent explicit emails to the woman he was having an affair with, including pictures, and another posted regularly on dark web forums. Two of the men had multiple complaints filed against them at previous jobs. Just a lot of shitty stuff that proved they were assholes with very little conscience."

"What did you do with the info?" Grant tossed the sliced carrots and zucchini into a pan.

"I was going to mail the packages to their wives and fiancée." Her mouth twisted, and she rubbed her finger on the edge of the counter. "And to Douglas's mother since he doesn't have a girlfriend. But I didn't want to blindside other women like that, so instead I sent copies of everything to the Digicore CEO and the top executives, as well as HR and the media. My guess was that the executives all had skeletons in their closets that they didn't want exposed. I was pretty sure they'd throw the Terrible Five under the bus in order to save themselves. I was right.

"Then, your father unknowingly helped out by cutting ties with Digicore, which threw everyone into a frenzy. If shitty moral character and allegations of harassment were enough to get five men fired and destroy a potential corporate partnership, then the entire Silicon Valley needed to get on the fucking ball and make some changes."

"You're amazing." Grant shook his head in admiration as he dropped the fresh linguini into the pot. "But I'm still kind of ticked off that I didn't get to beat those bastards within an inch of their lives."

She smiled faintly. "Honestly, I would have let you, if I hadn't known that a beat-down would backlash on you. Plus, I thought there was some poetic justice in using my cyber skills to punish them. For five IT experts, they did a lousy job of covering their tracks. I didn't expect the whole snowball effect, though, so that was an added bonus."

"Tough as it was to stay away from you for two weeks,

I'm incredibly proud of you." He leaned over to kiss her temple. "You've also given me a hundred more reasons for why I will never have social media or any other accounts."

"You're probably the least traceable man in the country."

"I plan to stay that way, too." He ladled the seafood onto a plate. After adding the linguini and vegetables, he set the dish in front of her.

"So, what's next for Rory Prescott?" He turned off the stove burners and leaned against the counter. "You quit Digicore and understandably don't want to work for Intellix. Do you have another plan?"

She nodded, her eyes downcast as she rolled linguini on her fork. "It's uncertain, unstable, and could be a complete failure."

"Sounds great. Restaurant work is the same way."

"Exactly." She looked up, a sudden spark lighting in her expression. "That's what I kept telling myself. That *you* did it. Why can't I?"

"You want to open a restaurant?"

She laughed. "Yeah, sure. The Gummy Worm Café. No, I want to design a software program that Hunter and Studio Twenty-Five, and other people, can use for the Mariposa Street renovation. Or any kind of architectural restoration project."

Grant blinked in surprise. "That's a fantastic idea. But I thought you didn't want to work on that kind of program because architecture and urban planning aren't in your wheelhouse."

"I didn't. And they're totally not. But neither was medical care when I designed the MedCure program. So I thought, why should I let that stop me? I have a direct line to experts with Hunter and the studio. Plus, the tech industry moves at a breakneck speed, so I'm always learning anyway. This time, I can choose to learn something different."

She popped a shrimp into her mouth. "Callie is going to connect me with the head of the architecture department at Skyline, and I've already signed up to take several online courses. I've contacted dozens of people about the project because I want to find ways to include both 3D and 4D technology for the planning, and then later for visitors. There's a lot of emerging technology for historic sites, but it hasn't been complied into a singular program for both restoration and development. That's how I want to change a corner of the world. A whole district, actually."

"You'll change much more than that." Pride in her surged through him yet again. "Are you going to work for Monarch?"

"No. Hunter said he would try and find the funds to pay me but, honestly, I don't want to work *for* anyone. Not even Hunter. I want to design a program for them, but I want to work for myself."

A tension Grant hadn't even realized he felt suddenly eased from his shoulders. Working for herself was exactly what would make Rory the happiest.

"What do you think?" She set her fork down and fidgeted with her napkin. "Like I said, uncertain and unstable."

"And unlimited." He put the pans in the sink and wiped off the stove. "I always knew you could do anything."

"I'm going to apply for grants, in the hopes that I can get enough funding for at least the next six months, if not the next year. Also, I'm researching venture capitalists who are *not* in the Silicon Valley, but who might have an interest in architecture and history."

Grant tossed the dishtowel on the counter. Wariness clouded his mind, but beneath it an idea sparked, bright and hot.

"Rory." He folded his arms, his spine tensing again. "It killed me not to do anything for you when you were in that mess. I wanted to go into battle for you. *With* you. I wanted to fight, and I really wanted to kick some ass. But I didn't because you asked me not to."

"I know." Her navy-blue eyes were luminous. "I also know how hard that was for you."

"And then..." He pushed away from the counter and paced a few steps. "You asked me to leave you alone. I fucking hated doing it but, again, I did because you asked me to. I'll do anything for you. Anything you ask. Even if it makes me batshit crazy."

"Grant..." She pushed off the stool and started toward him.

He held up a hand to stop her. If he touched her now, he'd be lost.

"I'm so sorry." She shook her head, her brow furrowing with dismay. "I didn't think...I mean, I knew you needed to do something, that you wanted to, but I felt like I had to take action on my own. At least, to try. It was so shitty, what happened at Digicore and stuff I'd gone through before...I had to prove to everyone, to myself, that I was as independent and smart as I'd always believed. I wanted to quit, Grant. You have no idea how much I wanted to just walk away and come back to you. I wanted..."

She paused and rubbed her throat. "I wanted to dive back

into the life we'd had together here, to make it last forever this time. I wanted to meet you at the Mousehole every day for lunch and to welcome you home late at night. I wanted to go jogging with you at dawn and have amazing sex and eat your food. I wanted to leave everything else behind and just be with you. But I couldn't do that because *everything else* wasn't going to go away."

She stepped cautiously toward him and rested her hand on his chest. His heartbeat quickened at the touch of her warm palm. "I needed to do something about it. The stupid game, the comments I'd tried to ignore, the dismissiveness, the propositioning... I'd gone through all of that alone for years. I told people—HR, my mother, my sisters, my friends—but ultimately I was the one who had to deal with it and then walk back into the fray because I didn't want to be beaten or stopped from doing the work I love."

She pulled in a breath. "So when I found that fucking scoresheet and was told to keep my mouth shut *again*, I knew it was the endgame. Somehow, I was going to take those assholes down by using my skills and my brain, and without anyone else's help."

Grant swallowed past a tightness in his throat. "And you did."

"Yes." She lifted her gaze to his, her expression both wary and hopeful. "I'm so sorry that it hurt you. I never meant to do that. But if you think you didn't help me, that you didn't go into the battle with me, that you didn't fight for me... you're wrong, Grant. You were there the whole time. You were part of the reason I did this...because I knew you'd had the courage to strike out on your own even when you could have taken an easier route. You were my role model. For two years, you've been so dependable, so steady and rock-solid that I always knew you were *right over there*. I knew you'd still be there, if it took me a week or a month or a year. You were like a lighthouse I knew I'd return to. You were my hero. You still are."

"Yeah, well…" He cleared his throat and rested his hand against the side of her neck. "Heroes don't get all sappy."

"Of course not." She smiled, her eyes glistening. "They just adopt kittens named Button."

"One more crack about Button, and I'm taking back the gummy worms." He tugged on a lock of her hair. "I meant it when I said I'll always do whatever you ask of me. So, feel free to get kinky with your requests."

Rory laughed and poked him in the chest. "I'll keep that in mind."

"As for your software design plan…" Tension threaded his shoulders again. "Applying for funding is a long process. It could be months before you know if your project will be approved or not. Venture capitalists are obviously no guarantee, either. God knows I'd lose my shit if you ended up dealing with another scumbag. Which is why…"

He took a breath and rested his hands on her arms. "I want to fund your software project."

Rory stared at him, shock darkening her eyes. When she opened her mouth to speak, Grant shook his head.

"I have money, Rory. Plenty of it. My parents established trust funds for me and Nathan when we were born, and I've never touched mine. But investing in you…I can't think of anything I would rather do."

"Oh, Grant." She eased away from him, and a tear slipped down her cheek. "I can't take your money."

Frustration lanced through him. He'd known she would say that. "Yes, you can. I'm offering it to you."

"What would your father say?"

"He'll probably be glad to know I'm investing in technology. In you. I want you to have all the support you need without worrying about money. If you want a contract, fine, but all that matters to me is that you have the resources to do exactly what you want. To do what makes you happy."

She wiped her eyes with a napkin and shook her head. His insides twisted.

"Rory." He stepped closer, willing her to let him do this for her. "I'm *asking you* to take this offer. Please."

Silence fell, stretching over the span of a thousand heartbeats. The air grew thick. His pulse pounded.

"I…" She drew in a shaky breath, shredding the napkin between her fingers. "How can I ever *not* do what you ask? I accept, Grant. Thank you so much."

Relief flooded him. He crossed to her in three strides and grabbed her up into his arms, kissing her thoroughly before setting her back on her feet. He ran a hand over her long hair, thinking a million years could pass and he would still need and want her every second.

"Rory." His voice came out hoarse. He pressed his lips to her forehead. "I want—"

"Oh!" She broke away from him, her eyes widening. "I totally forgot."

She spun and hurried toward the dining room. With a frown, Grant followed.

Rory grabbed a bag that she'd left underneath the bar and unzipped it. She took out Bob the Fish and placed him back on the empty hooks still embedded in the wall behind the bar.

Grant laughed. "You didn't burn him after all, huh?"

"Never." Rory slipped her arms around his waist. "Bob and I are old friends now. He sang me to sleep every night I was away from you. Thanks for entrusting him to my care."

He hugged her against his side. "Thanks for entrusting yourself to *my* care."

"Best decision of my life." Rory smiled and pressed the button on the plaque. Bob turned his head, opened his gaping mouth, and began warbling "Love Me Tender." The silver lights on his scales shimmered and glowed.

"It's still awful." She gave Grant a tight squeeze. "But I think it's our song."

"Good, because I love you tenderly, profoundly, excessively, and deeply...not to mention with great, epic passion." He pressed his lips to the top of her head. "I always will."

# EPILOGUE

*Three weeks later*

"*A* dozen women have already come forward, and the reporter is expecting more," Joanna continued in the voicemail message on Rory's phone. "*The San Francisco Tribune* wants to run it as a series of articles about discrimination in the technology industry as well as profiles of successful women. *The New York Times* is also investigating, and I'll be speaking at the Future of IT conference next month to announce the creation of the Women in Technology Foundation. We've received support from four of the largest tech companies already."

There was the sound of paper rustling before Joanna continued, "Rory, I'd like for you to be a board member in charge of the mentorship program, which you can handle from Bliss Cove. Edward is working on establishing the scholarships for young women seeking careers in IT, and he also wants you to be on the scholarship committee, but no pressure. We know you're busy with your own project. We'll talk about it when you and Grant come up for dinner next week. See you soon!"

With a chuckle of admiration, Rory set down her phone and returned her attention to her computer.

Shortly after the Digicore shockwave, Joanna and Edward —as the acknowledged pioneers of inclusion and diversity at Intellix—had challenged other tech companies to take viable action rather than issue statements about "new strategies." They had also contacted the media about the discriminatory issues facing women in the tech industry.

A number of reporters had jumped on the story, and Joanna was now serving as the go-between for women coming forward with their stories. She'd also announced her intention to create a foundation in support of women in technology, which was already off to a sprinting start—thanks to her considerable influence and widespread network.

Edward had been surprisingly enthusiastic about Grant's support of Rory's software design project and had offered his input and resources "if ever needed." In the two weeks that Rory had been back in Bliss Cove, she'd started consulting in-depth with Hunter and Studio Twenty-Five to make plans for designing the restoration and development software.

Grant converted the Mousehole cottage into an office for her, complete with a computer desk and a high-end, ergonomic chair; a reading nook, high-speed internet, and a supply of gummy candies, Twizzlers, and Sour Patch Kids. They fell easily into the life they'd established so briefly all those weeks ago, a perfect balance of the work they loved and the joy of being together.

One early morning in mid-December, they went for a run along the beach, where seagulls swooped overhead and sandpipers pecked at the shore. A newspaper-gray marine layer coated the sky, and whitecaps rolled over the ocean's surface.

Rory loved their morning jogs—the steady, rhythmic movement of Grant beside her, the sound of their breath mixing with the ocean's murmurs; the cold, salty wind. They ran along Pelican Beach toward the deserted boardwalk. After climbing the steps, they finished their jog near the Ferris wheel.

"Good one." Grant patted her rear as they slowed to catch their breath.

"We deserve pie after that." Rory bent to press her hands against her knees, her chest heaving. "Speaking of which, I still haven't had your famous apple pie."

"I'll make you one this afternoon. Apple pie for the apple of my eye."

"Says the owner of Button the Kitten." Rory grinned and straightened. "I think she's getting used to me. She didn't hiss when I walked past her yesterday."

"I'll have another talk with her." He lifted his arms for a stretch, and Rory unabashedly admired the way his biceps flexed and his shirt pulled over his muscular chest. The ocean wind pushed his thick hair away from his forehead, bringing into sharp relief his warm green eyes and the strong, masculine lines of his face.

Every time she looked at him, her heart gave a happy little jump at the reminder that he was no longer over there, but *right here*. That they were here together.

"Come on." He nodded toward wooden railing bordering the pier. "Let's walk."

As they continued walking to the end of the pier, anxiety tightened her belly. She and Grant professed their love every chance they got and multiple times a day in many different ways. Sometimes it was a quick, parting kiss and a "love you," and other times it was a deep, profound confession as they looked into each other's eyes and found themselves reflected there.

More often, it was in little gestures and flippant remarks —his brief kiss on her forehead, her spontaneous purchase of a cookbook she thought he'd like, the way he brought her black coffee with two spoons of sugar every single morning, her reminder to "think of me when you play the fish" as Grant left for the Mousehole.

No, Rory was never in any doubt about Grant's intense love for her, and she woke every day with the unbreakable knowledge that she wanted to be with him always.

He wasn't just *The One*. He was all the numbers put together. He was infinity.

So, why was she nervous? It wasn't as if he'd break up with her if the timing wasn't right. They'd talk it out and come up with a plan, and—

Rory shook her head to banish the worrisome thoughts. She'd been brave enough to shake up the entire tech industry. Surely she could do *this* without her knees trembling.

She and Grant paused by the railing. Seagulls soared across the gray sky. A cluster of sea lions lolled on a rock out in the bay.

*Now. Do it now.*

Taking a deep breath, Rory turned to face him. "Grant."

He glanced at her, his eyes crinkling with a smile. He did that a lot—smiled when he looked at her. In that moment, Rory's heart became a galaxy of stars.

"So, we…" She swallowed past another surge of anxiety.

"Even though we've officially been together for a couple of months, we've really known each other for two years. I told you I've loved you for longer than I even know, and in some ways I wish we'd crossed the line sooner so we'd have had more time together, but I'm also so grateful that everything unfolded the way it did because it all led us to *right here*."

Faint wariness rose to his eyes. Rory curled her hand around the old railing and forced herself to continue.

"I mean, I'd never really imagined myself being with one person for the rest of my life…not being a believer in fairy tales and all…but every minute with you is so perfect that now I can't imagine being alone again."

*Oh my god, Rory, stop rambling and get on with it.*

She dug into the pocket of her running pants and pulled out a little drawstring pouch. "I don't have a timeline or a plan, and I'm happy to wait as long as needed, but I really wanted you to know how much I love you and that I want to be with you forever, so…"

With shaking hands, she opened the bag and took out a men's ring—a simple, polished band the color of the foggy sky.

"Grant Taylor, I love you." She put the ring in her palm and extended it toward him. "Will you marry me?"

He looked from the ring to her. Shock descended over his features.

That couldn't be good. Rory's heart began to sink.

"I…" His throat worked with a swallow. He looked at the ring again and shook his head. "I can't believe it."

"I know it may be too soon," she added quickly, "and like I said, I don't have a timeline or anything, so it's not as if I want to go to Vegas tonight or—"

Grant laughed suddenly—a rich, booming laugh that echoed over the white-capped water and mingled with the cawing of the seagulls. Rory stared at him. Her heart hammered.

He grabbed her by the shoulders, pulling her to him so swiftly that their bodies collided in a rush of heat. He brought his mouth down on hers in a hard, fast kiss that sent a shockwave of warmth right to her toes.

*Well, that didn't feel like a "no."*

"I love you." He lifted his head, his eyes filled with tenderness and heat. "I've loved you for a lot longer than I know, too, but I'm positive that everything between us happened exactly the way it was supposed to. Including this."

He stepped away from her and reached into the pocket of his track jacket. When he pulled out a small velvet box, Rory gasped in astonishment.

"Rory Prescott, on December fifteenth, the anniversary of the first time we met..." He opened the box to reveal an elegant, white-gold band set with a rich sapphire. "Will you marry me, too?"

Rory couldn't speak. She pressed a hand to her chest and struggled to find the words. "You...you're kidding."

He grinned. "I'm most definitely not kidding. I've been planning this for a while now. I was going to ask you at the Mousehole, but I wanted it to be private. Just you and me. And since we're always alone when we go running, this seemed like the perfect time."

Tears flooded Rory's eyes. She pressed her hands to her face. "That's exactly what I wanted. On the anniversary of the day we met. I can't believe you remember."

"I've never forgotten. Well, I didn't remember the exact

date until you mentioned it, but after you told me, I knew that when I asked you to marry me, it would be on the same day."

"I can't believe this." She lowered her hands, staring at the sapphire ring in disbelief.

"I can." He took her left hand in his and slipped the ring on her finger. "Destiny helped me pick the stone. I wanted it because it's the color of your eyes, but she said it's also a symbol of power and kindness, and that it provides protection and great fortune. That was good enough for me."

"I love it." She spread her hand out and admired the ring through blurry vision. "I love you. Oh! Here's mine. I mean, yours."

With a laugh, she reached for his left hand and held up the silver ring. "I picked it out because it's classic, solid, and eternal, and it's made of this super-strong metal that I can't remember the name of, but if you were a ring, this is the one you would be. I had a special engraving put on it, too."

She turned the ring toward the light to reveal the grill fork and spatula, crossed in the shape of an X, on the inside curve.

"I love it." His eyes were suspiciously bright. "It's perfect. Like you."

Rory slipped the band on his finger. He took both of her hands in his and pressed them to his chest.

"So will you marry me?" He lifted his eyebrows hopefully.

"Yes." Rory smiled and threw her arms around him, hugging him close. "*Yes.* Will you marry me?"

"A thousand times yes." He tightened his arms around her. "And then a thousand more."

Their lips met in another warm kiss that contained infinite promises to be kept, wishes to be granted, laughs to share, and a powerful, unbreakable love that had found its forever home.

♥

**Ready for more Bliss Cove?**

When chirpy reporter Brooke Castle gets trapped in a snowstorm with grumpy bookstore owner Sam Donovan, the fire isn't the only thing heating up the cabin...

**Turn the page**
for an excerpt from the next book in the series:

**WORDS OF LOVE**
(Brooke & Sam's story)

∽

# SNEAK PEEK

## WORDS OF LOVE (BLISS COVE #5)

*H*e was late.

Brooke Castle peered into the darkened window of Title Wave Books and tapped impatiently on the glass.

Of *course* he was late. Unless he'd just decided not to show up at all today, even though it was ten o'clock on a Friday morning, and every retail business on the planet was open on Friday—except for Title Wave.

Brooke paced in front of the door and looked at her watch. Most of the residents in the California seaside town of Bliss Cove thought the bookstore's unpredictable hours were a charming little quirk—even if the grumpy proprietor was not.

Brooke had occasionally enjoyed the "quirkiness" of the store hours herself…except for now, when she actually needed to *buy some books*.

Taking out her phone, she scrolled for the Sierra mountains weather forecast. *Snow expected starting mid-afternoon through the evening, possible accumulation of three to four inches.*

It wasn't a dire forecast, but Brooke wasn't accustomed to driving in the snow, and she wanted to reach the Eagle's Nest cabin before the bad weather started. With a four-hour drive ahead of her, that meant she had to leave soon.

"Come on, Sam," she muttered.

She should have known that relying on the bookstore owner to open his business at a reasonable time was a dicey proposition at best, but her best friend Aria had offered her the cabin only a couple of weeks ago, and Brooke had been so busy with job applications that she'd neglected to order the books she wanted online until it was too late for timely delivery.

*No problem*, she'd thought to herself last night as she was packing for her trip. *I'll swing by Title Wave to stock up before hitting the road tomorrow. I'll be out of here by nine.*

So much for that plan.

This was not the most auspicious start to her New Year's retreat. Neither was her post-Thanksgiving discovery that her grandfather, Charlie Castle, editor-in-chief of *The Bliss Cove Gazette*, couldn't afford to keep her on as a staff reporter any longer...and that he hadn't intended to tell her.

A knot of guilt tightened her throat. She'd been working at the paper since she'd moved back to Bliss Cove two years ago. Though Charlie had given her a job right away, both she and her entire family had assumed her position would be temporary. She'd find a job with another newspaper or a magazine soon enough.

But after she'd crashed and burned so badly at *The New York Times*, she'd found it painfully easy to be back at home working at *The Gazette*, where speeding tickets and jaywalking filled the police blotter and a gingerbread contest scandal had dominated the holiday headlines.

*Take that, big scary world with your anxiety crises and disintegrating glaciers. I'm writing an article about the new baby otters at the aquarium.*

Brooke hadn't even considered that her staff position might be hurting the paper's already-strained budget...until she'd found out that her grandfather had been paying her salary from his own pocket.

The gesture hadn't angered her—helping each other was what her family did—but her guilt and shame had cut deep. She'd also been forced to admit that she'd stayed at *The Gazette* for so long because it was safe and she was with the people she loved, not because it was helping her move forward in her career or her life.

So in early December, she'd resigned from the paper and begun sending out dozens of applications and freelance article pitches to publications across the country.

Then the rejections had started rolling in, all of which had contributed to her feeling that she was too late. Her time had come and gone. She'd blown her one big chance.

But.

Charlie didn't call her "Sunny Side Up" for no reason. She was known both in her family and around Bliss Cove as being a woman who always looked on the bright side.

Unfortunately, you couldn't be "Sunny Side Up" without also sometimes surrendering to "Sunny Side Down." As her job prospects began dead-ending, she'd had an increasingly hard time being optimistic about her own life.

Seven years after graduating from college, she was still

paying off her significant student loans, and she hadn't taken any steps toward making extra money for IRAs and investment accounts. Not to mention, she was turning thirty this year. It was time to do adult things like get a real job not funded by her grandfather and to seriously plan for her future.

Or, rather...*start* her future.

That feeling has been solidified when Destiny Storm, Bliss Cove's resident fortune teller and purveyor of fate, gave her the Christmas gift of a Tarot card reading that foretold a time of immense *change, decisions, and new beginnings* in the coming year.

Brooke interpreted that as a message that it was time for her to take decisive action. Despite her usually chipper attitude, the universe wouldn't just hand over change and new beginnings. She had to work for them.

Like Gramps always said, a good reporter had to climb the stairs, pound the pavement, and knock on doors.

Speaking of which...

She rapped her knuckles on the bookstore window. Cupping her hand around her eyes, she peered inside again. No sign of life.

Well, she couldn't wait any longer. Maybe she'd find a bookstore on the road when she stopped for gas. Pivoting on her heel, she started walking back to her car when a tall figure rounded the corner at the end of the block.

Her heart thumped against her ribs, as it always did when she first caught sight of the ridiculously sexy...er, *strange* bookstore owner, who'd shown up in Bliss Cove a year ago with no explanation or apparent reason for being here.

A few weeks after arriving, Sam Donovan had taken over Title Wave, which had been on the verge of shutting down, and quickly roused the ire of the town council with his erratic hours. His tendency to open and close Title Wave whenever he damned well pleased offended Mayor Bowers' belief that all downtown businesses should adhere to a schedule.

In addition to making no effort to please the local officials, Sam had made it clear that he wasn't interested in getting involved in town events. He did attend all the festivals —though based on Brooke's observations, it was mostly for the food.

Despite the mayor's and councilmembers' disapproval, the townspeople were glad to have the bookstore remain open and, by unspoken agreement, they gave Sam both space and privacy.

He approached, an apple in his left hand and a folded newspaper section underneath his arm. He moved with a casual stride that belied the power coiled through his body. A shaft of sunlight broke through the gray clouds and burnished his dark hair with strands of gold.

Brooke suppressed a flicker of awareness. Despite his reclusiveness, a man couldn't *look* like Sam Donovan and not inspire female curiosity.

He was tall, well over six feet, with strong features and thick hair that was perpetually finger-combed. While he often wore faded jeans and old, flannel shirts, the worn clothing seemed to enhance rather than detract from his muscular physique. With his stubbled jaw and messy hair, Sam Donovan was a striking example of scruffy masculine beauty.

Between his looks and his tendency to be a bit scowling and anti-social, he'd been compared to everyone from Heathcliff to Severus Snape to Mr. Darcy.

"What are you doing here?" His eyebrows snapped together.

"Good morning to you, too." She gave him a bright smile, determined to be Sunny Side Up. "I'm here for the tango lessons."

He frowned and shifted the paper to his other arm.

"I need some books, genius." She indicated the window display. "Title Wave is supposed to open at nine."

"Says who?"

"The world. Including the mayor and the town council."

"Guess they're wrong." He pushed the door open. "We're closed."

"What do you mean, you're closed? You just opened the door."

"I'm not staying." He pushed up his cuff to glance at the old analog watch on his wrist. "I just came to pick something up."

"Well, can you spare ten minutes to actually operate your business?" Brooke lifted her hands in astonishment. "I need to purchase some of your stock. I'm a *customer*."

He expelled a sigh, as if wearied by the very idea of selling books. "Ten minutes. No longer."

Before he could change his mind, she hurried toward the shelves. She stopped by the Self-Help section and began scanning the titles.

Despite his erratic hours, Sam took excellent care of the store. The shelves were always well stocked with both new titles and backlist, there wasn't a speck of dust anywhere, and the displays were neat and organized.

Brooke loaded half a dozen books into her arms and veered around the corner to the Romance section. Due to the job search, the holidays hadn't given her much time for reading either.

She'd packed some of her personal favorite romance novels to bring to the cabin, but there were at least ten new releases that had been on her radar for weeks. She stacked them on her pile and made her way to the front counter.

Sam was logging in to the computer, both hands on the keyboard, the apple now stuck between his teeth. The newspaper lay on the counter, open to a half-completed crossword puzzle.

Clearing her throat, Brooke dumped the books on the counter. He took hold of the apple and bit into it.

Not once in her life had Brooke thought there was anything remotely sexy about a man eating fruit. But the sight of Sam cupping the apple in his big hand while he tore through the ruby-red peel and crunched into the flesh with his straight white teeth…

Her breath shortened.

Though she wasn't interested in Sam romantically, it wasn't the first time he'd had an electric effect on her body. Whenever she saw him at a town festival, a little zinging sensation went through her like a shock.

Which was all fine and good, but she'd learned the hard way that a *zing* could short circuit in a bad way. Better to avoid them altogether.

"You buying those?" Sam asked around the apple bite.

She tried to muster up some distaste for him talking with his mouth full, but the way he *rolled* the apple over his tongue and bit down again with a—

She had to get out of here.

"I am, indeed." She took her wallet out of her purse.

Sam wedged the apple between his teeth again and wiped his hands on his jeans before he started ringing up the books. His gaze lingered on the titles—*The No-Brainer's Guide to Self-Enrichment, How To Stop Screwing Up Your Life,* and *I'm Okay, but You're Still Meh.*

Heat rose to her cheeks. She hadn't told anyone about her current existential crisis, and she certainly didn't want Sam speculating about why she needed self-help books.

"I don't need a bag." She pushed her credit card across the counter and tried not to think about how much debt it was already holding.

He stacked the self-help books in front of her, took another bite of the crisp apple, and set the fruit on a paper towel. After wiping his hands on his jeans again, he picked up the romance novels and began scanning them while he chewed.

He was probably rolling the apple over his tongue again. His jaw muscles worked. His throat rippled. The sweet, fruity scent drifted to her nose.

Brooke unzipped her hoodie to let cooler air circulate around her body. Had it always been so warm in here?

Sam glanced at one of the romance covers, *The Pleasures of the Pirate,* which displayed a buxom woman clutching the legs of a shirtless pirate with an impressively unrealistic set of abs.

Why hadn't she been organized enough to order her books online? She normally didn't give two hoots what anyone thought of her reading choices, but it wasn't the first time Sam had made her kind of jittery and nervous just by doing…*nothing.*

Next, he rang up a copy of *Slave to You,* which bore a

particularly erotic cover of a half-naked man blindfolding a woman clad in lacy lingerie.

"These are for...uh, research," Brooke mumbled, heat crawling up to her ears.

*— End of Excerpt —*

Find out what happens next for Brooke and Sam in:

**WORDS OF LOVE**
*(Bliss Cove, Book 5)*
Available Now

# ALSO BY NINA LINDSEY

**Escape to Bliss Cove…**

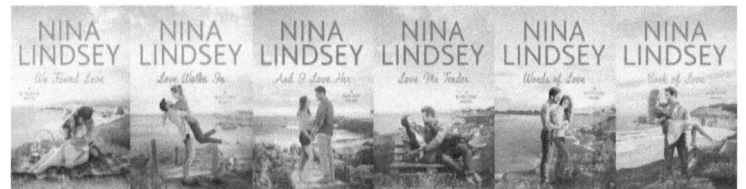

## WE FOUND LOVE

After Trevor's meteoric rise to fame in the chef world tears them apart, Kate escapes to a small seaside town to heal her broken heart. Determined to prove they belong together, Trevor seeks Kate out in Bliss Cove and risks it all for a second chance.

## LOVE WALKS IN

Shaking off her past mistakes, Aria Prescott is determined to start a new life with her latest venture, the "Meow and Then Cat Café." Then property developer Hunter Armstrong swoops in to take over the whole district. Who will win this war of both homes and hearts?

## AND I LOVE HER

An expert on the hot, wild tales of mythology, Callie Prescott leads a tidy life. And that, thank you, is exactly how she wants it…until action hero Jake Ryan arrives in town and wants some close-up action with the brilliant, beautiful professor.

## LOVE ME TENDER

Rory Prescott and tavern owner Grant Taylor make a deal — she'll be his date to his brother's wedding if he'll let her stay short-term in his cottage. But what happens when this fake relationship becomes passionately real?

## WORDS OF LOVE

When chirpy reporter Brooke Castle gets trapped in a snowstorm with grumpy bookstore owner Sam Donovan, the fire isn't the only thing heating up the cabin.

## BOOK OF LOVE

High school literature teacher Grace Berry has no time for romance. But when sexy, award-winning author Lincoln Atwood comes into her classroom, Grace is eager for his lessons in love.

Looking for even **more** steam & emotions in your romances?

If so, check out my **NINA LANE** books here!

CHECK OUT MY **NINA LANE** BOOKS!

In the mood for even **more** swoon and steam? With all the feels and a roller coaster of emotions? My **NINA LANE** books reportedly make some readers cry their eyes out... between fanning the sizzling heat coming off their ereaders. If that sounds like your cup of tea, go check 'em out HERE.

Born and raised in California, NEW YORK TIMES & USA TODAY bestselling author Nina Lane now lives in Wisconsin where the winters are freezing and the cheese is exceptional. Mom to two teens and a neurotic dog, half her life consists of laundry, Girl Scouts, horses, and football, while the other half is filled with hot, swoony alpha heroes and the women who bring them to their knees. Nina's a fan of popcorn, print magazines, working out, and checking the weather daily with her meteorologist husband. She holds a PhD in Art History and an MA in Library and Information Studies, but considers writing epic, emotional romances her one true calling in life. Thus, she is grateful and ecstatic to be able to bring the stories in her head to life for all her amazing fans. ♥

Learn more at: www.ninalane.com

AND CLICK HERE TO JOIN THE BOOK NINJAS!

# ABOUT THE AUTHOR

Nina Lindsey writes romances filled with heart, heat, and happy endings. She is delighted to introduce readers to Bliss Cove, California, a coastal town with an abundance of warm cookies, ocean breezes, and the ever-present possibility of love.

Nina loves all things spicy and sweet, with chili chocolates being at the top of the list. She is also a fan of glossy magazines, pop culture, Gilmore Girls, energy bites, Orangetheory, and the sound of silence.

She lives in Wisconsin with her meteorologist husband (yes, she asks him daily, "What's the weather forecast?"), their two children, an overly energetic dog, and a snail named Pipsqueak.

www.ninalindsey.com

facebook.com/ninalindseyauthor

instagram.com/ninalindsey.author

goodreads.com/ninalindsey

www.ingramcontent.com/pod-product-compliance
Lightning Source LLC
Chambersburg PA
CBHW051950240626
47153CB00005B/1702